Killing the Birds

Christopher Smith

BLACK ROSE
writing™

© 2015 by Christopher Smith

All rights reserved. No part of this book may be reproduced, stored in a retrieval system or transmitted in any form or by any means without the prior written permission of the publishers, except by a reviewer who may quote brief passages in a review to be printed in a newspaper, magazine or journal.

The final approval for this literary material is granted by the author.

First printing

This is a work of fiction. Names, characters, businesses, places, events and incidents are either the products of the author's imagination or used in a fictitious manner. Any resemblance to actual persons, living or dead, or actual events is purely coincidental.

ISBN: 978-1-61296-571-0
PUBLISHED BY BLACK ROSE WRITING
www.blackrosewriting.com

Printed in the United States of America
Suggested retail price $16.95

Killing the Birds is printed in Adobe Caslon Pro

For Ethan and Shirley

And always for my folks

Killing the Birds

CHRISTOPHER SMITH

Chapter One

They found him against a large red cedar down a steep drop twenty yards off the road. A father-and-son team was felling trees for firewood to sell in town, the son seeing the wristwatch reflecting the sun's light. Now, where the most prominent sound was usually the ever-present warbling of the cool-running mountain creek, the radios of the town's two squad cars intermediately came to life, the officers calling to one another, and the twilight had been invaded by red and blue flashing lights. The father and son were being further detained, so each facet of the force could ask them the same questions. By the force, I mean Richards, Ellerth, and the new guy.

Sergeant Richards had all he needed for now, and stood stone-still smoking his Pall Mall pensively. I, too, had gotten all the information I was going to get for now, and had begun arranging my notes. I kept glancing up to see if Richards had moved on, but he remained as one of the trees, letting the cool air slowly come to him and wondering what had happened here in the real light of day. He finally turned my way, his face scrunching in response to the sight of my still-present face. He bowed his head, and then began his short trip over to me. He let his rump fall onto my hood and spoke out at the woods.

"I see your radio frequency is still honed in to our business."

"My business too, Serge."

"Maybe."

"Do you know who he belongs to yet?"

"Dan, I know they don't pay to fill your tank. Why don't you spare yourself the footwork and wait for the press release down at the station? It's not like you can work that phone-camera of yours. No one's gonna want those out-of-focus pieces of shit."

"I come, I see – now I have pictures I can write about."

"I never understood why people want those types of pictures. They should just thank God it ain't their boy."

"I don't care why – I just supply."

He stepped away from my car so he could lean down to look me in the eyes. His soul narrowly made it through thin dark brown peepers.

"I'd just think you'd want to do something useful, Dan, like your old man."

"It doesn't look like the boy was raped."

"I'll see ya, paper boy."

"Puts the motive in the air, don't it?"

He just kept walking away. He waved for his partner and they drove off. Richards tried not to think about the hows and whys. Hell, he was most likely on his way to tell the parents that their son was on the other side now. He had his own concerns. It wasn't like he was a detective. It wasn't like I worked for a real paper.

I had been on that mountainside a couple of hours, had finished off my sandwiches and most of the article—time for the office and the keyboard. But just as I turned the key, the Feds showed up. (Well, if they weren't Feds, they were steely-looking insurance agents.) What the hell were they doing here? How the hell did they get here so fast? Richards came back when he saw the agents driving up the road, and then began showing them around the scene and imparting what information he owned. One of them, the shorter Federal Agent with the bulldog neck, finally pointed to me for an explanation. After getting it he strode over kind of awkwardly, due to his hard dick, I guess.

"You can go now," he said.

"I was just leaving."

"Good." He turned away.

"What are you all doing here?"

He ignored me and kept striding away purposefully. I took one last look down the hill. Whatever name that boy had been given at birth would be heard around this county for a while, in barber shops, at PTA gatherings, at high-school lunch periods. He did not die like the rest of us: bad health, a lake undertow, a drug overdose. No, he had an old railroad spike hammered through his chest and into his heart. People would talk about that.

I eased my faithful old Dodge Swinger down that logging road and onto Route 31 and into town. The evening pulled its darker shawl about itself, and I wondered how long they would hold the presses for me. I called in the bulk of the information over the CB so Boss Rogers could get started (cell phones worked about fifty percent of the time in this world of mountains.) At the police station I waited in the old cafeteria for the official press release, along with my competitor, Max Conner, from the other paper. We had gone to school together, played on the basketball team and had landed a few of the same girls. We were not close, but we had spent and continued to spend a lot of time together.

His paper made my paper look like the Washington Post. He mainly supplied the community and hunters who had come in from other counties with hunting and fishing tips. But he was in the business. His wife had an advice column, and she also offered recipes and pressure-cooking safety tips. They churned out three papers a week from their basement on Mondays, Wednesdays, and Fridays. On Fridays they even let folks know what was playing at the Rand Point cinemas.

Rand Point was an actual city.

"I bet you the father did it. The fathers almost always do it. They get afraid the son will tell. He was molested, right?"

"No, Max, he was not molested... not today, anyway."

"How do you know?"

"That's not the type of question I answer."

We played a little garbage-pail basketball, told a few dirty jokes, and bitched about the cops making us wait. Then Ted Wilson, a writer for the Rand Point News, slipped in, smiled, and began eating a bad-smelling turkey sandwich. I shivered to see him again; not the cold chill one feels when seeing a dead boy in twilight, but still deep with association. He played the situation like he had shot hoops with me yesterday.

Max said to him, "I thought this one might bring you down. Is that why they've kept us waiting? Only wanted to chew their fat once?"

Ted got his pad of paper ready, ignoring Max completely, and asked me, "Dan, can ya get me started?"

"I don't know who the kid is. Someone thought enough of him to hammer a railroad spike into his heart. He wasn't sexually assaulted. I'd say he's about ten, maybe eleven... twelve. He was barefoot. I did not see the shoes nearby. Richards wouldn't tell me if he found them. They kept me at a distance."

"No shoes," Max said simply.

"Was he beaten? Bruised?" Ted asked.

"Pants were dirty, maybe a scratch on his face. Otherwise he was just murdered."

Sergeant Richards came in and told us the rest:

Jimmy Wagner, eleven years old. Never reported missing, because at the time his body was discovered he was just late for dinner. He resided on the other side of the river about a mile out of town. The officer included some personal stuff he knew we might want: Average student but popular with the other kids, good at sports, oldest of three siblings. Richards also let it out that the parents seemed truly devastated. His bike was found a half mile up the road from his body. That's where they figured the original confrontation had occurred. They would continue to cover that area and the area where his body was found. The boy had gone out this Saturday morning to do his paper route – my paper, the Reverend River Herald.

The place I then went to make my deadline.

Rogers' secretary, Grace, leaned on my desk shaking her head. Belief had arrived reluctantly, but understanding might not ever make it. She played with her short curly hair and questioned a world she couldn't quite make out through her hazel eyes.

"How could anyone do such a thing?" And she shook her head some more.

. . .

I entered my shack of a house, put my "X" on the calendar and went to bed. I dreamt I was back with Melissa in Rand Point. We were decorating the house for Christmas. Things were nice and cozy. In the dream I slipped into the washroom to down some Valium and roll a joint, which I did quite often in those happy-go-lucky days. Melissa came in and we had a huge screaming match.

I woke up in the dark. After hitting the washroom I sat up in my bed seeing the ankles of Jimmy Wagner's bare feet.

. . .

My mom went to church every Sunday. Once a month she'd call and try to talk me into coming to the Lord with her. I made my usual apologies, to her and the Lord.

"Okay," she said. I heard her release air out of her mouth, along with the disappointment. "The Lord can wait on you. He's the One with infinite patience."

"I'm going shopping today, Mom. Anything I can get you?"

"Someone said the cantaloupe were good."

I emptied my overflowing cart onto the moving counter and smiled down at little Nell Hartman. My sister used to babysit her and a few siblings, and now Nell had her own bun in the oven; I stole looks at the swollen tummy. I attempted to relax as she added up the cost. I spotted The Herald and that was the first time I knew my story had made the front page—which is to say that it competed with the war.

"You shouldn't be bringing Lucas all this crap," she said to me while still ringing it all up. I did not answer. "You're still shopping for that colossal stoner, aren't you?"

"Well, that beer ain't for me," I said, on the wagon almost a year now.

"You should take advantage of his not getting out and bring him what he needs: rice, vegetables, a little meat. Look at this, two ten-packs of Ho Hos. Do you bring him his pot as well?"

"From the looks of your stomach, Nell, I'd say you already had someone to look out for."

"He's your friend," she said. "That's a hundred twenty-two dollars and sixty-three cents."

I glanced at the pimple-faced bagger as he actually hurried to complete the task. When he finished, he looked up, and I thanked him. He didn't know me, I didn't know him—I loved when that happened. Too much shit to carry into exchanges with people you know; nothing like a little "thank you" and "you're welcome" between complete strangers. But next time would be different. Next time we would have to up the ante, because we would be familiar with each other.

Lucas lived a mile off Main Street up the ever-rising Nog Hill Road. It was his mother's home. She made her life in Reno now, partnering up with a gambling cousin. They pretended to be helping each other out by sharing a place, but they were sharing a bed as well. The cousin had gone off to Reno to be the gambler he figured he was born to be. She went there knowing that no one there knew they were cousins, and they kept that to themselves. Lucas' father had gotten run off the road by a logging truck when Lucas was seven.

Lucas made his money off the phone and internet, selling everything from magazines and exercise machines to real estate in Florida. He could no longer fit through the front door of the two-floor house, so he had the back door customized to roll his wheelchair out onto the back deck through slide-open glass doors. He could still walk, but he didn't care much for it. He kept the front door locked. I had a key. His dealers knew to go around back and knock, and there was a note for UPS to deliver 'round back. He would not answer the front door; he had no use for people who did not know him and his ways.

Being Sunday, Lucas sat before the computer for fun's sake: some hugely violent video game. He waved and thanked me as I loaded his fridge. The obese man squeaked when almost having his head chopped off by one of Satan's helpers, and he constantly chided his enemies.

"Oh, you'd like me to come down there, wouldn't you?" he'd muse. "No, I'll wait behind this corner a moment; let you play your hand." He paused for a bite of a Twinkie.

When I had dispatched my chore, I took a seat nearest the large glass doors, pulled the string that opened the blinds, and watched some birds packing their October bags.

I said, "Another two weeks and the getting-around-town-without-sliding-into-a-ditch derby will commence."

"More like a month," he groaned while blowing a demon into carnage on a wall. "Front page!" he congratulated me. "Even in a one-and-a-half-horse town like this, you're almost a celebrity."

Another boy, not Jimmy Wagner, had delivered Lucas' paper. He slid it through the mail slot in the front door.

"Can you activate the radio? I want to stay in the game."

"It's Sunday, Dan. I don't feel like hearing all that crackling and boring-as-fuck cop talk."

"Lucas, I just lugged in your damn groceries."

"All right, all right, the trump card." He hit a switch and we had the police frequency in stereo. "But I'm keeping it low."

There was nothing coming over the airwaves but the sound of ocean waves shushing their children. I had a juice while Lucas began downing cold beer. At the half-hour mark Wells showed up smiling like an evil Santa Claus.

"Look what I got here, Luke." Wells unraveled a half ounce of green sticky bud that a mother skunk would mistake for her own child. "Don't even ask me where I got this; just be thankful I put aside a half for you."

Lucas smiled fully, beaming up at his supplier to assure that his gratefulness for this delivery shone through, so other deliveries would come through. He pushed his tinted glasses up his nose and took a closer look at the weed. I had to admit that Mary Jane looked good today. Wells asked me if I were in the market.

"No, thanks," I said, ever the polite recovering addict.

"And you're drinking juice," he said. "Don't tell me you're still on that unbelievably fucking boring wagon."

"Yep."

"How long?" he asked.

"I'm not sure."

Lucas laughed while crunching up a bud for rolling, and then explained the chortle. "Knowing Dan, he has it marked on the wall, or maybe 'Xs' on a calendar."

"It's almost a year," I said. I always feel silly being on the wagon in front of my old partying buddies. Not only are you making a direct comment on their lifestyle choice, but you also feel like a boy who can't handle the heights jumping off Tweaky Boulder into Reverend River. And that was the truth. Not that I couldn't handle the heights, but that there was no room for anything else in my life but handling those heights. Or maybe I couldn't handle the heights. That's what A.A.

says.

After making fun of me for a few moments and more bragging about his pot, Wells asked both me and Lucas, "Did ya hear about that kid getting killed up Golden Top? They say he had a wooden stake jabbed in his heart, like a vampire, for Christ's sake!"

Apparently Wells didn't subscribe to The Herald.

"No, I missed that," I said, mocking ignorance.

Lucas smiled and said, "It was a railroad spike, and Dan here did the front-page story on it."

"Cool," Wells cooed. "Did you see the body?"

I just looked at him. The price of fame, I guess. How could I make this guy's day describing this poor kid bent against a tree, a spike in his heart, no shoes on?

"The cops wouldn't let you see it, huh?" he offered.

"No," I lied, "they wouldn't let me see it."

Lucas held his tongue and puffed a smoke into life. I drifted out back until that was done with. I wanted to leave but felt I had nowhere else to go—untrue of course. And besides being my best friend, Lucas knew a little about everything, so talking to him provided an entertaining and informative time-kill. In fact, he helped me with a lot of my research. Thusly, my reputation grew and that's how I got the Rand Point gig back when. These days I don't even go to the movies in Rand Point; I drive the extra miles the other way to New Port. I avoid Rand Point and the people that town owns—bad memories, bad vibes.

Wells hurried off for more business and Lucas and I shot the breeze a good while. Just as I was pushing myself up to leave, voices came over the radio.

"We got another one on Bell Road, just beyond the hotel. Some lady called. Serge, you got that? Over."

"This is Richards. Another one? Over"

Lucas looked at me. We were both thinking about another kid with a railroad spike through his pump.

"It's a 214, Sergeant Richards. Over."

"I'm there. Over."

Both I and my enormous friend relaxed. A 214 was a vagrant, a homeless person. Now and again they floated down from the hills, or off of roads of accepted ill repute: gambling shacks, open field gatherings -- dancing naked around fires. Then I had a thought: "Why did he say 'another' one? Why not straight to 214?"

Lucas never shrugged his shoulders when you presented a puzzler to him; he immediately went into deduction mode, trying to beat you to the answer.

I said, "They must have had some ruckus earlier with one of them. What is it, three of them now?"

"Three regulars, yeah. But ya know, it's possible they had orders to round up those three. You know, a kid gets killed, round up the degenerates. So they got one of them down at the station, Ellerth spots another one."

I was out of my seat and heading toward the door. "It's a good enough guess to check." I hurried out the back just to stick my head back in a second later. Without my asking, Lucas answered.

"Bell Road, just beyond the hotel."

. . .

They already had him in the back of the patrol car, a mile from the hotel. I parked and waited to follow them to the station. Driving behind at a safe distance, Richards' partner, Larry Ellerth, still noticed my old Dodge Swinger and gave me the finger out his window. I waved when I saw Richards check his rearview. I'm not quite Philip Marlowe, am I?

At the station Richards let Ellerth take the "suspect" in and came over to deal with me as I approached him. I went straight for it.

"You found some old shabby, dirty fabric on the Wagner boy, and now you're rounding up the vagrants three. Or are they just the usual suspects?

"There's a fourth now," he said. "Remember that old logger from Washington, lived up on Baldy? Well, he's dead but his son and wife are still up there, living on God knows what. He's been coming into town lately."

"How many garbage pickers ya got in there? I know at least two."

"Remember what Einstein said: 'When you know something, you stop thinking.'"

"Maybe I want to stop thinking. Speaking of thinking, none of these vagrants have the wheels to drive the boy up Golden Top."

"Dan, you have to start thinking to finish. They all got feet, all familiar with long treks. One of them could have been up there when the boy took his ride up."

"Why the hell would he ride his bike up that logger's road?"

Sergeant Richards sighed out his share of the world's weight. "Why do I bother to keep you informed, Dan? His dad said the boy liked to tackle these ant hills one by one. Sometimes he catches a ride to a particular hump just to try to conquer it. Usually makes it about halfway."

I shook my head. These weren't like the Rockies—no snowy peaks and sharp points poking the sky in the eye, but they weren't hills, either.

"So, can I write for tomorrow's front page that you are gathering together the raggedy men in relation to the Jimmy Wagner murder?"

He shook his head and scratched at his full mustache, saying, "And then the two bums we don't have disappear on us. Gee, Mr. Holdsworth, you are so helpful."

"All right, I'm willing to work with ya. What can you give me?"

He looked on me sadly, like my father does sometimes. "If you need to supply the town with blow-by-blow accounts of this grisly affair, you can say we are interviewing witnesses and possible suspects.

Don't say who they are. I don't want any of these poor homeless wrecks attracting any more community prejudice than they already do."

Richards turned to leave. I called after him for some more info, but he kept on. Just as he opened the door I asked, "Why are the Feds looking into the Wagner boy's death?" He stopped and stood there a moment, scratching his beer belly, his head then twisting back to reveal a face that had certain sweet thoughts about me. Then the small police station swallowed him whole.

Being Sunday, I entered an office that was empty except for my boss, John Rogers, who was simultaneously editor, owner, and one of the printers. Everyone had their Monday stories done by Saturday in this small burg. The sports guys were in and out, or phoning theirs in to Gracie, who now was probably running after John's food cravings or off for the day. John wasn't Lucas, but he wasn't starving. I plopped myself down into the welcoming arms of the chair across from his desk.

"Any follow-up on the Wagner story?" he asked.

John was from this wood mill called Reverend River, but that didn't stop him from thinking himself a genuine newsman. He'd seen a lot of movies, his favorite being Humphrey Bogart in the newspaper drama Deadline USA. That's why he sought to give his hometown a real paper, not just hunting, weather and coupons from laundry mats. And he had come by his skills honestly: education and an interest in his community.

I was still wondering why I hadn't followed my brother Joe back to Chicago.

"Well, for your ears only, Boss: they're pulling in all the vagrants. Until Richards finds all four, we're to be mute on the subject. He gave me a generic, 'they're interviewing possible suspects.'"

"That's something, Skip. I bet Max took the day off. We'll have this story all to ourselves tomorrow. Wait – I thought there were two or three vagrants. There're as many as four now?"

"You have to keep up with the Homeless Herald, boss."

"Can you do a quick one? The remaining staff would like to leave for the warm bosoms of their loved ones."

"Being Sunday," I said.

"Being Sunday," he said.

"Sure," I said, coming to my feet. "It'll be quick, because there's not much to say. And the scoop ain't always the prize, boss. Max will likely have a tear-jerker of a story on what a great kid Jimmy Wagner was."

Rogers asked, "You got some of that tear-jerker stuff, right?"

"I did not bother the family, but yeah, I called a couple of teachers I knew from the school. I can fill the thing out if you got time."

"Sure... but hurry." Then he called after me, "You're covering the funeral Tuesday."

The newspaper was being replaced by news sites on your computer, accessible from you phone, but paper people kept on, like a dignified chicken stalking about with its head cut off, before the final step has been truly taken.

I said the office was pretty much empty, but it never really did bustle. One of the two sportswriters sat in front of a couple of TV screens in his basement den watching and eating. If you hadn't caught the game, he would let you know how it ended up. He delegated the high school games and other community competitions to the writers on the student paper. Old Randal Weinhart claimed the other athletic pen. He never divulged his actual age, but he wasn't kidding anyone; he had acquired Mickey Mantle's rookie card during Mickey Mantle's rookie season. The elder provided grand stories from the previous generation's sports world when reminded of them by a happening in the new generation. He stood them side by side – rarely to make a point or to say which held the day, but just to do it because he could. The hunting and fishing writer came in when he pleased. If his article came up short, Rogers would fill it in. The boss man knew his way around nature, and had killed a lot of it. John Rogers' wife took care of style, local school theatre and such, and she created a crossword puzzle twice a week. The puzzles' themes ran from trees and history to old popular TV shows. She also had a celebrity column where she simply pinched all her info from Entertainment Tonight. She faxed in all her work. Boss Rogers and Gracie handled all the loose ends: the TV guide, obituaries, and so forth. The big stories around the country came in via the AP wire. And then there was me. I covered any local events that took an extra amount of footwork. Every now and again the boss called me an investigative reporter, in front of the others to boot. But I was just an ear that heard, a mouth that talked.

CHRISTOPHER SMITH

Chapter Two

Reverend River: a town born of its namesake, heir to the trees that seduced the wood mills into being. Main Street claimed one side of the river, with the smallest bar immediately there, and across a small "street" the pool hall and the rustic hotel. The biggest wood mill in the area sat on the other side of the river from this action Mecca. The county's unemployment rate floated at about fifty percent, a number the majority of the country would never comprehend. But the fact remained that most of the area residents showed up early for the government's free cheese drops. You worked in the wood mills that were shrinking, or you got along on your wits: hunting, selling firewood to the retired folks; or maybe you were Lucas, working off the computer in your room. Like life itself, survival in Reverend River took many forms. Not everyone could write for the Reverend River Herald.

A hundred years ago it was all Indians and French trappers. And other than the lumber and mining industries, it remained a home suitable to only that type of savage or extremely resourceful human who could deal with the weather and the mountains. There were some descendants who just never thought enough to leave. The late Sixties and early Seventies ushered in a crop of hippies escaping societal conflicts. My mom and dad left Chicago as thirty-year-olds certain that the hell that had broken loose was nothing compared to the hell that was about to break loose. He and Ma loaded their kids into a station wagon donated by my mother's father and got the hell out of Dodge. In this instance: Chicago. For them it made sense that if they went somewhere brutally beautiful, they would have a healthy, proud, simple life, and not many neighbors to bother them. More people left Reverend River than moved there.

Our bigger brother, Rand Point, started out as a timber town, with plenty of silver mines, but as time passed, someone thought to build museums there for the tourist trade. A part of that would have to do with Northern Pacific's building a railroad station there in the late 1800s. A city sprung up along Pend Dreille Lake. Reverend River has a few Native Americans selling trinkets on the roadside, but no museums. Some towns just don't grow much beyond their first incarnation. Hell, this whole area was no stranger to ghost towns, having been mined of all its silver.

Rand Point is where I and my girl ran off to. We packed out things and got the hell outta Dodge. In that instance: Reverend River.

. . .

Early Tuesday morning I picked up Gabe at Mrs. Rhoads' boarding house. He had his own car, but we were heading to the same spot, same story. He was waiting for me on the porch that needed paint-chipping and paint, fidgeting with some sort of ball. Then, as I pulled to a complete stop, I saw he was trying to spin it on his middle finger like a basketball. I had to show off, demonstrate the proper technique. I shoved my car in park and sprung from its grasp.

"Let me show you how that's done," I said with open arms.

The little fella tossed me the ball without smiling. It was denser than I expected, and painted black with an eight in the circle of unpainted off-white.

"An eight ball," I said incredulously; an eight ball the size of a small volleyball. I spun it haplessly. Then I adjusted and spun it but good, the ball avoiding gravity on the tip of my right index finger due to its motion. He did not smile or congratulate me on having such a useful skill. I tossed it back to him and he carefully placed it in a bushel basket on the porch.

I maneuvered my old Dodge Swinger south out of town toward the funeral site. Sitting shotgun was the paper's only photographer, Gabe Teplitz, a Jewish man in his thirties who had been passing through photographing the Northwest's intimidating loveliness on both film and the digital variety. It was a special occasion indeed when Gabe would give you a straight answer. As to why he stayed in Priest Pond? He once had told me, as straight as if he were telling me his favorite condiment was ketchup, "I'm on the run from the law, and this place is just so not on the map."

It's true: If you were going to really go for it, Alaska, that's where you went. It boasted itself Northern America's final frontier. So it was on the map. Reverend River never said a peep about itself to the rest of the country.

The riverside mountains were a part of the river, thus a riverside road had to be made room for. This resulted in some of the finest walls of rock cuts, some shooting fifty yards straight up from your car window; slabs of granite with stories to tell. The road and the river swerved in between the mountains' toes. I never tired of speeding along this magical route.

Again, these mountains were not the snow-peaked kind, but they were countless in number.

Boss Rogers let me take my own photos when out digging up a story, but when covering a county fair or funeral, the pictures could be more important than the words. So the paper finally hired a real photographer. Up until then the boss covered the sight stories, only slightly better than I did. Gabe had all kinds of equipment in the two nap packs slung on his shoulders.

"Hey, writer, slow down," Gabe said.

"Come on, Teplitz, an outlaw like you shouldn't think twice about this speed."

"I'm not an outlaw. I'm a Jew with a camera. Now slow down."

"You know not to get caught taking these pictures, right?"

"Discretion; got ya."

"Hey, really, Gabe, why aren't you in a cab in New York instead of risking your life here with me? Someone whose goal it is to one day plunge his old Dodge into the river?"

"I killed my brother in the rage of a love triangle. This was the worst self-punishment I could think of."

It began to drizzle as we soft-footed our way toward the small gathering. Gabe whispered for me to stop. He screwed a part onto his camera that made it reach out like Pinocchio's nose, and then, using my taller and wider body as a hiding place, began clicking to capture the sad faces of a boy's soggy farewell. Snap, snap.

I guessed who the parents were but would have to confirm it before I left. The mother had the surviving nine-year-old daughter pulled to her side. Their youngest boy must have been at home. The woman cried; the girl looked at the casket blankly. The father kept digging his good shoes into the ever softening earth, his face down with his shoes or up against the rain, never at the casket or his family. The preacher told us what a powerful shame it was to lose a child, and our souls motionlessly nodded in agreement. He said the boy was with God now, and I could see in my mind a smiling, playful boy walking hand-in-hand with an old friendly man dressed in a long, flowing robe. I could see it, but I didn't believe it. My mom could more than see it; she lived it, breathed it. For me the kingdom of Heaven was what most of the world thought about Reverend River: beautiful, brutal, and way far from where they lived.

That makes it awkward for me at Alcoholics Anonymous. Their main philosophy was that you have to find a Higher Power outside of yourself that could save you, because it had become obvious that you could not save yourself. The A.A. book said that your Higher Power could be anything at first: a tree, the open sky, a thought, but every meeting ended with the Lord's Prayer (you did not have to join in), and the Big Book they referenced used the "Him" word so many times that there was no chance they believed in a female god. But they encouraged you not to let that bog you down. The main idea was that you had to go outside of yourself for the answer. There was something I appreciated about that concept, and yet I firmly believed that the universe resided within me. I kept going to the meetings—not as often as I was supposed to, though.

The casket sank and the voices in sad song faded along with those that owned them. I approached the preacher. He nodded that they were indeed the father, mother, and sister. He also pointed out the uncle, who sped away in an old blue pick-up truck. He never asked why I needed to know or who I was. He lived "the life" to give what he could. When I asked more than he knew, he just smiled and shook his head. The drizzle became rain, but he would have stood there answering my questions a while longer. He represented God; he would not be caught trying to get off work early—not when the earth had just inherited an eleven-year-old boy.

"That was a lot of fun," Gabe quipped as we quick-footed back to the car.

As I opened my door I saw a tall shape in the trees beyond the graveyard. His back was to me as he walked away, but I saw enough to guess that the ragged image represented a vagrant.

On the ride home Gabe offered this: "Hard to imagine nothingness."

"I've never been able to do it," I returned.

"Hard to imagine a god, though, as well—one that hears all our prayers."

"I've never been able to do that, either; how about yourself?"

"Well, I always feel like someone's looking over my shoulder."

"It's called paranoia," I informed him.

"I know the difference."

"God?"

"I don't know who or what it is, but the way I can't imagine nothingness is the same way I know something is there. They're congruent somehow. Or you know: two halves of the one thing."

"Buddha with a camera," I said.

I looked over at the small-framed Teplitz as he removed the Pinocchio lens from his camera and packed them both away, his boyish face buried beneath a thirty-year-old man's beard. We'd driven all over this northern country together this past year, and I still didn't know who he was.

I dropped camera boy off where he boarded and picked up those cantaloupes for Ma. On the other side of the river the paved road provided more bumps and sharper curves. Fifteen minutes out of town I turned onto Boyko Trail, a dusty road of pebbles that ran along wide-open spaces for a few miles, mostly hay growers, a few horses and cows, mountains ahead and behind. Then I turned onto Mom and Dad's road, one of our first jobs when we arrived here all those years ago and found that flat area just at the foot of hard-life alp—a perfect spot to build a house. But we needed a road to connect us to a road that eventually led to a town full of supplies. We cleared trees and stone and anything else that got in our way, only occasionally conceding to an impressive stump or boulder. Thus the path curved here and there toward its destination. Each year we made the path a bit more serviceable. Each winter took its toll on our work, and repairs were needed. Once Mom tried to talk Dad into asking his current mill boss for the use of a Caterpillar, or some such miracle-working machine. Pop was never much for borrowing, but by the end of the second summer its wonderful noises sang an expedient song.

She was at the well pumping to her heart's desire as I pulled up, her slim, aging frame still an applicable machine itself. She did not turn when she heard the car. She either didn't care who it was or knew it was me.

I said as I approached her, "You know, I've heard tell of folks who have running water inside their houses."

She said nothing; just finished filling her five-gallon metal tank and then lugged it toward me, then beyond me, as I tried to take it from her.

"Come on, Ma."

"You bring those cantaloupe I was expecting Sunday?" she asked, and then struggled up the stairs and into the house. She saw I had the cantaloupe.

I watched the screen door slam and then I slowly followed her into the home that had taken all the Holdsworth family had in their hearts to create. Some days I had thought I might run away just to keep from the non-stop regimen. My dad, for all intents and purposes a good, kind man, never smiled gently at my childish complaints. I had to rise to his determination, for he feared a liberty would soften us all. I had just signed up for another year of Little League in my sweet home Chicago when Dad and Mom came into my room with their life-changing news. After working all that first summer in the Sticks, we spent the first winter at the Reverend River Hotel. I was Jimmy Wagner's age.

Now I stood watching Mom place three pots of water under flame on her propane stove. She had finally given in to progress, leaving the woodstove as a counter most of the time. One flame had to be for herbal tea, one to heat water for dishes, and the other... maybe she was going to wash her hair. The less she had in the form of running water and such luxuries, the less she would need from society. That was the plan way back when we came back to nature and Mom was the last soldier standing at our outpost. If hell broke loose and she could get no propane, well, the woodstove was not that out of practice. I placed the fruit in the old-fashioned ice box—just a steel, air-tight cupboard, really. She lived mostly off the fruits she had pressure-cooked and jarred for storage and the vegetables she grew, those outside and those in the greenhouse.

She finally turned to me, took a breath, and said, "Some tea, dear?"

We sat quietly for a bit in the living room minding our tea as she pushed back the strands of long, brown hair that had escaped her braid and were attacking her forehead and eyes. (I said brown, but it was mostly grey now. I think of my mom the way she used to be quite often, like she lived in parallel realms.) I took to thoughtfully looking out the window.

"Let me have that jacket of yours. I'll patch it up some for you."

"Thanks, Ma, but for now I can't spare it. When I put the old winter coat on for the season, you can have this."

"You can stay for dinner?"

"Sorry, I have to get my story in."

She shook her head lightly, her long face disturbed. "You drive all this way just to turn around and go back. You'd think that town held something of interest."

"It's my job, Ma."

She sipped her tea and then tried to sneak a question in matter-of-factly: "Have you seen your father?"

"I dropped by to see him at the mill about a week ago."

"Is he still at Randolph's?"

"Yep, splitting the bark off for the same pay he got ten years ago. Sergeant Richards implied that that's what I should be doing, that that was an honest living compared to what I called a job."

"How is it you were talking to Sergeant Richards?"

"Mom, I write for a paper; I talk to the cops a lot."

She said disappointedly, "Oh, humanity still up to its same old shenanigans? My sweet Lord, how can you stand to be down there?"

I knew she liked the town and its people. I tried to change the subject:

"How you been? Getting the last of the crop in? How are the pot plants?"

"You know I don't smoke anymore."

"Just kidding ya, Ma. How was this year's take?"

"The Lord was generous, as always, though your father only came up a few times to help, a couple of more times than you. Actually, your father accomplished quite a lot, as always.

"Oh, by the by," she began, "the Lord asked after you while I was working His soil. He asked directly about you; I could feel it; none of that crazy talk, like I heard a baritone voice coming down from the sky; just through my own mind He asked about you. I told Him that I was a bit concerned, but that you always seemed to land on your feet. I thanked Him for keeping you sober. You're still keeping to the vow, aren't you?"

"Yeah, I'm making it so far; you know, one day at a time."

. . .

The half-hour ride back to town was filled with mythic images of my old home, of all of us working as a team to have a roof worth living under before the second winter. Dad had made a couple of friends in town and they were out to help on and off all summer. Often I was forced away from the real work site to keep my brother Joe and sister Ellen out of harm's way, but my dad could only handle my babysitting for short spurts. He'd send Mom down after a while, wanting me at his side. At the end of these incredible, hard-working days, Mom and Dad would smoke their dope and smile about the day's progress. During victorious times like those, they loved to talk out loud to society.

"Do you miss us, world?" Mom would begin. "Are you fighting in the streets without us?"

Dad spoke with a political edge: "Are you crying about not getting your share, little children of the government? Well, we decided to take responsibility for ourselves. So don't come call us with your problems. We don't have a phone anyway."

We kids didn't really know what they were talking about, but we took from it the feeling that we were kind of special—Swiss Family Robinson, that type of thing. Sure, I cried when they dragged me away from my little league team, from TV, from the Chicago Cubs, but it's funny how quick your faith turns into another religion. I was Barefoot Country Boy before the first summer ended.

That first winter had tested the family's resolve, but the second summer arrived as a hard-working paradise once again. Every day and night was a camp-out, and that got to wearing thin—no roof, little comfort—but we stayed alive and moving, like the mighty Reverend River, reminding us that we were never far from our ancient selves.

Each summer brought us closer to having a house at the foot of the mountain, the house and the mountain in turn merging with us. Then we settlers were settled, and we were just us.

The fifth summer, Mom found God, and an awkward feeling emerged between the troop's two leaders; an argument in slow motion; a different kind of hell than fighting in the streets. Some changes are harder than others, as there are different faces of struggle. We kids took to God's sharing our bunks just fine, but Dad contended with it endlessly, only to realize he could not stay in a love run by someone other than him and his wife. Six years with Mom saying God came before Dad and he finally left. He did, I credit him, make it until we kids were grown.

. . .

Back at the office I endeavored to bring my column out as informative and communal. I was not Mike Royko (Growing up I read the Royko books of columns my dad had brought from Chicago). All news did not sift through my sly wit, or personal perspective and righteous indignation. I was the true paper boy, delivering the facts: "Just the facts, Ma'am." But halfway through the funeral article, I snapped. Writing about a boy being stabbed through the heart with a railroad spike, speaking respectfully about his wet farewell, remembering the preacher's faith in God... I really did just snap. I began rata-tat-tatting my words until they sailed on my blood through my veins. I could not stop myself. My editor (Boss Rogers) had dropped by to tell me it was getting late, and I pushed him from existence with the wave of a hand. Ultimately I wrote some sentence that sounded like closure. I was done. I handed the article to John and did not stop for his input, telling him, "Print it—don't print it. Change it if ya like. I'm going home."

I found myself parked in front of the smaller of our two taverns, just ten yards from the river: a pool table, a juke, stools and tables. They called it Athens. Up the hill a few blocks and north was The Ranch, where they had bands Fridays and Saturdays—a much bigger place than Athens, dance floor and everything. I had spent an uncountable number of hours at each watering hole in my time. Now I sat in my car with the radio playing, looking in the window at strangers, old friends and a nemesis or two. I envied every drink they swallowed. I gripped the steering wheel hard for a moment and stared out at the whispering river. Next thing I knew, Max leaned against my old Dodge.

"Are you coming in or not?"

"I don't know what the hell I'm doing."

After a pause he said, "I read your article on the cops questioning folks. Too bad ya didn't know who they were. Then there would have been a reason to write that story."

"Fuck you."

"Not in much of a mood, are ya, Danny boy?"

"I leave more out of my articles than you know to write about."

"What the hell does that mean?"

"It means I know who the suspects are. I was asked to keep it under my hat for certain reasons."

"Richards asked you?"

"No, your mother asked me." I turned the engine over. "Thanks for chasing me away."

As I drove off I heard him shout, "You'll be back. They all come back eventually."

Max was right about most of us addicts: Whether just to visit or to start the ridiculous circus all over again, we always returned to the scene of the crime.

Chapter Three

My funeral article didn't make the front page the next day. Gabe's pictures were there, a few words from editor John Rogers, maybe a couple of mine. I went into the office easy, remembering I had told him to do what he wanted with it—but still, I had expected to see a version of my article it. I sat across from his desk until he showed up smiling, a doughnut in one hand and coffee in the other. He lowered himself carefully. We each tried to stay cool the longest, him grinning, me tapping a handy pencil.

"Maybe you should just read what you wrote," he finally said.

"I wrote it. Isn't that enough?"

"Then you should be grateful I didn't print it."

"Why should I—"

He cut me off strongly. "Maybe you should just read it." And he tossed me the very pages I had handed him last night.

The article started off professionally enough, but then slipped toward the emotional side. The second half informed the reader of the dramatic happenings that caused me to leave Rand Point. My mouth hung open. There was a slight connection between Jimmy Wagner's death and the crazy crime of which I had been accused, but why did I write about what I refused to talk about?

"I don't remember drinking that," I said.

"You don't remember what?"

"I said that I don't remember writing that."

"You said, 'I don't remember drinking that.'"

"No I didn't."

"You certainly did, Skip. Speaking of drinking..."

I stood up quickly to leave the room, but stopped at the door and turned back. "It's been almost a year," I said. "I haven't fallen, not once. It's a record."

"So what's up, kid? People usually know what they're writing. The funeral get to you?"

"I felt all right—not giddy, but all right."

"Now you're starting to remember writing it, aren't you?"

I re-took my seat. John granted himself a break to enjoy his coffee and a big bite from his doughnut. If I had anything to say, he would wait for it.

"John, you ever been accused of that bad a crime?"

"Not even close, whether you're talking about the Wagner boy or your personal happenings in Rand Point—I was accused of cheating at cards once."

I tried to keep my eyes in his general direction while speaking.

"Once you say it out loud, you know most people will at least entertain the possibility that you did it. And though my folks, my brother and sister, swear they never thought twice about such ridiculousness, it took me a while to feel normal even around them. I mean, people, regular-looking people, have done such nasty things— why not me?"

"Because you're one of the good guys," he said.

"I'm a selfish drunk who schemed and stole to keep alcohol in my blood, my mind in the finest and lowest forms of drugs."

"Do you want me to think you did it?"

I just bowed my head.

"Listen, Skip, no one knows everything about anyone. And maybe we're all capable of anything, and then you decide who you trust. I'd trust you watching over my own on a stormy night with all the lights out. And I'd be right to."

"More people felt that way before the incident."

"Oh, I see, you want to change the past. See Kelly in sports. He's still trying to get the '84 Padres past the Tigers."

I sat silently. He finished the doughnut, then the coffee. Then he said, "You should hit a meeting tonight." I nodded in agreement. He asked, "Can you find one tonight?"

"Even in a town without a movie theater you can find an A.A. meeting seven nights a week."

"God bless America."

. . .

John told me to take the day off for a little R & R. I stopped by Lucas' and sat in my usual chair, mostly quiet for the first half hour as the big man sold Nordic Tracks. I broke my silence in the form of musing:

"What were the Feds doing up there?"

"Up where?"

"They were at the crime scene on Golden Top."

"You didn't mention that," he said, spinning his heavy wheelchair deftly to face me.

"Didn't I?"

"No, sir—not on the front page, either."

"So whaddaya think?"

"Murders in another state connected to this one, most likely."

"Yeah, that sounds right."

Lucas made us turkey sandwiches and then I fell asleep on his couch. I seem to remember dreaming about building the homestead again, only I was an adult. Dad kept telling me to stop screwing around. I got quite mad, because I was working so hard. Lucas' voice merged with the misty vision.

"Dan. Dan!"

"What?"

"Your phone; somebody loves you."

I rubbed my eyes as I cast off sleep.

"Hey, John: What's the rumpus?"

"Obviously you think a day off means you don't check your cop frequency. They're headed up to Baldy to get the lumberjack's kid."

"I thought he had been down in town of late."

"They can't find him, so they're figuring he went back up."

"I guess I should meet them at the station on their return. They won't like it if I —"

"Bullshit. I called Teplitz. He's waiting on you. Let's document some action. When will we ever get a chance like this again? You never know when you'll get footage worth money on Scoop TV or The Insider, or, you know: When Fugitives Run. Here are the directions I got from their transmission."

Rogers had sold some of Gabe's past footage to the Rand Point TV news station, but he was thinking bigger with this story.

. . .

Teplitz was tossing that hard-rubber eight ball when I pulled up. I called from the car, "Let's go capture real life!"

The days were dying earlier now in October, and with the heavy clouds it was quite a spooky twilight. We rose slowly up Baldy, eyes peeled for logging trucks coming down—though there were fewer and fewer of them each year. It amazed me that there was enough room for them and my Dodge Swinger at the same time, but I had slipped by plenty of them in my time, so I had carnal knowledge. I also had the knowledge that that's how Lucas' father died. We were surrounded by northern trees engulfed in moist air: pine, furs, and cedars. Gabe fidgeted with his video recorder, then his camera. I talked to myself, trying to remember which vein off the logging road led to the cabin I sought.

"God damn it! I know it's on this side. Damn! If an offshoot doesn't come—wait a minute. Let's try this."

This led to an open field near the top that held an old platform and roof for when the rain tried to ruin an outdoor get-together. I retraced my steps and kept going south.

Gabe said, "Maybe we missed it. Maybe we should —"

"Gabe, if ya just knew what you were talking about, I might think to listen. Wait! You hear that?" I pulled the car over and killed the engine. We heard a voice filtering through a megaphone. "It's up ahead," I said.

We turned up a path which my Swinger had no business traveling. It had no business going down most of these roads forty miles south of the Canada border. I never would have bought this car, and I didn't: Lucas' mother left it behind when she ran off with her cousin. After a few good jolts to the shocks, I decided to take the bumps at about two miles an hour, the front hood sinking and rising in dramatic fashion like a ship on stormy seas. Then we were climbing and I had to hit the gas to make it. Suddenly the scene revealed itself: two squads, lights flashing, parked twenty yards from the house. The Feds had parked closer, keeping their vehicle between themselves and the cabin for protection. I pulled over to one side, Sergeant Richards' two good eyes following me with no great pleasure. As I came to a halt, he shook his head back and forth as if to say, "You ain't staying, pal." I flashed my Dennis-the-Menace grin and casually got out.

"Get right back in there," he said, striding toward me. Gabe was still in process of slipping from the passenger seat with all his equipment. I could hear the megaphone's voice:

"This is your last warning! Then we will have to enter your home by force, no matter which loved ones you are putting in harm's way!"

Richards turned back toward those words, then back to me.

"I ain't got time for you, Holdsworth. I got to keep those hard-ons from killing anyone."

"Hey, do your job, Serge; I'm doing mine. Start shooting, Gabe."

Gabe took a few shots with his flashbulb, then raised his video camera and pointed it at the agents. Richards was about to go into a tirade when the cabin's front door opened. Teplitz aimed his lens at a tall, muscular man with dark red leather for skin. His hair went up instead of down—a white man's afro. He actually kept his beard short and trimmed, which seemed incongruent with the rest of his appearance. All together he stood as an impressive example of the human animal.

The Feds called out their directions: "Put your hands up and walk to us slowly." The lumberjack's kid, looking to be about thirty years of age, moved down the steps easily, never raising his hands. "Raise those damn hands now!"

He did not. He stopped to look back at a figure in the window, as he addressed the agents: "That's my ma looking on in the window. Don't go shooting her."

"Raise your fucking hands or I'm going to shoot you, your mom, and your fucking dog!"

The mountain man raised his arms but did not move forward, instead choosing to begin his defense. "I didn't do nothing! I bet you think I kilt that boy, but I didn't. I didn't do that terrible thing."

The agent who had chased me off Golden Top now shuffled to the big man while the other covered him. Richards went to them.

"Easy does it," Richards said. "He ain't armed."

The agent told the suspect to bring his arms round back, and then cuffed him. "Whoever's on the other side of that window, we're taking this man in to be questioned. No harm will come to him."

Suddenly the front door swung open and a small woman brandishing a .30-06 stepped out. "You vigilantes ain't taking my boy nowheres!" Both agents turned their weapons on the mother and began shouting:

"Drop the weapon! Drop the weapon now!"

She called back, "Get off my property! You ain't taking my boy!" And then she foolishly let go a warning shot into the darkening sky. The agent closest to the son was about to shoot, but the lumberjack's son kicked the pistol from his hand, sending it flying. He followed that with a roundhouse kick that sent the agent to the ground and momentarily out—all very impressive, seeing that the suspect had his hands cuffed behind him. Now the mother began shooting the Feds' car, sending everyone for cover, and sending a cold chill down my frightened spine. The other agent and Richards knelt down behind the car. I had leaped behind the trunk of my Swinger. The lumberjack's kid remained standing between his ma and the law, a government official dazed at his feet. Where the hell was Gabe? From his belly he kept recording the events, not behind anything, but just where the property slanted down off to the side, the video camera going from mother to son to the law behind the car. I really did not understand my Jewish friend.

"Ma, go in the house and put that gun up!"

"They think you're some sort of animal, Son! They ain't got no concern for your well bein.'"

"Mrs. Barde! This is Sergeant Richards! I promise you that we all realize your son is innocent until proven guilty! You have my word he won't —"

"Your word?" she called back as he finished his vow. "What would I know of your word? I ain't got no faith in no stranger's word!"

"Mrs. Barde! This is Special Agent Perez. My partner is on the ground with most likely a broken jaw. I don't care what you think of my word, but I do promise you he won't be lying there long! This is a violent vow!"

"Boy, the only reason your body ain't on the ground, your soul ain't gone to meet its maker, is I decided it to be that way!"

I glanced at Gabe turning his camera from one talker to the other. He remained smooth and task-oriented, adjusting the focus and such.

The son purposefully turned and hurried to face his mother closely and directly, his arms cuffed behind his back. We could not hear his words. The mother bowed her head, then her weapon, then mourned her way into the cabin. The son then faced his accusers.

"If you go to take my mother, I will make it a matter of you having to kill me."

The downed soldier clawed his way off the dirt. Perez moved out into the open with his gun clearly aimed upon the son.

"Reynolds, you okay?"

The husky but short Reynolds rubbed his jaw. "It's not broken, but that lady is coming down."

"Re-think," Perez said: "One thing at a time. Let's get junior here while the getting is good." Perez took a moment to assure his partner by eye contact that there was time enough in this world to retreat and return.

"Okay, Barde," Reynolds said, waving the son over. "Let's go for a ride and talk this thing over. I doubt you did it myself, no shit. Let's just let the wheels of justice roll along."

I think I saw Barde grin; Gabe side-stepped toward me as he kept shooting. He whispered clearly to me: "Let's go before the Feds take this footage from me."

"Why would they do that?"

"Come on: First off, they're Feds; second, no one in their biz wants footage of them being knocked to the ground airing on the TV show, When Feds Get Kicked to the Ground.

I got behind the wheel and turned the engine over. With that I saw Reynolds and Perez look our way. They exchanged quick words on who would put the prisoner in the back seat and who would confiscate the camera, but I was gone.

Teplitz smiled from his shotgun seat, which is like a laugh for him. He said, "This might get interesting."

Though I had not done anything wrong, I pushed the Swinger to escape mode. This was the wrong road for that; we bounced and hobbled until I'm sure I did damage to the old girl. I eased up, seeing that no one was following. Out on the gravelly logging road I still told myself to take it easy... just heading back to the office, not running from federal agents or anything like that.

Then the government agents appeared in my rearview. I also saw in that trusty mirror that Barde did not occupy any part of the back seat. They hurried upon me and I pulled over. As Agent Reynolds freed himself from the front seat, I called back to him, "Hey, I was in the flow of traffic, wasn't I, officer?"

Gabe then did the damndest thing: He jumped from the vehicle and ran into the woods, up a deep incline of dense brush and trees, lugging that video camera and a backpack. Reynolds pursued. Perez asked me to get out. After a minute of standing there together he shouted for his partner, who then shouted back: "I can't find the little bastard!"

"Come on down here, partner, before you get molested by a bear."

Perez was handsome, in shape, and sounded educated.

We listened to Reynolds thrash his way through the brush, back to civilization. No doubt: Perez fit into his suit like a runway model, as opposed to his partner, whose body fought the idea of that type of garment tooth and nail. Reynolds appeared from out of the thick and came directly to me. His fist turned my fine-tuned machine of a mind into a vibrating, out-of-whack film projector. All images and sounds were interrupting each other as I fell to the hard earth in a heap. Then he kicked me in the gut and I began a scary search for my breath. I think I heard Perez tell him to stop. "One more for luck," Reynolds said, and gave me another swift kick, and I grasped for breath again. As I regained precious air, I heard Sergeant Richards' patrol car roll up over the many pebbles and stones. I pushed myself up to a sitting position, leaning back on the Feds' car. I saw Barde in the back seat of Richard's patrol car. Richards got out slowly, calmly. Ellerth got out with a puzzled expression on his face, which soon creased into a smile.

Richards said, "Well, now! What's going on here?" His tall frame hovered over the agents.

Reynolds shot back, "This guy was refusing to stop."

"I pulled right over, ya fucking goon!" I wiped blood from my lip.

"They had no business taking video of our procedures," Reynolds stated as a professional frothing dog.

Richards asked, "Where is Cecil B. DeMille?"

Reynolds squinted, confused by the reference. Perez jumped in for him. "The guy ran off into the woods with the video camera."

Richards walked up to me and offered down a hand. I took it and became a standing man again. Ellerth smirked at me. I gazed up into the woods in recognition of the Herald's brave photographer. Reynolds was then in my face again.

"I want that tape!"

Perez said, "Tape is over, partner."

"If I do not get that tape," Reynolds spit into my face, "or disk, or whatever the fuck, I will arrest you for obstruction!"

"You gotta be kidding me."

"No, paper boy, I am not! Until this case is over, I will not have any information released that does not first filter through me or Agent Perez."

I looked to Richards, who returned a shrug.

I said, "What you say may be all well and good, but you had no business fucking hitting me!"

"I want that..."

"Footage," Perez said.

Then, out of pure, stupid anger, I announced, "I'm going to make sure you don't get that footage!" Then I shouted at the woods: "Good job, Gabe! We'll rendezvous soon, brother reporter!"

Reynolds spun me around, and before I could say "your mother," he had the cuffs on me. "Until I get that tape, you're under arrest. Perez, grab those keys to this piece-of-shit Swinger. Let's see if Video Boy can make it back to town alive."

Richards stepped in front of Perez. "Boys," he began almost softly, "you all have your ways of doing things, and I swear that I am here to be of service, but that fellow out there is a nice little guy. We won't be leaving him walking down this mountain in the dark. Wait here for him, or you leave him the keys; we're not playing hardball just yet."

The two agents paused, then Reynolds dragged me to his car and pushed me in, making sure I didn't hit my head, the thoughtful mongrel. He would have to wait for a better time to mistreat me—like whenever Sergeant Richards wasn't around. From the back seat I looked across the road to Barde in Richard's back seat. He was already looking at me. Then he smiled, and I swore we were in third grade heading down to the principal's office.

KILLING THE BIRDS

Chapter Four

I have been in this cell a few times, in each of these three cells parked in the back of the station, out of sight, not out of sound, never sure if I was out of reach; a slow night; just me in my cell closest to the exit door, and Barde in the cell to my right. The big third cell that usually housed a collection of drunks and vandals held no one. We two were in recovery mode, I already having passed my loud swearing phase a few moments earlier. Barde had said nothing during my declaration of independence, and it seemed he had given up sharing fellow-victim grins with me as he stared straight ahead.

So I sat there going down Memory Lane.

My first stay at the Hotel Prisoner had come about due to my being drunk and walking out on a restaurant check. I had walked in knowing I was broke. Lacking funds didn't seem too important when I was drunk and hungry; drunk, young, and dumb – an unfortunate combination; sixteen and in love with beer and freedom. Then there were a couple of fights throughout my latter teenage years that brought me back to La Cage Retreat. Had I mentioned that school was a memory at age fifteen? I don't know what I said about it then, but it was just too hard to get that high every night and make it to school in the morning. One of them had to go. I told the folks I was staying over at Lucas' a lot: you know, studied, shot some hoops, hit the hay, awakened bright and early for school. After all, Lucas lived a mile from school, as opposed to old Living-in-the-Bush Holdsworth. What we really did was spend all our time scrounging and scamming for beer and pot money. And you know that all led a couple of Hendrix-loving freaks to LSD and magic mushrooms. Woo hoo! We missed the 60s, but we caught up, in our way. We tripped our brains out, sat on top of Lucas' roof, Rainbow Bridge blasting out the house windows. Now tell me: School or that?

Lucas never ended up in jail. Not once. He was usually there when the gang was making mischief, but he never got caught doing anything. I remember one time we were partying while walking the tracks. We stopped to throw rocks at a switchman's shack. (I tell myself now that I thought it stood abandoned, but no, I was just a drunken prick. The cops were suddenly there on foot, the sneaky bastards. I turned to run away, but a young recruit, Richards, came from the other end. I reeled around, staggered a few feet, just in time to see Wally Sims getting grabbed – but no Lucas. The second Lucas saw the flashlights he dropped to the ground, which was not where they were shining their lights at that moment, and he rolled into the ditch—a smelly, wet, mosquito-infested ditch that night. He lay there hushed throughout the raid, and then walked home when the coast was clear. Lucas, always quick-minded, had made up for his slow feet. Of course, his ditch-rolling days have long gone by.

I looked over at Mountain Man Barde. They had stripped him of his boot laces to eliminate the tasty option of suicide. He seemed to be missing other pieces of himself as well. The most memorable of the missing items was his vest. I remembered because it had a cool drawing on it of a river flowing between the mountains. After an apprehensive reticence, I pushed out words.

"You were at the funeral," I said to Barde. "That was you, out in the brush."

The big guy didn't even bat a lash. I throw out this great piece of deduction and he doesn't even flinch.

I continued, "You knew Jimmy, didn't you?"

His head jerked to stare at me, his eyes wide and piercing. I waited for words but they never arrived. I looked away. Under my breath I said, "Maybe you did do it."

He rose with a heavy sigh, moved over to the furthest corner of the cell from me, and leaned against the bars as if he intended to sleep that way. I decided to counter by finding sleep before him, and then snoring him into submission. I curled into a fetal position on the plank of painted wood and had a positive thought about Gabe's getting my car home safely. John Rogers was going to throw a party in our honor at the office; true reporters we; true to the bringing out of truth to the public. Then I heard Barde snoring from his standing position. He had to be faking, but the longer and louder he snored, the clearer it became that he was the king of finding sleep. Still, seeing it, hearing it, did not covert me; how could anyone sleep while standing? Was he part horse?

I woke to the cell's being unlocked, squinting up at Richards. Barde sat calmly, staring forward. I made it to a sitting position.

Richards said, "Good to have you back after all these years, Holdsworth! I hope it was everything you remembered it to be."

"Am I leaving?"

"Yeah, I got hold of your father just before he left for work, like you asked. Perez and Reynolds are out looking for Gabe."

"He's a slippery fellow."

"And I'm sure Gabe's already downloaded it and selling it to the highest bidder. Still, those agents are desperate to avoid embarrassment, you know, for the whole high school to see, so to speak. Funny how afraid we are of what other people think about us."

"Am I still charged with that obstruction bullshit?"

"For now we're running it through, but it'll all go away soon enough. And, Dan, you were never one to worry about causing yourself trouble. I'd call you downright self-destructive."

"I'm not as young as I used to be."

. . .

Dad and I walked quietly to his '90 Ford pick-up and remained mute for the first half of the ride to my place. I could see he would rather have been around the sound of loud saws and the smell of cedar, instead of getting his son home from lock-up.

"Do you want to hear about it?" I asked.

"You fell off the water wagon?"

"No. It's been almost a year. This was work-related."

He examined me doubtfully. "Doing your job doesn't land you in the hoosegow."

"You don't wanna hear it." I took in the scenery and cussed him out in my mind for being such an honest citizen.

He eventually said, "Okay, tell me."

I told him the whole story. I could see him trying not to react, trying to show that there were no more surprises in store for him from this world.

"So ya see, Pop," I said as we pulled up to my single-floor dwelling, "I was just doing my job."

He nodded and waited for me to get out. That really pissed me off. "C'mon, Dad, let's hear it!"

"There's nothing to hear. You want to play this gossip game for the sake of peek-a-boo entertainment, you get what you get. I'm not judging you."

"Bullshit. You and Ma have no respect for what I do. You know there's a lot of romance in being a reporter."

He looked over at me, carefully turning his mind's cogs to a place of perspective at which we might meet.

"I get that, Son. And I really hope it brings you happiness." He shook his head lightly, a small smile born of the search. "It's just hard for me to understand, that's all. You know that about me. Why are you upset? I have no taste for reading about humans committing the same old mean, sad, frustrated acts over and over again. I have a hard enough time keeping track of my own folly. I traded the newspapers for peace of mind. But I do respect you, Dan. I'm glad you haven't been drinking. Just don't ask me to join in the keeping-score game. I know the score. I was in that game a long time. I get to be away from it as much as you get to tangle with it."

I absorbed his meaning, then opened the truck door and slid out. I had made it halfway to my door when I heard his friendly voice:

"Hey, Dan: how about some fishing this weekend? It won't be long before the hindering weather."

I nodded up and down: "Sounds good, Dad." He drove off.

The man loved to fish. And he would talk about the world, his Chicago days, there in the cool wilderness, but not politics or current events. He preferred to reminisce about my grandparents, when they were young, when they were his parents, what they were like when they were alive. He loved history. He'd talk about who were the first ones to conquer this harsh area of the country: the Nez Perce Indians, the French trappers. How they survived and what they did for fun. But when it led to the silver mines and when Clarence Darrow came up in 1905 to defend labor organizer William Heywood, who had been accused of bombing and killing Governor Frank Steunenberg, the governor who was helping the companies to squelch the union rebellion, then Dad would trail off. I'd want him to tell me more. I'd say how those first unions had to be violent or things would have never changed, that maybe some things were worth dying for, that there was a bigger picture. Then he'd start talking about fishing, his grandkids, or something else. My mom said not to challenge my dad's beliefs, or his sanctuary from beliefs. She said to me once, "He fought for change; he doesn't want to fight or talk about fighting anymore."

I have never fought for anything. I drew glorified images of my recent actions as being arrested for keeping footage from the Feds as noble reporter first amendment stuff, but it was Gabe who ran into the woods; I got arrested because of Gabe's actions, and because Agent Reynolds had just been kicked to the dirt by a suspect in handcuffs.

As I opened my front door it occurred to me that Agents Perez and Reynolds, one or both, might be tracking me. They could have been out there waiting for Gabe to show up with my Swinger, which I did not see anywhere near my home at the moment. I eased into my supposedly empty home with eyes on alert. I checked every room and closet. Then I noticed my old message machine's blinking light.

"It's Gabe. Meet me where the fat man surfs the computer waves. And see if you have the capability to come alone. This is interesting, isn't it?" Click.

I stepped out my back door and paused. The clouds were lower than yesterday's. The wind blew harder, but no rain. I advanced down a path that led into the woods out back. I found a tree trunk to squat behind and looked out at the clearing from where I came. What do you know: that mutt Reynolds appeared from nowhere, hurrying after me. This would be so easy. This wasn't one of those Indian trackers, or even one of those Native American trackers. I could lead Reynolds anywhere and end up on the other side of him, which is exactly what I did. By the time he came out on the other side of the woods, which opened directly into an abandoned wood mill, I had hitched a ride. It was just a matter of making sure he heard me when I wanted him to hear me, and not hear me when I needed that. I left a piece of my shirt on a branch right in the middle of the path for him to find, to keep him salivating and moving forward while I doubled back.

When I entered Lucas' place, Gabe and the big man were in the midst of another violent video game. When I tried to interrupt, they hushed me in unison. I raided the fridge for a sandwich and a Coke and had a seat.

I said between bites, "It won't be long before they find out who my best friend is. We better get to work. Gabe? Gabe?"

Gabe sighed and turned on his stool, his eyes shaded from lack of sleep. He handed over the still photos. "There." Then he remembered something else. "Here's a disk with the video footage I already sold to Scoop TV. It'll probably be on the tube later this evening. I'll give Rogers a cut if I feel like it."

"How much did you get?"

"None of your fucking business, paper boy," he said, and then laid down on Lucas' couch for a nap. "I'm going to hide out a little longer."

I said to Lucas, "I guess I'm going run down to the paper to write a story to go with these pictures. Hey, Gabe, where's my car?"

"It's around back here," he answered from behind his eyelids.

"I got something for ya," Lucas said. He picked up a computer printout. "Two years ago in Northern California, a camping ground, a kid had a stake you use to secure a tent to the earth jabbed into his heart. He was nine, I think. Five years ago in Oregon, a kid was stabbed through the heart with a crow bar." I winced. "I guess he had to hammer that home, whoever the sick fuck was that did it. Lastly, seven years ago in Wyoming: This time it was a cattle prod of some sort."

"How'd you find all this out?"

He bowed toward his computer. "Work this puppy right and you can travel the world."

"You are something, Luke. But what the fuck does all this mean?"

Gabe rolled over and seemed to be listening with mild interest. Lucas only paused a moment to scratch his massive belly.

"I'd say this crazy bastard is trying not to kill. He moves on from the place that holds the memories of his madness. But a couple of years in the new place and the old madness returns. He really must get off on it. That, or he's purposefully doing these killings in different places, different times. There could be a pattern, could be a reason."

I said, "I guess we can't be totally sure this is the same guy."

"All the kids were missing their shoes," Lucas said simply. We took turns looking at one another.

I asked, "Why is he taking their shoes?"

Gabe said, "That's easy: Memorabilia."

I raised my brows. "There goes the escaping-bad-memories theory."

"You're right," Lucas replied. "There it goes."

. . .

I handed over the article to Boss Rogers and he held up the photos that went with it, and he smiled. "This is some sweet work you and Gabe did."

"I'm glad it makes you happy. Hey, you might make some money again in this dying newspaper market."

"Oh, I never made money, Skip. No. See, I always wanted to be a newspaper man, but the Mrs. and I never wanted to leave this wonderful homeland of ours, so we try not to lose too much money, break even as often as we can. I never told you that?"

I just shook my head.

. . .

I drove aimlessly about town and by the river, feeling celebratory, feeling like a real newsman, but also feeling sad for wanting to celebrate with a drink, and feeling sad for the lack of a lady by my side. Then I noticed the Feds tailgating me. I pulled over and got out with a friendly smile on my face.

"Agents Reynolds and Perez, I pray you well."

"Where's that video friend of yours?" Reynolds asked, refraining from getting in my face this time.

I turned in a circle with my arms open wide to say that I did not see him anywhere. Reynolds saw the disk on my dash, but I grabbed it first; the disk had no meaning, Gabe had already downloaded it off the camera and sold it, but it was my disk and I was a newsman. And why was Reynolds grabbing for it? Well, he kept using the word tape, so he was as lost in the past as I. We struggled over it and he elbowed me in the face.

. . .

I again sat in the cell next to Barde. I sprang to my feet and commenced to ranting, which, I've already said, is what I do first in lock-up, a kind of tradition.

I took a break and then checked out Barde, who seemed sure I had lost my mind. I asked, "Ever been to Oregon, you fucking animal? Ever been to Wyoming? Ever been to —"

I stopped because he had said something. I asked him what, but he sat quietly. I threatened to scream for the next twenty minutes if he did not repeat what he had said. Then the words came out of his mouth:

"I've never been out of Reverend River."

I was staring at him when Agent Reynolds and Sergeant Richards walked in. Richards asked, "What's with the screaming?"

"You know I scream, Serge."

"Yeah, I know you scream."

Reynolds asked, "You didn't think you were going to outsmart the FBI, did you, paper boy?"

I could not wait until the agents saw the happenings at Barde's mountain retreat on TV tonight for all to see, but all I said was, "This man's never been out of Reverend River."

Reynolds laughed heartily. "You don't think so, huh? Well, I guess just that old deerskin vest he was wearing has been catching Greyhound," and he leaned toward me, leaving less than an inch of space between the thumb and index finger of his right hand, "... because teeny-weeny, itsy-bitsy parts of it have been to Wyoming and Northern California."

"What about Oregon?" I asked. Richards and Reynolds both looked surprised by my knowledge, knowing of the dead boy there.

"I'm impressed," Richards said.

"Yeah, I guess the guy isn't too bad at this game," Reynolds said, feeling magnanimous from the vest evidence. "Well, no traces of Oregon on the vest, but that's okay: he'll fry hot enough for his trips to Wyoming and California."

No electric chairs out this way; Reynolds watched a lot old movies, I'm guessing.

I attempted to crawl behind Barde's eyes to find the truth of his mind. I guess all those drugs I did in my time made me think I could do that. But all I saw was a dirty, tall, human animal.

Reynolds chuckled and said, "Well, we got what we wanted from you, paper boy; you can run along home now."

I said, "You found evidence of the boys on the vest, but have you found evidence of Barde on the boys?"

Reynolds smiled. He seemed to almost like me for a moment.

"That DNA will take another day or two, but we got the fucking animal we were hunting. Even without that evidence, we got enough."

Again I looked at Barde, who focused quizzical eyes on the agent. My mouth hung open as I grappled with this man who had said he had never left Reverend River, a man who looked like he rarely left his mountain. Richards' voice broke through my thoughts:

"Come on, Dan, back to the real world of covering PTA meetings and pie-eating contests."

I gave Richards a sporting smirk. Then I smiled fully at Reynolds, and almost asked him if he would still be in town tonight, and could I come over and watch TV with Perez and him, just to see their faces if they happened on Scoop TV.

KILLING THE BIRDS

Chapter Five

When my mom said that Dad had done his time on the front line fighting, well, we are not talking Abby Hoffman or the guy who ties himself to a tree. He didn't scream at the top of his lungs spreading the new word. He was just another person who felt fairly sure that the wars since WW2 were fear and greed based, the masses being manipulated by the powerful few. He wrote some letters and attended some meetings and marched for peace in Chicago and Washington.

He was there when a particular crowd, filled with numerous young folks, called out their anger to the surrounding authority. Dad had gone to this rally for his two friends, Dave and Bill, two musicians who played quite a few protest rallies, and the old man tagged along just to keep an eye on his childhood pals. Long story short: They ended up in jail, all with minor wounds. Dad never told me all of it. He just said to beware of large groups of people who want to get together and shake their fists at another group of people. His old friend Bill told me more when he visited our mountain retreat. He said they had tried to leave when the rock-throwing started, but couldn't get through the mass that had become one long snake wiggling to and fro. When the snake finally did get cut in half, they were tossed ringside where angry cops—most of them—were fervently pounding any heads that they could access.

I was six years old then. Four years later we left Chicago. My folks just wanted to raise children, and wished for an end to the inner tug-a-war, between helping and being involved, and being mellow and happy.

. . .

I stood out front of the R & R police station, first pacing back and forth and kicking dirt up with my old work boots, then lowering my rump onto a cement pillar that kept cars from driving off into the steep ditch north of the building. It was only a mile-and-a-half walk to the paper, and another mile further to where we left my Swinger, but I wasn't ready just yet. I contemplated going back in and annoying Sergeant Richards, but he came out instead.

"Want a ride, Dan?"

"Serge, a deerskin vest can't kill anyone."

"You're right. They'll have to find something to go with it. And you know they most likely will. He'll have left some trace in one of those towns."

A drizzle lightly christened the earth yet again, and we both let it touch us. I wanted something from Richards but I could not say what—maybe one last quote to bring closure to the final Wagner-boy-murder article I had begun writing in my head... the last one until the trial, if anyone cared by then.

Richards asked, "Why do you find it so hard to believe he did it?"

"I just don't think he ever got off Baldy much, let alone hitched to Wyoming."

Richards offered me the ride to my ride again and I took it. I watched the windshield wipers going back and forth obediently, bringing momentarily clear sight—ever momentary. He said, "So, you'll put yourself in this next story, tell how you spent another night jail next to mountain man Barde."

"The people would like that," I said.

He nodded and smiled.

When I got to the office my fellow news people clapped and whistled. Some went so far as to pat me on the back. "Tell us all about it," Kelley, the sports guy who was born after the Vietnam War, said. The elder sports scribe waved from across the room and shuffled endlessly toward me as he fastened the top button of his Bing Crosby sweater, and said, "You nosed your way into the bigs, kid." His ancient eyes sparkled as he touched my shoulder, and I filled a cup with black liquid speed. Gracie toed up to my right ear to whisper, "Are you okay, Dan?" I told them to read my article tomorrow. I did not see Boss John, but went into his office all the same and took a seat. I pushed the chair back against the wall and closed my eyes. I awakened five minutes later as he moved by me to the worker's side of the desk.

He combed his thin, grey hair with his fingernails and said, "I have information for you—information that no one else has. He tossed a file over to me. "Don't just sit there; we're holding deadline on you." He loved saying that.

Most of the information was stuff Lucas already had: names of victims, places and times, but one thing jumped off the page: the reason the sick bastard took off their shoes. He drew on the bottom of their left foot a type of bird, that particular state's bird. Well, he did not draw it truly: he carved it with what must have been a delicate, thin carpenter's knife.

He had left his mark and kept the shoes for keepsakes. What a sweetheart.

I typed my experiences with the law and the case into a reporter's presentation. I went long, but John was thrilled with the copy and just let it exist. We had beaten the whole country to the story, the Feds' having gone mute on the old case, afraid their known presence in Reverend River would tip the killer. The nation's papers, magazines, and TV news programs were calling us from coast to coast for pictures and more background—and of course, sent them running to their local

FBI contacts. The story not only kicked the war off our front page, but Chicago's Tribune, the Washington's Post's—you name it. Agent Reynolds' being kicked to the ground by mountain man Barde played for packed audiences in front of their TV sets everywhere over the next few days. Gabe never revealed what he got paid.

Everyone wanted to know about the man who killed boys and drew birds on their feet... so they came to Reverend River.

They stood outside Mrs. Barde's home talking into cameras, saying things like, "In this small cabin atop a rugged mountain, alleged killer Kenneth Barde planned his next trip of death. What state was he planning to visit next? Stay with us for full coverage."

The townsfolk were making money they could have never foreseen. The hotel and boarding houses had extra clients. Folks were paid to show the press and other visitors up to the Barde cabin or to other worthy backdrops. And believe it or not, Scoop TV paid me ten grand for my exclusive accounts. After all, I had been in the cell next to the famous "Bird Man" not once, but twice. Lucas said I should have held out for more, but I've never had ten grand at once before. These were good times for those of us who could profit from the killing of boys.

The Scoop TV correspondent, Ty Riggs, came into my living room after all the technical lighting and camera duties had been completed. He introduced himself like a football star and went right into the questions. Here are some of them:

"How did it feel to be that close to the devil? Do you always keep track of the police airwaves? Did Barde tell you why he killed those boys? Allegedly, I mean. How's the fishing here in the spring?"

My brother called from Chicago, my sister from Tennessee. She wanted to make sure I was still coming with Mom and Dad for Christmas. (The folks still had no problem traveling together to see their grandkids; the two who carved out a life here remained family.) I said Christmas in Nashville just could not be missed, and all here would have settled down by then anyway. My niece and nephew got on the line to ask what it was like to be in a cell next to a killer, especially a killer so specifically crazy. I said that everyone was innocent until proven guilty. I don't think they bought it.

Mom called to insist that I come up to talk with her.

. . .

The clouds were hanging low again, creating a ceiling that made the whole countryside intimate. It had been raining for days; all the back roads were muddy, soft and slippery. I had just put new tires on the Swinger, so I felt safe. Lucas laughed that I should buy a proper vehicle with the TV money. I held tight to that money, though, not sure when I might really need it. However, I did begin repairs on my snowmobile. Winter in Reverend River without a snowmobile was for chumps.

Mom hugged me hard, having hurried out to the car to greet me. She even got misty-eyed. Goofy, strong, not easily pushed around by this tough world – Ma Holdsworth. Yes, I took note of her shaking limbs, her firm grip. I had been out and about sparring a bit with a serial killer, getting beat on by FBI agents, all of this surely leading back to the alcohol consumption that sought to consume me. Shelly Holdsworth was strong, but vulnerable where her children were concerned.

She made me tea and fried zucchini and we talked about the strange events. I tried to change the subject. For example, was she excited about the Christmas trip? She kept bringing the conversation back around, though.

"Dan, I know this is a dangerous planet no matter where you turn, but seriously, of all the peaceful mountain spots, you're up Baldy while the police are confronting a nut."

"It wasn't a Bruce Willis movie, Ma."

"You're running up Baldy to get some stupid story that the people who need to hear, the families of those boys, will get without you. Is it really that important to be in on the comings and goings of crazy people? Do you need to be part of their lives?"

"Come on, Ma. I usually cover carnivals and government legislation. This was a once-in-a-lifetime deal."

"So you've got a taste for it now? You'll be searching out more of this type of investigative work? You'll be running off to LA to cover the underworld of the movie business?"

I laughed so hard I nearly fell from the old wicker chair. Ma eventually joined in. She said through a smile, "And I don't want to hear that you're a war correspondent across the seas in that sad place." She smiled at the planet's magnitude and then laughed to release her concerns—a silly girl's giggle, really, but with years under her belt. I looked into her long, lined face and saw the woman who needed that humor to survive out here—to continue anywhere, I guess.

She took away the empty plates, replaced the tea with cold water, and played her Fender acoustic guitar; John Denver, of course. This "hippie" runaway always preferred Denver to Bob Dylan. And man, could she sing his songs. Alive! She came alive with his words falling off of her tongue. While she was singing "The Eagle and the Hawk" I moved about the old Holdsworth home. I scrutinized the stairs that for many years used to be a ladder leading up to our bedrooms. I remember that when Dad finally built the stairs, he cut into that huge tree that ran across the house. He wanted the stairs to join perfectly with it, but he couldn't get it even, so he kept cutting into the house's largest beam. My mom became very nervous, saying that that was a very important load-bearing tree. Finally she screamed for him to stop carving into it, and instead he cut into the bottom of the stairs to make it even. "For Christ's sake, John, use your brain!" My dad's nostrils flared. Shame came. He realized what an idiot he had been, that she clearly had the brains that evening, but when my mom started laughing, he gladly joined in, as did we kids. We had survived another growing pain, another challenge to build onto our lives.

Now she resided in the house alone: two kids across the country, one married to the town and a husband who wanted to be in line before God.

I slept over at her request. What a shit I would have been to say no, as I had done so many times. She read me some of her poetry just before lights-out; lovely phrases groping for Earth's breasts and the spirit's brawny will. She kissed me on the cheek and climbed those well-connected stairs. I slept on the couch when I stayed over; I snored and did not like to disrupt any peaceful dreams she might be having in the country's pure dark.

I stayed on the next day, helping with chores and taking a hike up the mountain at whose feet our cabin was nestled, but it was too muddy to keep that up, and we retreated to harvesting the last of her peppers and onions. We pressure-cooked some peaches and then we swept and mopped the floor. Dinner contained sprouts, fried zucchini and homemade applesauce.

Then, without the sound of a car, came a knock at the door, only a pause, and then the entry of one of our long-time neighbors, Milton Wesley. I could see he was surprised—and disappointed—to see me. He smiled and chuckled. We exchanged pleasantries. Talk turned to my adventures as a news man. Then I said I had left some things undone, kissed my mom hard on the cheek so she would know I meant it, and jumped into my Swinger. Mom was not as alone as I had thought. I was glad, I was sad.

. . .

Day's sight had completely vanished by the time I got to Lucas' with his groceries. He appeared happy and sad himself; happy to see me, a little sorrowful that I might have forgotten about him.

"I thought you were dead; you know, the way things have been around here lately."

"Sorry, Luke—spent last night and today with my mom."

He adjusted his darkened spectacles and scratched the skin hiding beneath his ever-growing beard. "That's nice. How is she?"

"Real good—I think she has a boyfriend."

"No."

"Widower Wesley, about two miles south."

"Well, that's good, isn't it?"

"Yeah, I guess it is."

I looked over at him and I could see the goose bumps, the pleasure sensation of fresh consumables being placed into his fridge, and by his best friend to boot. He and my mom were alike: neither wanted to venture too far out too often, and so enjoyed a visitor.

We watched a DVD I had rented and then played some video games. Then another seldom-heard knock was heard upon Lucas' door. I opened it to see a woman with dark hair, blue jeans and a sports jacket. She smiled.

"I'm sorry to disturb you in the evening. I was looking for a Dan Holdsworth. I was told I might find him here."

"That's me," I said, not offering her entrance.

She flashed credentials. "I'm a journalist from the Boise Tribune. I was hoping we could talk. My name is Rosa Baline."

"Oh, come on. There's nothing more that I can say about all this. Besides, I think my contract with Scoop TV prohibits me from going on record with any other media group for a couple of more days."

"I didn't want to talk about Kenneth Barde. Though that did story did bring someone to our doorstep with a story about you."

"Listen, I really haven't —"

"You'll want to talk to me before I write this article. Can we go somewhere and talk? It's about what happened to you in Rand Point."

My blood ran cold. Could she be referring to the incident? Of course she was. Please, Lord, not that horror getting connected to the Kenneth Barde story!

All I could manage to say was, "Please."

"Where can we talk?" she asked.

I stepped back and let her in. "Lucas, this is Rosa Baline. She's here to ruin my life."

"It's about time someone got around to that little chore," Lucas quipped, not picking up on what I meant. "Would have done it myself, but you can see I'm not in the best of shape." From his chair he reached out his hand to Rosa, who took it graciously. Lucas had had several beers, so nothing was tightening him up too badly. I, on the other hand, stood in the middle of the room in sober prayer. I heard my voice offer her a drink. She asked me if I were sure I wanted to discuss this in front of my friend. I informed her that my friend knew more about me than even clever reporters. She took a seat on the couch and asked for a Coke.

After handing her the beverage, I said, "Spare me the suspense and let me know what you know."

"It's about the child molestation charge."

"I was never charged," I said strongly. Then softer, "I was never charged." I sat down shaking my head, trying to make it go away, and looked over at Lucas. He had come around to my grief and embarrassment.

He said, "You have nothing to be ashamed of, bud. Don't let this drag you down all over again."

Rosa said, "Look, tell me your side. I don't want this piece to be apocryphal."

I squinted at her. Lucas explained, "Apocryphal: not genuine authorship." I nodded. Then he said to Rosa, "That word is more about counterfeit than about getting facts wrong."

"I took liberty with it." Then she continued: "I'm not out to hurt anyone. I was just doing background on this Bird Man story and came upon this claim against you. I mean: the guy who breaks the news to the country about the Bird Man, accused of child molestation—it's not diurnal."

I stood up and sighed heavily. "Di-what?"

Again Lucas chimed in as my human dictionary. "Diurnal: a daily happening."

"Lady," I said, then paused, "skip the college words; I'm not a fucking thesaurus. Unless you want to talk to Lucas here, dumb it down some, okay? I'm just a small-town writer. We all didn't graduate from Boise-fucking-U." I stalked the room trying to calm down. Then I said, "What did Melissa tell you?"

"It wasn't Melissa—it was her brother Pat. From what I understand, the only reason he didn't go to the authorities back then was that his sister had begged him not to."

"But a good story gets around all the same," I said with a sneer.

"Dan... may I call you Dan?"

"If you're going to humiliate me from coast to coast, I'd prefer that you called me Mister Holdsworth." I opened the fridge, gazed seriously at the beer, then slammed the door closed, leaving my old friend behind. I sat down and sulked.

Lucas reminded me, "They can't get to you if you don't care what the world thinks."

I stared a hole through him. He raised his arms and retreated. The reporter then got down to business, pulling a small recording device from her jacket, and then removing the jacket from her person. I could see that Lucas had nothing against the view.

"Mr. Holdsworth, why don't you just tell me what happened those many years ago?"

My eyes found hers as I asked disdainfully, "Those many years ago?" Then my eyes found the wall beyond the TV. "Well, those many fucking years ago I lived in Rand Point with the lovely Melissa Ryan. She had a five-year-old boy named Colin. Colin's father had joined the Navy and had only been back to see the boy once since he was born. Anyway, Melissa waited tables a few nights a week. She got back around eight in the morning, sometimes nine. I was sleeping on the couch this particular morning. Colin comes out to wake me and ask me for breakfast, and he's naked as a jaybird, as he always was in the morning, a ritual for the free boy. I'm wiping the sand from my eyes, the boy standing next to the couch bitching for breakfast, when Melissa's brother Pat knocks and enters in one beat. He pauses, and then asks if his sister is back yet. I inform him that she has yet to return from work. He says something clever, like 'Oh,' and exits stage right."

Rosa then interrupted me. "That's all he said, and then left?"

"Yeah, because he knows that Colin ran around in the morning nude. He knew nothing was going on."

"But —"

"Let me finish, Rosa, darling. Pat hated me. Before I came along he had been the main man in Colin's life—his sister's life, too—but more than that, he thought very little of Writer Boy Me. So he tells Melissa that he caught me with Colin nude. She says that's no big deal. But then he adds that Colin was under the covers with me. I find all this out almost a month later. The two of them co-existed with me while they thought I might be a molester of this sweet kid. So they do what stupid fucking adults do when talking to a child about sex: They talk around it. 'Did you and Dan play any games... games that involved parts of your body?' After a day or two of this, sweet little Colin says, 'We played a game where the alligator bites my weenie.'"

I stopped. I rubbed my forehead hard.

"Was there such a game?" Reporter Girl asked me.

"When I used to cook for him, if he was impatient, he would start to talk silly to me. I would get silly with him in return. And one time we got to talking about animals sneaking into our tent, like we were camping—ridiculous animals, eventually, not animals from around here, but the ones he saw on TV. I'd be making him breakfast, and I'd say, 'The Rhino has me by the toe, buddy Colin. Better come over and help me.' He'd say, 'A tiger has me by the arm. Better finish cooking and come help me, buddy Dan.' Well, you heard it coming down the street: He said, 'An alligator has me by the weenie.' And for the rest of the morning, every animal that ever existed had him by his weenie. You don't know how that kid and I laughed. And then one day Pat points a rifle at me and says, 'You fucked Colin!'"

I had shouted, and Lucas and my new friend Rosa both shivered for an instant.

I blurted the rest feverishly: "I rumbled out of the apartment, leaving many valuables behind. I would wake up in the hotel where I went to stay and swear Pat was across the room from me, holding that damn rifle, a figure in the dark. Even when I made it back to Reverend River, I waited for him and his weapon, adjusting my eyes to the dark of whatever room I was in, squinting for the man with a gun."

Rosa's dark eyes actually seemed transfixed, as if by the truth of a moving story. Lucas had his head bowed.

"Of course I called Melissa to ask her if she could believe such a thing of me. You know what the love of my life said? She said she didn't know. She said, and I quote, 'But Pat saw you.' Well, I waited for the cops to come, but they never did. I was thankful for that, if I was thankful for anything at that unbelievably painful time. But I had to tell people, people I cared about, and wanted them to still care about me; I had to tell them what caused the breakup, Pat said he saw me under covers with Colin. Of course, any smart person could do the math. I am seen molesting that boy, and still living there weeks later. But still, to have to say it? To know that Pat told every single fucking person he knew? And now Rosa from Boise gets to decide what she believes. Well, have fucking fun with your stupid fucking story!" I turned to storm out, but reeled back around, leaned in toward Rosa, and said, "I know it's too good to pass up."

I then did storm out and made it as far as the road, but I retraced my steps and squatted on Lucas' front steps. Hot tears scalded my cheeks. A few minutes later she pushed open the door, stood over me, then found a home down on the porch beside me. She just sat there a full minute, looking out at nothing. I too remained still and quiet, wondering where this might go. She finally said, "I believe you."

Chapter Six

Rose Baline climbed down into her small rented car and took off on an hour drive to the hotel in Rand Point. The story would not hit the papers, I believed; I believed Rose believed me. I also believed Lucas when he said that as long as I did not care what the stupid fucking world thought, I wouldn't go crazy. But none of that stopped me from going directly to Lucas' fridge and throwing back a beer. I was pissed at the world and they were going to pay for it, even if I had to cover the tab by hurting myself.

Lucas went through many emotions that showed clearly on his fat face as I remained standing by the sink, hurrying through my second beer: first, plain surprise. It had been so long that he had finally accepted my sobriety. Then he began to giggle; his old drinking buddy was back! Then a somber, world-weary sigh, for hadn't my drinking and drugging almost killed me in the past? Then a new concern: Hey, he's drinking all my beer! After my fourth, I dashed to my car for a beer run.

I returned with two cases.

"Hey!" Luke exclaimed. "Where's the party?"

"This thing may go on a while and I don't wanna to be running for beer when I'm drunk."

"You've always been wise, in your way."

I put a few choice CDs in his player that could hold five at a time. The first was Johnny Winter. I rolled out Lucas' golf rug and searched out the putters. This is one of the only motivations that pulled Lucas from his chair. The list also included getting up to go to bed, rising from his chair at the bathroom door, getting up sometimes when he cleaned up around the place—which I mostly did, by the way—and golf. At these times his legs would tremble at the knees first, and then reveal that they could still hold the weight. Always he grabbed hold of a part of his body where his insides reacted to the rare movement. Where golf was concerned, I had to pick up all his balls.

An hour of golf and then we were just kicking back and talking about old times. Smirking, laughing, and bitching. Our eyes opened wide when we recalled with disbelief the truth of our old daring ways. Our craniums nodded softly toward the folks that had departed one way or the other, or the times that had departed, the days that had died. Ultimately the demon that liquor attracted popped into my head.

I pulled out a wad of cash.

"Luke, while I was out, I figured I should visit the ATM—money for pizza or whatever." He danced his excitement from the chair, his arms and chest roving in search of funk. "But look at this," I said innocently. "This is way more money than we'd ever need for ten pizzas."

He retrieved a joint from the counter next to him. "Well, this is one of my last."

"Give Wells a call," I said. "And while you're talking to the guy, see what else is floating around."

My old drug buddy beamed with excitement. "We're going to be bad, aren't we, Dan?"

"It's all in how you look at it, Watson: perspective, elementary, coo coo ca choo—Sammy Davis Junior and those not as talented."

Lucas giggled as he texted.

His man got back to us twenty minutes later. In the middle of the conversation Lucas lowered the phone to consult with me. "He's got the bud and some blow, but I thought maybe you were thinking about something more abstract as well. I mean, if I know Mad Man Holdsworth."

"Tell him to bring by a half ounce, a ball, and to make a few calls to see if Timothy Leary is about. Or if the parlor has some of those special pizza toppings."

The wheels were in motion. The least on its way to our den was pot and cocaine, but we held out hope for a return of the Sixties: acid, magic mushrooms. Everything a mind climber needs to venture up and monumentally inward. Peace, love, and Jimi Hendrix.

Wells showed up a very different-looking person from when I saw him a week ago. (Was that only a week ago?) Last week his long, heavy-metal hair was washed, cologne wafted—probably in the name of his girlfriend—and his clothes were clean. Today the hair clung to his scalp in clumps from the grease. His shirt had a ketchup stain and he smelled as if he hadn't bathed during that week. My nose also detected urine fumes, like he had pissed his pants the last time he had passed out and had taken no notice of it. Speaking of noses, his was running, and he kept wiping at it with his sleeve. He talked a mile a minute.

"I couldn't come up with the shroomies or the acid. But look at this bud!" He threw a half ounce of skunk bud at Lucas. "I might be able to get in touch with a guy in Rand Point if you guys want to take that drive." Lucas and I looked doubtfully at each other. "Wait till you taste this blow. Let me get things started. But here." He tossed a tightly wound baggie of blow at Lucas. Wells, shaking, took his own stash out and began breaking some up on a CD cover, never taking a breath from talking. "Fucking stuff is as uncut as I've ever scored. And I didn't cut yours. I wanted you to know what the real stuff is like, for once in your fucking miserable, pathetic lives, but next time you call, well, I have already cut the rest. Hey, that's blow biz. A guy's got to make a living. But hey, I only cut it some, ya know. It's still killer blow. I mean, ya know, the thing is, well, you all been there, you know. I don't have to tell you. You know what I mean?"

He made me uncomfortable. I was once again in the underworld: jittery dealers doing too much of their own product, late-night attacks on your own body, and a less-than-zero morning coming up. For the sake of your fix you're keeping company with an incoherent fool, but you nod your head like he's really onto something, a drug scene Mark Twain.

He continued on. "Mary left me. Ya believe that? Bitch! No, I don't mean it. She's in rehab. Ya believe that shit? She just couldn't handle her drugs. She had to go all the way down to Boise because I kept calling her and she kept falling back into my bed—my bed of dope." He guffawed. Then he looked suspiciously around the room, at the doors and windows. "She's going to be staying with an aunt down there. The aunt talked her into leaving me and going into rehab down there. I call her the anti-Wells." He looked at us to confirm him the Grand Master of drug dealers. We smiled pretentiously. After a few more minutes of Rapid Wells, we all dove down for some lines.

Oh, the immense pleasure! The mind orgasm! Look, Ma, no hands! Look, Ma, no brains! I've watched movies in which the characters do blow and just go right back to rambling. When that stuff hits my mind's sweet spot, I just want to lean my head back and wade in the pool with the endorphins. From my pleasure dome I peeked at Wells cutting out more and then snorting. He did not have to hold his one nostril closed to get it up the other. Me? That almost wasn't good enough. I must have a small passage up there or something. I have to close off the one nostril, and even then it's a life-and-death struggle to get a good line up there in less than three tries. But at this moment I would say it was so worth the effort. Wells' babbling did not annoy me at the moment; just a distant TV program I wasn't watching. Lucas lit up a joint and we took turns being Humphrey Bogart.

After a few lines, a lot of psycho-babble and a round or two of golf, I felt the need to begin drinking again. My nerves were now unprotected by normalcy. The euphoria of the first holy lines had become a pattern of keeping above water. Less than zero awaited our arrival, but alcohol would help all that. Good old fucking beer—then another line. They shouldn't call this stuff cocaine. They should call it more! Why hadn't I picked up some Wild Turkey or vodka? Our little-town liquor stores were closed now. I would have to drive to Rand Point if we needed more provisions. And with Wells starting to drink our beers, well, there might be no choice.

Wells received a text and Lucas and I held our breath. This was most likely just one of the many calls he would get at this hour of the night: drunken customers thinking of how they could keep on drinking with the help of Joe Blow. And a customer it was. My psychedelic hopes deflated. But hey, maybe Wells would leave then, and stop drinking our beer. I would take that. And I really should not be driving to Rand Point. I had never gotten a DUI, and considered myself lucky. Wells told us how sorry he was that he couldn't stay longer. We expressed our disappointment. Then he got another call. In the middle of the conversation he lowered the phone to ask, "You guys want to drive for some really good shrooms? Think about it, cuz we ain't taking my car. And if I play middleman, you guys are going to have to throw me an eighth."

My eyes consulted with Lucas. He tried to be my friend by saying, "You better not, Dan—maybe tomorrow."

But I knew opportunities. If we didn't do it now I might never do mushrooms again. This peddler would have his phone off the hook the rest of the week, the rest of my life. That's the way addicts think: since I'm never ever going to do this again, well, bring out the dancing bears.

"Tell him we're on our way, Wells."

I hoped to get out of town without seeing whoever was on the night patrol, Ellerth or the new guy. I slid down Main Street absorbing the town's after-hours feel. The mill across the river asked, "Where ya going, Dan?" I ignored it. Then my tires massaged the riverside route doing fifty, the recommended speed for this area of it. I started to feel good. A night drive, the radio on. I even cracked my window to let the cold night air wash my face. The dark river kept pace with me and rock cuts directed my Swinger sternly. I was legally drunk, but the blow kept me wide awake. I giggled out of nowhere and Wells joined in. He said, "Like old times, eh, Danny?" And he was balls-on accurate about that, for better and most certainly worse, both sides always. The world used the heads-or-tails question to arbitrate an answer, but it's a canard.

I got nervous again as we came to the lights of Rand Point. I hadn't been there since the incident and a shiver jolted down my spine. I had not prepared myself for that. It was less sleepy this time of night than old R & R, and I felt even more conspicuous. I said a prayer that no authority figure would find my Swinger worth pulling over. (For an agnostic, I prayed a lot.) I drove along perfectly, but that didn't mean anything. Your DUI could come all the same: a tail light out, a yellow light, a little swerve to miss a pot hole.

Finally Wells pointed me down a side street.

The exchange went smoothly. The guy let us, but then had us wait there. As we waited, a child in Star Wars pajamas slept-walked through the hall to the kitchen for some water. With the glass in his hand, he stopped to recognize our existence. Since we were nothing he hadn't seen before, he continued his journey back to his room.

"I'm only selling halves," the kindly peddler said. "I hope you have the cash, or you wasted your trip. That's one-twenty."

I handed him the funds and he handed me the baggy. Wells went to make some old-time talk. The man wearily smiled and opened the door for us to leave. Next stop: liquor store for some Wild Turkey and vodka. That would just about tap me for the night.

On the way back on the winding riverside road, I uncomfortably asked Wells, "So, you got a customer to take care of?"

"Fuck him. He still owes me money."

"Maybe he'll pay you back."

"No, he told me on the phone he just had enough for his much-needed sixteenth."

"Aw, don't leave the guy hanging."

"Well, maybe you could drive me down there, wait for me, and then we can get back to partying."

I searched for the right words for half a minute. Then I just had to say it. "Wells, I'm going to give you a fat eighth, but I gotta tell ya, when I trip, I can get self-conscious. You know, unless... unless..."

"I know what ya mean, man. Don't worry; we're going to have a good time."

"Wells, I just want to trip with Lucas. I'm sorry, really. Please don't take offense."

His brows furrowed and then they rose. "Oh, you don't want me around talking on and on. Don't worry, man; I'll be cool; we'll have a good time."

"Look, I haven't done any of this in a year, longer for the shrooms, and hey, we have already had a good time. But I just want to talk with my best friend for a while. Please understand."

"I understand, Dan. I mean, you've always been kind of—no offense—a weenie, but don't leave me to trip alone."

"Look, I'm going to make this fat eighth. You can drop by like Santa Claus somewhere. God, can you imagine how happy you're going to make that lucky son of a bitch—maybe this guy who wants the blow. But I'm not asking you, Wells, I'm telling you: I'm going to trip with just Lucas. When it starts to get weird, well, me and Lucas..."

"I got ya, man. Don't sweat it. I didn't mean to get bogged down at your place anyway. I was just bringing you guys the goods. I got things to do."

"And God bless you for coming by—really, thank you."

All was shaping up for a good old Lucas and Dan Mind Meld. I would get to Lucas' place, Wells would get in his car, and I'd lock the door behind me. I turned up Nog Hill with a smile in my mind. Then I saw the lights flashing behind me. I pulled over and said another prayer.

I had one thing going for me: It wasn't the new guy, who was a stranger to me. Ellerth stepped up to my window with his overgrown flashlight.

"What are you up to now, Holdsworth?"

I tried to act casual. "Hey, Ellerth, ya mind not flashing that damn thing in my eyes?"

"Kind of late for a ride, isn't it, paper boy?"

"I'm just bringing Lucas some supplies." I cocked my head toward the brown bag in the back seat.

"What is it?"

"Provisions."

"You're going to make me reach back there?"

"It's a bottle of Wild Turkey and a bottle of cheap vodka. Lucas is having a few guests over tomorrow."

Ellerth had to lean back fully to release the mirth. After cackling, he pointed the flashlight at Wells. "Oh, I see; it's the candy man. Who's going to bail you out this time, Wells?" Then he put the light back into my eyes. "Little Dan is off the wagon. It's a shame... a real shame. You must really like that cell, Holdsworth. You've been gone, but you're out to make up for lost time."

I shifted into the plead gear. "Man, Ellerth, I'm three blocks from a safe parking job. You know me: I'm out to hurt no one; I've never cracked up. I'm a nuisance, maybe, but come on..."

"I just wonder what you all got in your pockets. I mean, what other kinds of provisions did you bring back from Rand Point? I was having a burger when I saw you all taking the route out of town."

"Just the booze, I swear," I said.

I have to give credit to Wells: He knew enough to keep his mouth shut. Ellerth did not like him. One word, civil as could be, and we'd both be in lockup.

"I just know there's something good in your pockets," Ellerth said with a grin. "You boys skiing the powdery slopes? Maybe you got something green in your pockets, I don't mean pot; Mister Scoop TV here, making money off our work."

I said, "Man, I got ten bucks, but it's all yours."

"How about Mister Wells over there?" Ellerth asked with an aggressive smile.

Wells bowed his head and said, "Oh shit."

I said fast under my breath, "Hand me something. I'll cover you tomorrow." He looked me in the eye. I hissed, "Damn it, I'll cover you!" He handed me three twenties, which I handed to Officer Ellerth, who then tipped his cap and went back to his car and drove off.

In front of Lucas', I said good night to Wells. He was worried that Ellerth might pull him over. I told him that Big E was off to Bell Road for a money girl. Wells said something out of the corner of his mouth as he drove off, something about us all getting old fast. I shook there for a moment from a lingering fear from the moment with Officer Ellerth, which then became tingling relief.

Inside Lucas' fortress I deftly split the mushrooms in half and we ate them all. Folks always complain about the pungent taste. They taste like dirty mushrooms to me. But most folks are wimps anyway. We sat back and smiled at each other, anticipating the warm, fuzzy, hilarious feelings coming our way. But like Hunter Thompson said: You usually wait, thinking you're not getting off, and then you begin planning revenge on the scum that burned you, and the next thing you know, the walls are breathing.

First, though, with mushrooms, you invariably begin to feel tired, yawning. You swear you're coming down with a cold. You make jokes to your partner that maybe you'll just go take a nap for a while.

Next thing I knew the walls were breathing, and the floor was, too. I began chuckling. Lucas joined in. I couldn't believe how hard it was hitting me. I have had a few fantastic laughing trips, but I never got the colors or breathing walls like my friends had. An hour into this and it was a hailstorm of colors. Sparking green traces running around the bathroom door. Blue flame spurts coming off of Lucas' green t-shirt. The floor had waves like a little lake. My face felt rubbery as God's warm hand patted my head.

I said to Lucas, "Man, I heard about it being like this," stopping to laugh, "but wow!"

His smile threatened to break his face in half. And again, invariably, on mushrooms, as was now the case, my head fell back as if I had passed out. My nose snorkeled for a moment as a snore. And then a common occurrence commenced:

It was as if my mind and spine were in it together to make me a tree. And in my mind I saw tree trunks, some ripped from the ground, leaving huge holes in the earth. I swore that I—sitting in that chair—was partaking in a gathering, a universal truth dangling before me. I popped back up to see Lucas with his head plopped back like I had just been. I burst out laughing and did not stop for a full minute. A newcomer to the room would have had no other choice but to think me insane. Well, give me insanity… sometimes. The warmth oozed as God hugged me thoroughly. I laughed and wrapped my arms around myself.

When I let my head fall back again, the visions in my brain were of melting and collapsing. Whatever image came into view immediately began falling in on itself—earth, tunnels, houses, me—melting, caving in; we were returning to being the one thing; I did not altogether like that. I felt the inevitable ending of everything, of me. Then I had a thought: that the world was trying to be infinite by knowing when to end and start up again, thus always keeping the main fire fed. I laughed a molten heat. I felt blessed and insightful. The opposite of collapsing commenced; all was light and rising. The tunnel led up with colors sparkling and then bleeding. Infinite truths to the Being Puzzle came and went like a stage hand telling me there were ten minutes until show time, then five, then two. Again, the house fell in on itself slowly. Tree sap ran down the tree as the tree became sap and vanished into the ground. The tunnel led me up not toward light, but toward more tunnels. Tree branches became tunnels, tunnels became tree branches. Then an astounding thought had me laughing with my head facing the ceiling: Death and life but one ball rolling on forever.

This all went on for a good while. The best while, really. There's kissing a girl, which is just the best feeling. Knowing your mother loves you: that's all-important, but to love yourself this way... it's a miracle. It's the only thing that has made me contemplate God in a serious fashion. Put plainly: this fungus was a true phenomenon in its specific effect on the human mind.

Then the blasting climax fell back as a wave that would not make it beyond the cusp of the shore, let alone across the ocean. This ushered in a very grand time as well. We poured alcohol on it and talked and smoked pot, which led to more hysterical laughing. But now there were two people, and a more practical bent to the humor. The alcohol, pot, and mushrooms were in love. Lucas and I talked until our tongues were tired.

I said, "Let's put a comedy in, pass out, get up in the morning, start drinking, then finish the blow."

Who was I kidding? We did the blow and power drank the hard stuff, babbled, and then watched a Bill Maury movie, *Quick Change*, eventually passing out—but only for three hours, since all the chemicals would not allow much sleep. We awoke, had a bite to eat, and began drinking, smoking, and shooting golf. And God's in his Heaven and Jesus is holding.

This is what Lucas and I called making a proper stew, using your skull as the pot and the mind as the main meat and fat. We stirred and mixed and added more of what we had left. We had done this so many times in our relationship, in our time together. We never died, though. The ones who had died were just pussies, I guess. Or maybe I had taken my year off just in time. Maybe I was that close to joining the great passers-on. Either way, we were alcoholic drug addicts, and I could never explain what it was to be that to anyone, even myself. But as painful as it is to be what I am, honestly, that's how much fun it is as well.

There is so much pleasure to be balanced against the pain and risks, so much power at our disposal, in our hands, and maybe for some to have the fate of another's life in your hand is the greatest power—the doctor who saves the life and the killer who takes it.

CHRISTOPHER SMITH

Chapter Seven

We entered the third day with tired bodies and foggy eyes, our minds' wires severed and spurting electrical sparks, our blood a thick tomato soup. I didn't even bother to call in sick at the paper. In the middle of this last day of our debauchery, we sat out on Luke's back porch, me in a lawn chair, him in his wheelchair. A light flurry fell, autumn in Reverend River. The low, solemn clouds kept our voices from floating off into outer space. When was the last sunny day? We talked about everything: childhood, teenage life, early adulthood and the ever present. The one thought on my mind that never made it out my throat was how Lucas had once been the best athlete among us—big, slow feet but fit as a fiddle. Glory stories were shared, but never, "What the hell happened, Lucas?" We had been over that territory so many times. The first words out of Lucas' mother's mouth over the phone would always be, "So, have you lost weight, dear? We want you around, honey." Advice concerning the proper mass-alleviating procedures, the perfect diet for him, came flowing into his life via family and friends. He knew how to lose weight; he just didn't know how to make himself do what he had to do.

Lord, though! This guy had thrown the ball so damn hard in baseball practice that no one wanted to toss it around with him. He could out-dribble you in basketball and refused to be tackled in football. Now he just refused.

KILLING THE BIRDS

. . .

I awoke in my bed, which was in the living room these days, due to a ceiling leak I hadn't gotten around to fixing in the bedroom, a constant binging of drops into the various receptacles when raining. Again I did not bother to call in at the paper. I didn't even want to hear the voices on my answering machine. I left the red light beeping its summons. I turned the volume off to insulate myself from any new incoming calls. I ate, watched some TV, and then got back into bed. I had the shakes, and the world outside was not welcome. I felt bad. A sorrow no pleasant daydream could remove, for all matter one way or the other took a pointless form. It would take another day or two just to feel halfway normal. I started to recall ending up at Athens tavern after Lucas had fallen asleep the night before. I could hear my newspaper competitor, Max:

"Welcome back, Dan. I knew it was just a matter of time. Hey, it's all over now. No more: no more Scoop TV, no more calls for interviews. You're just one of us again. Drink up! Drink up!"

I rolled over in my bed and pulled a long slug of water from the large jar. I didn't mind falling off the wagon, Lucas and I had had a good old time, but I was frightened of living at Athens again. I knew the possibility of many drug runs to Rand Point loomed large with me flush with money. I said aloud to myself, "No, no, no." I truly pleaded with myself. After a couple jars of water and a few trips to the bathroom, I found sleep again.

I had all kinds of crazy dreams. One of them had me, Lucas, and Max up in this old cave we used to go to as a last resort for private drug and alcohol gatherings. We'd borrow my father's old nylon-bulb lantern, fill up a five-gallon drum with water, get the more important supplies from our local peddler, and then drive up Calf Mountain. Calf, one of the smaller ones, you see. In the dream, Lucas was quite fit, and talking about how he hadn't been in a while. He hopped around the outer edge of the cave after each drink of beer, yelping his happiness for losing the great weight. I smiled, too, overjoyed for him. In the background I kept hearing running water. I checked to see that the water drum was at my side. It remained there. So what was with the running water? I asked Max, who was now my father. He said, "Dan, when will you learn? There's no running water in a cave; maybe a pool of some sort deep inside, but no faucet." He shook his head, disappointed.

I opened my eyes and immediately heard the running water. However, it did not register absolutely. Then I saw a tall shape standing in the kitchen doorway. I pushed myself up and against the wall on my bed, calling out in a terrified shrill, a sound that perpetuated my own inner fear: "Who are you? Who the fuck are you?"

He just swallowed down the water like a parched animal.

"Barde?" I asked. "What the hell? Am I still asleep?" I knew I wasn't.

He walked over to look out my front window. I waited for him to swivel around holding his latest weapon of choice—maybe an old Nez Perce spear. Instead he said softly, "You ever hear of the Blue Reality?" His beard had been removed, but it was Barde, all right. The orange prison jumpsuit was a dead giveaway. The hands that clutched the dripping glass of water were cuffed, but not together; they had separated and each wrist had a dangling chain. The feet were different. One ankle had no evidence of ever having a cuff on it, but it was wrapped around the other ankle with the other cuff still holding tight to that ankle.

I said, "I'd say you didn't get written permission for this outing you're on."

"I escaped. The Blue Reality, ever hear of it?" He struggled with his own voice, and then ran the last of the water through it.

"You escaped?" My voice conveyed disbelief, but my eyes could see.

"I was just wondering if it was something my dad made up." He filled the empty glass and meandered into my living room. "Pop used to always go on about the Blue Reality. Sometimes I understood what he meant, most times I didn't."

"How did you get here all the way from Boise?"

"I knocked a guy down as he got out of his car in a shopping parking lot, took his keys and took off.

"The simplest explanation was that the sky looked blue from Earth, but wasn't really any color. So when you looked up at the sky and saw blue, you were in the Blue Reality." He turned and smiled at me. Then he sat down on the floor and crossed his legs.

He looked peaceful on my floor. I still had a heart overloaded with fear. This man babbling before looked to me like quite serial killer suddenly, and maybe this Blue Reality was his demented mantra— though I knew what his lumberjack father meant.

"Why are you here... in my house?"

"I was hoping you'd do me a favor. I'd really owe ya." He waited for me to respond.

"What is it?"

"I was on my way to see my mother. Then I realized they might think I would do that and be waiting on me there. But I really need to tell her something. Would you tell her for me?"

I nodded that I would.

"I'm going to Alaska. There's a lot of open space where I won't be bothered. I'll let her know exactly where I am when I find a place to build on. If she wants to come then, well, I'll send for her. Would you tell her that? Don't tell anyone else, though. They'd most likely come for me, wouldn't they?"

"They would." I wiped the sand from my eyes and scooted over to the edge of my bed. I took a break to have a drink of water. Suddenly a natural sentence slipped out of my mouth, one that didn't take safety into consideration. "Barde, why would you trust me with Alaska? What makes you think I wouldn't tell?"

After a puzzled expression, he said, "Well, you don't think I did it. You're the only one. Even the lawyer they give me thinks I done it. I can tell by the way he looks at me, always wants a guard nearby. You're the only one—you and my mother."

"You're sure I don't think you did it?"

"I can tell by the way you looked at me in the cell. Do you think I did it?"

I said, "But you did know the boy."

Barde smiled, and it took me off guard, such a sweet expression. "Jimmy rode his bike up my mountain. He told me he wanted to see what the bald spot looked like from on top, not where he always saw it from a distance. You know: the spot where the fire had been. When he first saw me he looked scared, but I think me picking berries gave him enough to ask how far he was from the top."

I had to rub the insanity of this moment from my forehead. The sun broke free from the clouds and a streak of its light painted the carpet a foot from my feet. The remaining birds chirped their gladness for the rays' warmth. I could see my small one-floor shack of a house from outside, sitting on a small street-road surrounded by mountains and trees, a river running through it. I could see Jimmy Wagner looking off at Baldy from a ways. Then he's on top seeing firsthand the dead ground from the fire ten years ago, and the new growth of grass and bushes breaking ground, the stuff he could not see from his Blue Reality life off the mountain.

"Barde, where did you get that deerskin vest you had?"

"There was a cold spell in late September. I came into town for toilet paper. Me and Ma, well, we could get along without it, but we both like it a lot. In the parking lot of the store, this man gets out from his pickup and stops to look me over. He looks happy to see me, though I don't know him. Then he hands me over this vest. He says that I need it more than him. I suppose that could have been true. I had just forgotten to take my coat with me when I left that morning. I do that. It'll cold, but I just walk on away from the house, not going back for a coat. And this was a big vest, covered a lot of my chest and stomach.

"What did this man look like?" I asked. Barde just shrugged at my inquiry. "Was he young? Old? Tall? Short?"

"He might have been fifty. His hair was graying, and not so much of it anymore. He was a nice man."

"This nice man just dropped evidence from a killing on you."

"I don't think so. This was a kind man."

My smile grew wide, and then the laughing started. Barde squinted at me. I asked, "How the hell did you escape?"

"Oh, that was funny. They were moving me, me and some other fellas, from the Rand Point lockup to the Boise county prison. I was sitting in the back of this truck wondering how what had happened could ever really happen. I adjusted my left leg because it was falling asleep, and I felt the one cuff on my left leg come undone. See?" He raised his right foot to show that he had shoved the left foot's cuff into his right foot's sock. "I figured right then that I might never be free again. So I decided this was my only chance. I started banging against the back doors and screaming like a hound who had been skunked. I can see now that that was kind of unrealistic, but my dad always said I was unreal strong. Well, I couldn't budge it. I kept trying, though. They pulled the truck over and opened their doors with their guns pointed at me, screaming that they was gonna beat me so bad I wouldn't have strength to make such a fuss. I kicked at them, leaped on top of them and then ran down the road, then into the thick mountain brush."

"You're lucky to be alive, Mountain Man."

"One way of dying is better than one way of living."

"You're deep, Barde. But then you did have a lumberjack philosopher father."

"Lucky for me those guards were lousy shots, or I would never have made it into the woods."

I said, "And how about that one cuff never really being cuffed."

"That had to be God," Barde observed. "But I had to do my part in escaping, and then coming across a country home with an ax in the yard for wood chopping. But I couldn't chop good between my wrists with my wrists being cuffed, and finally the old feller that lived there came out and chopped it for me; he must have gotten tired of watching me from the window."

"You should have changed out of that orange neon sign you're wearing at that point."

"Yeah, I suppose you're right."

Then a thought hit me: "Barde, how did you find this place? My home?"

"It wasn't easy. I asked folks, figuring you were kind of famous, writing for the paper and all, but no one knew you. And those that recognized your name didn't know where you lived. A couple of people just ran when I went to talk to them. I tried to hide the cuffs with this rag I found, but I guess the orange jumpsuit gave me away. This girl at the grocery store knew where you lived. She just asked me not to hurt her." He paused. "Why would I hurt her?"

"You idiot; your face has been on TV for the past two weeks."

"It has?"

I had the words on my tongue to tell him to change into some clothes of mine get the hell on to Alaska, but the patrol car came screaming up the road, then skidding to a stop at my door. Another car pulled up as well, and who got out but my old pals Agents Reynolds and Perez. I actually chuckled, although every hair on my skin was dancing. Richards, Ellerth, Reynolds, and Perez all had their guns out. They were not fooling around. This wasn't a harmless deer they were hunting. Barde popped to his feet, pulled up by a rope it seemed. He looked out the window and frowned. "I guess that grocery girl told them."

A shot rang out. At almost the same time, my window crashed and crumbled onto my carpet. I covered up on the floor. Weren't they supposed to announce themselves and their fucking intentions? I guess the sight of Barde standing there in plain sight was too much for—I have to assume—Reynolds. Barde now stood off to the side out of the window.

He said to me, "What a lousy shot. Are all guards and cops this bad of shooters? You'd think they'd have had special training."

Richards' voice boomed through the megaphone. "Dan, if you're in there, I'm sorry. Shit-For-Brains here forgot what we in law enforcement commonly call PROPER PROCEDURES! Are you okay?"

I screamed from the floor. "No! I'm not here! Good thing, too! Because I might have been killed by that asshole!"

"Does Barde have a weapon turned on you?"

I felt I was betraying Barde by calling out: "No, he's unarmed!"

Ten seconds later Reynolds burst in the door, followed by Perez. Barde kicked the gun from Reynolds' hands, and without bringing his foot back to the ground, Barde re-loaded and kicked Reynolds in the face, the agent falling back into his partner. Barde took advantage of this collision to take Perez's gun from him, like candy from a federal agent. He then elbowed Perez in the jaw. He executed every move promptly but unhurried; fast, but not lightning—just fast enough. He picked Reynolds' gun from the floor and told the two agents to stay on the carpet. I'm thinking Richards saw them lying on the carpet through the doorway.

Richards' voice boomed again. "Dan, are those agents all right?"

"Yes, Richards! They're unarmed now, so we're all safe! Hey, I got an idea: How about no one else barging in here? You know, Barde has all the guns he needs now!"

Barde opened the back door as I came to my feet. Ellerth had the drop on him. Richards had likely told Big E to cover the back. The officer trembled, as did his pistol.

"Don't move! I'll kill you!"

I decided that with Ellerth and that shaking gun, I'd be better off on the floor, and from there I witnessed this:

Barde tossed one of the agents' guns softly in the air. Ellerth's eyes followed it. Barde kicked the gun from Ellerth and punched him in the face. Ellerth took the blow well. He wobbled for a moment, and then recovered. The suddenly brave officer lunged at Barde. I guess he figured if this human creature could unarm him, he could manage the old turnabout-is-fair-play bit. Barde took the force of the attack and swung Ellerth headfirst out of my sight. I heard a thud and then saw Barde relax, so Ellerth was no longer an issue for him. Perez and Reynolds scurried across the floor in desperation for the gun Barde had tossed. Barde kicked them both and ran out the back door and into the field, all guns in his possession, his big hands having no problem holding them all. The agents groaned, each in his particular fashion, Reynolds wrestling the floor haplessly. Ellerth crawled into the room and leaned against a wall. He looked at me but said nothing. By the time I got out the back door, Richards was aiming his rifle at Barde's back. This particular shooter was not about to miss; he'd won every turkey shoot for the last fifteen years. I almost went to grab at the gun. Then I was going to scream, "NOOO!" But instead I simply said to Richards, "He didn't do it, Sergeant. You're about to shoot an innocent man."

Richards kept the sight up at his eyes. I could see his mouth move. He muttered something to the effect of, "How the hell do you... what am I supposed to... oh for Heaven's sake." Then he lowered the rifle a tip. "I'll try to get a leg." By then Barde had made it into the woods. Richards glared fiercely at me. "That man kills somebody, it's on your head, Holdsworth." Sergeant Richards jogged off after Barde, which was a joke, but the man was doing his job. Perez stumbled out, then

Reynolds. They looked off at Richards as he disappeared into the woods, then at me.

Perez asked, "Where does that wooded area come out at?"

I said, "An abandoned mill. Right, Reynolds?"

Perez turned to his partner. "Our best bet is to drive around the other end somehow."

Reynolds sneered at me and they carried their weary soldier bodies through my house and to their car. I sat down on the back stoop. Questions ran around my brain and back out my ears. I wanted to solve this, but I really wasn't that smart. Lucas! Me and Lucas together! He could be Sherlock and I would be Watson.

I asked myself again why I was so cock-sure Barde was innocent. Then I wondered if Scoop TV would give me another ten grand for my account of what had just happened. Too bad Gabe wasn't around with the camera: that's what made the story travel, those images—and not just rocky footage by an amateur with a cell phone.

Still, you never knew what story would pop, and they would pop for different reasons. The Cubs were a game away from the series a ways back, and a fan kind of got in the way of a foul ball being caught by a Cub in Wrigley Field for the third out, putting an end to the opposing team's rally, and thus holding onto the lead. Not only did the fans blame that little fellow on the Cubs' curse continuing by having that inning continue into a classic Cub debacle, but the story popped, the hysteria complete, and the media had helicopters flying over his house, and Mister Foul Ball was endlessly hassled at work or wherever he was recognized, until he had to move to another state to find peace.

So funny and sad: there were so many real reasons that the Cubs lost that night, but this innocent enough foul ball ignited the hysteria in the human mind.

CHRISTOPHER SMITH

Chapter Eight

It was quiet again. I pondered, sitting up on my bed. Mostly I just let the room be still. It had been moving so fast just a half hour ago. Let it be still. Soothe my mind so my heart slows down. The jangly, drugged-out nerves will vibrate for days, but let the room be still, at least for now. Then I broke the silence by breaking the rest of the window that had been fatally shot, the shattering sound awakening my home from its convalescence. I swept up the mess and drove down to the hardware store for the specifically-measured glass and some window putty. On my way out and in, the neighbors watched the one who had attracted the Bird Man, but they were decent enough to whisper and point, rather than shout or question. That would all come later. As far as the window, I had originally found a piece of plastic to tape over the hole, but Dad's voice rang in my ears: "Why tape over a broken window when the hardware store is open?" He is wise in his way.

I still had the ringers turned off on the cell and the landline, so whoever heard about the happening already would just have to assume I was all right. That was lousy of me. So I called my mother and then went down to the mill to have a chat with Dad. I'm sure Lucas had not heard; he would be in a dark room for a while longer.

The talk with Mom filtered through my hangover depression. Every step my thought process took resounded inside me. I was half empty and half full with endless drunk and drug chatter.

. . .

The cedar scent jumped through my nose as the winding saws ate wood, a gnawing ballad. I used to work here. Actually, I had worked here a few different times. I had mostly graded the one-by-twos that had just been cut, putting them into piles representing their worth. The pieces with no knots or bad marks were premium.

I watched Dad a few moments without his knowing. The early November snow flurries fell around him and the platform on which he moved about. He shoved a twelve-foot-long log through four times until it claimed to be a beam, claimed that it had been one all along—just a distant cousin to the tree. I waited for Dad to take a breather, to wipe his brow.

"Hey, Dad."

"Dan, come back to the wood side?"

"I came to tell you a story."

"Only if it's about a boy and his dog and their adventures in the South."

"No, Dad. This is a story of a boy and his pet serial killer."

His head fell for two counts and then his eyes found mine. He pointed for us to have a seat on a pile. He barely expressed himself in any manner as I went through the morning's events. I left out the three-day drinking and drugging binge; he would not have enjoyed that. Inside him I knew there was clinching afoot. He certainly did not enjoy hearing of a bullet spitting through my window, but you can't bury the lead. Again, it was not his way to be knocked back by life, but I definitely caught a strong wince. Dad knew that living in the country provided no protection from life's sorrows and frustrations, but it went a long way toward eliminating certain stimuli. Still, he accepted his share of the folly and harshness with his portions of the good meals and friends.

The story having been told, I waited for his reaction. I told him I had come down just to let him know so he wouldn't have to hear it from someone else and worry, but now I anticipated his response.

"Are you all right, Son?"

"Yeah, I am, Dad."

"Good. I have to get back to work now."

. . .

I craved red meat and sugar. Nell the cashier stood at the same place she must have been standing when she told Barde where I lived. She giggled, and her small, almost perfectly circular face glittered with the extremeness of the day. Nell said, "I see the cops got there in time to save your skin."

"Oh, yeah, the cops were my saviors. Could you ring me up, Nell? I'm in a hurry."

She did not touch any of my purchases.

"I heard there was shooting," she continued. "Someone told me they killed him. Another said he killed one of those FBI guys and escaped. What happened? Is Sergeant Richards okay?"

"I'll tell you after you ring me up." That was un-cool of me.

She went into action, lightning-fast. Then she attentively blinked her eyelids. I said, "Richards is fine, watch the news for the rest. They know everything."

She called out something nasty as I made my retreat. I nodded to the bagger. His eyes expressed disappointment for not getting the lowdown.

When I pulled up to my home, there was a crowd. Added to the neighbors were Max, Ted Wilson—the Rand Point reporter—a couple of other reporters with their notebooks ready, and a TV news crew whose van claimed to be from "Rand Point's Number One News." They all advanced on me, blurting out questions. "Is the Bird Man a friend of yours?" "Why did he come to your house?" Not one of them offered to help with the groceries. I could see Max smiling from ear to ear. This was all just too amusing to him. I did not answer one question. The neighbors with their cell phones high in the air trying to get a good shot, well, they were just more reporters, I guess. I made it through the door and locked it after me, took a breath, and then jumped a foot when I saw someone sitting on my couch.

Rosa Baline said, "I hope you don't mind me letting myself in."

"Man, you news people."

I hurried to the fridge to put the goods away and then began frying a steak with vigorous and hostile movements. Rosa eased into the kitchen.

"I don't eat meat, Dan. Could you rustle me up a salad?"

I wheeled around to let her have it, the whole day's craziness with both barrels, but she was smiling—not idiotically, but like interesting women do. She knew that in our way we were related, and felt confident that I appreciated her not being with the others outside. And Boise Girl had not run that article about me being a suspected child molester, so I kept my mouth shut and made her a big salad. Yeah, I had salad fixings; I was my mother's son.

In the middle of our lunch conversation, she proposed a thought:

"I think you are apt to believe his innocence because you have been accused of a crime which you did not commit."

"You talk pretty, Rosa, but that's not quite it," though maybe she had something there. I went back to the steak and fries covered in ketchup.

"What is it, then?"

I tried to ignore the question and enjoy my meal. She relented to this cause and we finished in silence, other than her salad-crunching and my pleasure-filled meat-gnawing. She insisted on doing the dishes. I watched her and that gave me great pleasure. So I rewarded her.

"The sound of his voice when he said he had never been out of

Reverend River, the sound of his voice when he told of the man who gave him the vest."

"I read about the mysterious stranger who gave him the vest. His lawyer offered that to the press." She turned to me while drying a dish and leaned her voluptuous bulk against the sink. "Dan, what is he supposed to say? That he did it? Thank you for your time, and now where's that needle I've heard so much about?"

"That's why it's about the sound, Rosa. It isn't what he said, but how he said it, the way he talked about Jimmy."

"He talked about Jimmy?" she asked with great interest.

"Yeah, they had met when the kid was riding up to the top of Baldy. I guess that will be in my next article, or interview with Ty Riggs. The kid liked to conquer these mountains."

"And Barde and this boy talked."

"Yeah, they did. And it sounded like a nice, friendly meeting. One more time: The sound of his voice."

She looked at me a moment, placed the dish carefully on the stack on the shelf and sighed ever so slightly. "People can lie very well."

"That's true, but you believe what you believe."

"Well what did he say this guy looked like who gave him the vest? Maybe another vagrant?"

"No. Sounded like a regular, middle-aged man. Funny thing is, Barde doesn't think that the guy who gave him the vest is the killer."

"Yeah, because he knows he did it himself."

"No, he just thought he was a friendly guy."

"Right, Dan. I know: he trusted the sound of the guy's voice."

"Anyway, I know what I have to do."

"You're kidding," she said.

"No."

"You can't be serious."

I said, "I'm going to find the mysterious vest-giver."

"How?" she asked.

"That is such a good fucking question."

We stood in my living room, which darkened a little more with every passing moment. The day was dying—that much we knew. We looked at the lights out on my lawn. Cameras pointed at attractive people with microphones, my home their backdrop.

Rosa said, "It must be funny being on this side of the story."

"Ha ha," I replied.

The plan Rosa and I hatched was simple. We would go over to Lucas' and brainstorm. His computer could access practically any information we needed. We would put Lucas to the test. But leaving my home seemed just too daunting. Suddenly the sea of people and lights parted. Richards, Reynolds, and Perez pushed through. I opened the door and smiled, but Perez and Reynolds took hold of me like a criminal and I had to twist around to call back to Rosa. "You know where to meet me!" She nodded her head. I had uncoiled and was about to say something to Richards, but wrenched back to Rosa, who had kept her eyes on me, and I smiled so she would know I was glad to not be alone. She smiled back. I think she knew what I meant.

. . .

The police station's lunch room served not as the press release area this early evening, as when I had last sat in this same chair—the only chair with arms—but as a place of interrogation.

"What do you and Barde got going?" Reynolds asked through a devious grin. "You two shop for clothes at the same place? That is to say, the kids' section?"

The ridiculousness of the moment did not ease my tension. My eyes reached toward Sergeant Richards in the hope of confirmation of said ridiculousness. He wasn't there for me. I immediately thought the worst of him for not backing me against the Feds: that he made a great leap with the old story of my Rand Point child molestation situation and my now being "pals" with Barde. After shaking my head at the stump called Reynolds, it occurred to me that maybe Sergeant Richards was just disturbed because Barde had gotten away. He had that clean shot and I had snuffed it out with words. The Sergeant lived in a small town with small glories, but that did not quell a large sense of pride and duty. It would be a while before I left the residence of his dog house. It meant something to me that Richards knew me well enough after all these years. Still, once a possibility is brought out about someone, however unbelievably gross or horrifying, it's hard not to consider it. I mean, look at the brutality of nature; see the strange tornados that reside inside us all.

Perez rose from his chair slowly, pointedly. I was on his shit list as well. Within his even motion I saw water boiling. He so wanted to hit me. This guy saw a molester before him. The water boiled over. He spoke as though God had handed him the words.

"Your type runs fast. And really, you hide more than you run. You're cowards, but when you come out, you leave a stench, and society just cannot tolerate it. So it's off to the garbage dump with you. It's just a matter if it's to the executed section of the dump, or the lifer plea-bargain section."

I said, "Listen—"

"Fuck you, 'listen'!" Perez shouted in my face. "I'm waiting around for you to get wise! I want all of it! The Rand Point deal, where you diddled your girl's little boy, and what you and Barde were up to!"

I screamed, "I never touched Colin!"

Perez straddled over me now, both his hands firmly on the arms of my chair. "Now which poor little boy would that have been? The one in Oregon?"

I just shook my head while he eyeballed me. "I'm waiting!" Perez shouted, and the day's coffee spit into my face along with some of his saliva.

I said through grinding teeth, "You don't know what you're talking about."

He lifted me a half foot from the chair by gripping my shirt. I ripped his hands off as Richards pulled Perez from me completely. The Sergeant attempted to be heard over all the profanity:

"That's it! Now! Now!" Richards glared at Perez and then lowered his voice, saying, "I don't know how you do it elsewhere, but that's not how we do it here."

Reynolds jumped in menacingly, "We won't be here much longer. Neither will the paper boy."

Richards glanced at me before choosing his next course. "Listen," he said, "we'll put Holdsworth on ice for the time being. His dad is already on the way down. Then we officers of the court can talk about the evidence. Again, I don't know how you all do things at the federal building, or want to do things anywhere else you go, but the law needs some concrete facts—not stories and a visit from an escaped convict."

"The sergeant here told us what you told him on the way in," Perez said blandly to me. "Barde wanted you to look in on his mom. Come on. This Barde woman would beat most of us here in a one-on-one wrestling match. Maybe he had another message for her, like where he was heading. Maybe you're not in as deep as I think you are, but you're lying to us, and that lying shit will not set you free. Only one thing will set you free." Perez unbuttoned his collar and pulled out a cross that hung from his neck. Now he looked like a runway model from the Vatican. "What is it that will set you free, paper boy?"

. . .

I sat on the hard bench in the cell wondering why I hadn't told them the truth, that Barde wanted me to let his mother know that he was Alaska-bound. This guy might have killed children, and I'm covering his tracks. And even if he were innocent, as I truly did believe, Agent Perez was right about the truth: it's the best thing going.

A fat, drunken man snored away in the cell next to me. A young American Indian sat cross-legged off in the corner of my cell. (I know Columbus was lost when he named the Native Americans "Indians," but old habits die hard.) My Native American roommate had traditional artifacts hung about his person, but sported blue jeans and a heavy brown flannel. I sighed wearily and he took that as a cue to speak to me.

"The Nez Perce tribe believes that a sigh is a bridge to the next emotion. Most times, though, there is no need of such a bridge. Other times, the sigh is an absolute necessity."

I nodded and smiled.

"My grandfathers tell me there used to be gold all over these mountains and streams."

"Yes," I said to my friend, whose name I hadn't caught yet, "and silver. The place used to be loaded with silver. I've gotten good and screwed up a few times in the abandoned silver mines."

The young man scooted on the floor to better face me. He spoke up to me in knowing tones.

"Oh, you like to soak your brain in the alcohol, the drugs, too."

"Yeah, I've put my liver to the test, not to mention millions of brain cells. What do your grandfathers have to say about that?"

He took hold of a wood-carved wolf's face that had been swaying from its string. "My grandfathers say that alcohol causes too much trouble for its pleasure's worth. Still, they believe that it is like the rain, the hard winds, and the white man: something you just have to accept and deal with the best way you can."

I asked, "Do they—I mean: do you think the hard winds are more trouble than their pleasure's worth?"

"I am not very smart. I am only eighteen. I shall ask my grandfathers."

I took to nodding and smiling again. Then after about half a minute he said, "My grandfathers say that you make a good point about 'worth' being a tricky word. They will from now on only say that liquor causes a lot of trouble."

I stared at the young man for a moment. "You can communicate with them, your grandfathers?"

"Fellow prisoner, I have so many voices in my head I don't know how I hear them all with any clarity. It's when I scream at them and tug at them that I end up locked up in one room or another. I wish I could just keep it all to myself. You missed the fuss when they dragged me in. I never wanted to be anyone's burden, but it's not so easy."

He smiled at me and his eyes shone a good soul's hello. I liked him, but he made me nervous.

. . .

My dad came and I stepped behind him as we made our way through the station; I was a free man, with one omission: Richard said: "Don't leave town, Holdsworth." I was suddenly going to tell them that Barde had taken off for Alaska, but it wasn't like they were ever going to find him anyway. I kept my trap shut and followed Dad to "freedom."

In the pickup I quietly watched the lights lead the way through darkness. Dad asked if I wanted to spend a couple of days with him or my mom. I told him to drop me at Lucas' place.

"Do you think this is all over now?" he asked.

"How would I know? This is not something I'm making happen. It's something that's happening to me."

"I know," Dad said easily, "but when something keeps coming back to your front stoop of its own accord, like a stray dog, your interest in it grows. Richards told me you talked him out of shooting down this Barde fellow."

"Dad, I just don't think he did it."

"But I bet you are wondering if he did, wondering if you helped a murderer to his liberation."

"Yeah, but—"

"So that might lead you to think that you had better find the real killer." He glanced over at me. "Or am I a character in a movie now?"

"Really, Dad... such an imagination."

I looked straight ahead, anxious to get with Lucas and Rosa and play Scrabble with the facts. Dad would have been a great help. He has a keen mind. He just doesn't play Scrabble, or most other games.

Chapter Nine

Rosa's car held her slumped body in the front seat, her head leaning against the window. I stood and watched a small pool of saliva form on her lips and then fall in drops onto her blouse. I had time, and watching a woman sleep always entertained me. I knocked softly and she slowly came around before jolting. She rolled down the window.

"Your friend didn't answer the door."

"Yeah, he doesn't do that."

"Why?"

I had to ponder that just a moment: "Because he doesn't want any new friends." I pulled keys from my pocket and dangled them before her.

Inside I announced loudly that I had entered and had brought Rosa, the writer from Boise. He called back that we should make ourselves at home. I heard his bed squeak to the movements of his serious weight, along with the moans of a man forcing himself awake.

Rosa asked me, "Any problems down at the station?"

"They love me down there. Oh, they think I might be a child molester. I guess Melissa's brother has been talking to plenty of folks, clinging to the big story, but you know, that's not a problem." I whispered sweet nothings to the remaining beers in Lucas' fridge, but swung the door closed empty-handed. I said to Rosa plainly, "They don't think I told the truth about why Barde came to see me."

"Did you tell me the truth over lunch?"

"No."

After a pregnant pause, she said, "Come on, we're on this case together now." Pause. "Aren't we?"

As much as she had proven herself, I still struggled with this private information. She played with the lining of her black skirt and I lost my train of thought. I blurted out the facts of the matter.

"Barde wanted me to tell his mother where he was headed. Don't ask. It doesn't matter where he went. But one day I will make my way up to Old Lady Barde's cabin to tell her."

"Why didn't he just go up? Oh, right."

Lucas limped out with use of his cane. His body quivered through the chore, his knees on the verge of buckling. He lowered himself carefully toward the chair at the computer until gravity pulled him down in a sounding plop. He looked us both over suspiciously, scratching his beard, his eyes then searching mine for an answer through lightly shaded glasses, just dark enough to fight off the computer screen's rays.

"Hey," I said, "guess who came by to see me, Lucas: the escaped murderer, Barde. No kidding. He sends his love."

I told Luke the whole story. His mouth opened here and there, he laughed hysterically occasionally, and a couple of times he just shook his head in disbelief. He surmised his feelings with words:

"This thing just keeps on going. Man, bullets through your window." He chuckled again.

"Bullet," I corrected, "as in, only one."

"Dan!" he shrieked. "It's another ten grand from Scoop TV!"

We both rejoiced. I bounced over to his chair and slapped him five. He asked if I could lend him a couple bucks when the check cleared. Then I caught Rosa shaking her head. I took a moment to pace the room.

"Well, Luke, old buddy, I had this other plan."

"Let's have a beer and talk about it," he proposed.

I fetched him a beer and he took note that I was back on the wagon.

"Okay," he said, "out with it."

"We're going to try to figure out who the real killer is."

Each word he replied with had a full breath before the next word:

"What... in... the... hell... are... you... TALKING ABOUT?"

Rosa chimed in. "We're going to brainstorm, use your computer for research, information."

Lucas nodded his head respectfully at Rosa and then glared at me.

"Come on, Luke," I pleaded. "You're great at puzzles."

"Yeah, I'm working on one now: When did you quit your job as a writer and become a detective? Take the money and run, Dan. Hell, Barde most likely did it."

"No!" I shouted. Then sanely I said, "No, he did not do it."

"Why do I get the feeling detective work was not involved in that deduction?"

"Will you help?"

He took a long slug from his beer. He hit the switch to the computer beast and it hummed into life. "Things in common with each crime," he said. "That's where I think we should start."

Rosa began diligently running through a thick, compact yellow notebook. Lucas said he was searching for information on each town where the other murders had been committed. Rosa called out the name of each town. I poured myself a soda on ice.

"The most recent, two years ago: Big Creek, California. Five years ago: Blue Ridge, Oregon. The first murder—the supposed first murder: Kotter Hills, Wyoming."

Lucas called up tourist literature and printed it all out. He did not read any, but handed them to me and kept searching. Rosa and I traded sheets of paper as we finished perusing them.

"They're all small towns," Rosa said. "The smallest is Reverend River. The largest is Big Creek, California."

"So he's not doing them in order of size, because Big Creek, being the biggest, was the one just before the smallest."

Lucas, while typing and peering at the screen, said, "The order, I don't think is important, but the size? That seems too big of a coincidence to ignore. I mean that they are all small towns." Rosa and I ventured inward to muse. Silence filled the room for a few minutes.

"Okay," I said, trying to keep things rolling: "let the small-town queries simmer and volley back and forth some other facts. How about the birds, the state birds: What's ours?"

In the time it took Rosa's brows to furrow, Lucas voiced: "Mountain Blue Bird."

"Okay," I said, having no idea where I was going. "Anyone got the Oregon state bird in their noggin?"

Rosa shook her head and said, "No, but we have the computer."

As the words fell from her tongue, Lucas said out loud to his phone: "What is the state bird for Oregon?"

A woman's computer voice, a female Stephen Hawking, responded: "The state bird for Oregon is the Western Meadowlark."

"Nice trick," I said. Does it sit up and speak as well?"

Rosa said, "California?"

Now Lucas sat mute. He remained still and silent in his chair, not seeing or saying anything, just ruffling through his file-cabinet mind. I said, "All right, Miss Phone." But he just kept thinking, taking to making sounds by puckering his lips and blowing out. Finally:

"California Valley Quail."

"No," I said out of disbelief, not out of knowledge. Rosa just smiled widely, believing him. "Check it," I said. The phone lady confirmed it.

"There's one left," Rosa said: "Wyoming."

The woman who lived in Lucas' phone said it was the Meadowlark, but not a Western Meadowlark, as with Oregon.

We went round and round with what the birds might mean. Except for the Wyoming Meadowlark, the others all had places other than their state's name: Mountain Blue Bird, Oregon's Western Meadowlark, California's Valley Quail. We deduced that a mountain is up, a valley is down, and all these murders were committed out west. And the reason Wyoming's Meadowlark didn't have a direction or place was because the other Meadowlark had already taken care of that.

Rosa said, "This is all adiaphorous."

I gaped her way. "Now you're making that word up." I turned to Lucas, who was squinting, but only for a few moments before he came up with it, though his definition had a question mark next to it, awaiting Rosa's confirmation:

"Neither helpful nor harmful?"

She nodded proudly.

"Hey!" I declared: "English from now on—English."

We went back to work. Since a state bird represented the state, we delved into other state facts. When did they become states? Oregon was the 33rd, California the 31st, Wyoming the 44th, and ours the 43rd. So we played with the numbers. I said, "It all seems adiaphorous." I was pleased with my ever-increasing vocabulary.

We moved on to flowers. Golden Poppy, Syringa, Oregon Grape, but nothing added up to significant.

Then Lucas said, "Hey, all these states border our state, except for California."

"Yes…" I encouraged him to continue.

"Well, what state would link them all together?"

I prayed the answer would come quickly so they wouldn't see that I would need about fifteen seconds to bring the image into a reply. Luckily, Lucas wasn't really asking a question, just beginning his point.

"Nevada would connect us to California and Oregon. Montana, Washington, and Utah are the other states that touch ours. Along this line of thinking, there's too much ground to cover to guess where the next murder would be—so not really helpful."

Rosa jumped in. "California is connected to Idaho by Oregon. So I think Nevada would—"

"Wait," I said. "This is nowhere. All of this is nowhere. Forget the Sherlock Holmes crap. We have to find something more concrete. Okay, he's terrorizing the Pacific Northwest. He does it with at least two-year intervals. He likes birds."

"The two-year interval part is interesting," Rosa said. "It goes toward the personality of the person doing it, don't you think? Is it a thought-out pattern, or is it he can't get up the nerve for a while again?"

"Or," Lucas joined in, "he is trying to stop each time and eventually gives in again."

I tried to be a part of it. "He moves. He isn't killing from one place. He moves. Maybe he's trying to forget the past."

"Yes," Rosa said.

"No," Lucas said. "I mean, that might be true, but he could still be a rover. Since he moves, why not further away? Why always in the Pacific Northwest? It seems more like an animal hunting in his territory. It's a large area for an animal, but we're talking a human animal."

My head hurt.

Just then there was a knock at the door.

"Don't answer it," Lucas said. "I don't want any more company."

"I have to, Luke. It could be my dad or someone. I'll talk out front."

It was my boss, John Rogers. We eased out close to the road.

"Dan, tell me the reason you're not down at the office writing this story about Barde's coming to see you, with the shooting and the chasing. It's because you've just finished it up right here, right?" I did not respond. "Oh, Dan: shoot! Come on down with me. The printers will be gone, but you and I can do it."

"Boss, I'm kinda busy."

"Don't do this to me. The biggest story—hell, I have ways of making a killing off of this. This is... well, this is huge."

I said, "Look, we live in a small town and we run a small paper. What's the point?"

"What the hell are you talking about? What does size have to do with it? I'm a newspaper man! What are you? Tell your friends you'll play with them tomorrow."

I went back in and informed Rosa and Lucas that I had to go. I suggested that they keep working. Lucas immediately appeared uncomfortable about being alone with Rosa. She had a weary countenance as well.

"Okay, get some sleep at my place," I handed Rosa my house keys, "if you don't mind the possibility of a crowd still being there." She took the keys. "Lucas, we'll be back here tomorrow. Keep your thinking cap on. Fuck these clues. Try to come up with a better direction for us. We're not going the right way, I don't think."

. . .

The streets were wet now, the last leaves clinging to them. Rogers laughed and chided me about being the Bird Man's bitch. He also went on about cashing in on all of this; more money from the dead.

Expecting the offices to be empty, my skin tingled a bit when I saw Gabe passed out sitting up in a chair, his head bowed in reverence to the Dream Angels.

"What's he doing here? We're not going out, are we?"

"No. He's had a long day," Rogers said through an elder's smile: "Poor little tyke had your place staked out, got some great shots."

Gabe rustled a bit, but I couldn't tell if complete consciousness had arrived. I said, "I didn't see him at my place."

"Well, he sure as heck was there. The pictures are great! He covered the whole scene; not just you, but the overview; the press, the neighbors, all in single shots. It's front page stuff! We're going to be on the map! Job offers for the three of us."

"Like you would ever leave Reverend River, boss."

"Hey, Skip, I guess you never know."

"Wait a minute: overview?"

Then I heard Gabe's voice. "I operated a drone from across the road and such; had it flying all around your place, hovering in one place for still shots; even caught that Boise reporter climbing in through your back window."

"A dark-haired woman?"

"She's the one. Don't worry. You can have that picture. I'll keep a copy for my files, of course."

I just stood there marveling at Gabe's creativity and dedication.

I asked, "Both video and pictures?"

"Of course."

Rogers grabbed my shoulder and told me to get to work, chop-chop, double quick. We were famous again. We might knock the massacre at the St. Louis mall off the front page. Maybe we would just share it. Either way, Rogers had plenty more than his usual amount of calls coming in. The story had legs, mostly belonging to Barde.

I tried my best to be a good little journalist. Keep the story in focus; keep me off to the side, but damn if Mountain Man Barde hadn't made that impossible. The people would want to know how I felt; I had to enter the story. The lines were more than blurred; they were gone. With each pause after a paragraph, the detective in me showed his face. Who did this? The killer gave Barde the vest. He framed him; this all happened in Reverend River. The killer could live here, as Lucas had said, as well as in any of the crime-scene towns, a hunter trapping his territory. Why hadn't he framed anyone before? Maybe he truly wanted to retire.

I handed in my article, told Rogers he could print without me, slipped on my jacket and then noticed that Gabe was still occupying the same chair, his eyes closed, his head against the wall.

"Gabe?"

"Yeah." Only his mouth moved.

"If you were trying to figure out a crime, and you thought that the murderer was local, how would a big-city Jew such as yourself go about that?"

"Well," and he removed himself from the wall and glanced about the empty room, "if you're talking about a serial killer, the Bird Man specifically, I guess I have a direction for you." He stretched his arms and yawned. "They're always quiet, the neighbors say, but a lot of them have had little run-ins with the law. That is to say, if you're a busy bee going about killing people, you're going to have some close calls. And your mind is not what we call thinking properly. Look at Dahmer. A kid escapes from his apartment, tracks down a cop, he's bleeding a bit, a cut, and Dahmer convinces the cop that the doped-up kid just needs to get back home. No arrest was made, just I believe a report. He killed all those people, but he almost got caught once. If I were an investigative reporter, such as yourself, I'd check out strange police reports that didn't add up. Or go through our past editions for any strange articles about Reverend River characters giving the place a creepy atmosphere. No vagrants this time."

"For instance?" I asked, slightly doubtful.

"Like some nut arrested for shooting birds. The Bird Man?" he led. "But it doesn't have to be that obvious."

"I don't think the police are going to accommodate me at this point in our relationship."

Gabe got up and put on his jacket. "So go straight to weird articles in our paper, or Rand Point's. Me, I got better things to do." He saluted and left.

By the next hour, I had gone three months back into the Herald's past. Sleep kept crawling up my sleeve and shoulder and into my eyes.

I was just about to give up when a picture caught my eye. Gabe had taken it at a rally of the local chapter of the National Rifle Association. A man stood at a podium set up on a gazebo in Rand Point Park. His mouth was wide open as he enthusiastically called out the cause. His last name was Wagner, the uncle, I guessed, for it wasn't the father; the thing that caught my eye was the deerskin vest that he wore. Damn if it wasn't the same vest Barde had claimed to have been given. I found my magnifying glass on Grace's desk and took a closer look at the picture. There it was, the small, circular design I'd seen on Barde's vest: a river flowing beneath a mountain. It had probably been burn-carved into the material.

I printed the picture and hurried out the door, at first actually driving toward the police station, then changing directions, heading to Lucas' place. I needed to know that this evidence rang as true for someone else before I walked into the den of the wolves of authority. That, of course, was bullshit: I just wanted to hang onto this moment, share it with my friends, and be calm beside the river that never resolves until it is the ocean; feeling for the moment that I was beyond the river, beyond the rush—which again, was bullshit. We were all a rush; we were all explosions with house payments.

I heard voices conversing as I turned the key in the door. Rosa jumped to her feet when I entered. She was disheveled, her hair a mess, her eyes shadowy, and her shirt un-tucked.

"I think we're on to something!" she explained. "Lucas came up with a very interesting angle."

Lucas corrected, "We came up with it."

I asked, "Does it involve the Wagner boy's uncle?"

They both turned their heads, indicating that it did not. I handed Rosa the picture connected to the article. Her mouth opened slowly. She asked, "Is that the vest?"

"That is the vest. See that design? It's the same one I saw on Barde's vest."

Rosa handed the picture over to Lucas' awaiting hands. He read it and began smiling. "It says here that this Wilford Wagner is one of those guys who has a fort for a home stocked for Doomsday, a compound: food, ammo, guns, and more. He's one of these militants who thinks he's his own state."

"Yeah, he's a character, all right," I said, by then pacing a bit. "I didn't take this straight to Richards because I wanted to make sure you all thought this evidence is as strong as I do. Hell, after what I've been through with the Feds and Richards, I guess I wouldn't mind some company down there at the station. Rosa?"

She acknowledged hearing me, but her mind remained deep in thought. She paused, scratched her chin, and then released a harsh breath.

I said, "You don't have to come. I just thought—"

"No," she said, "that's not it. I just had another thought. Yes, we're going to let the police handle this from here on in, but wouldn't it be something to get some footage and an interview with this Wagner fellow before we drop the dime on him?" Drop a dime; she was talking like Reynolds.

"He's not going to let us—"

As she interrupted me, I heard Lucas making a quip about the outdated "drop the dime" phrase, and then saying to himself as much as Rosa, "You're an okay broad."

"Listen," she said. "We call him and say we're doing a follow-up on the NRA rally and his beliefs about the government, a follow-up story. Then later, after he's busted, we have footage. We would all make a good dollar selling the footage and our stories, and I can finally get above the lower level of this occupation. Dan, your glory just grows, mine gets started."

I had stopped pacing, my mind taking in this interesting idea and feeling its shape. Lucas boomed: "Nancy Drew and the Hardy Boys! Forget about it! This guy will bury you in his yard and plant our state flower over your bodies! That's the Syringa—a lovely flower, if you ask me."

Rosa shot back, "Why would he see through the follow-up story?"

"Because he knows he framed this Barde guy," Lucas said with arms flailing. "He—" Lucas halted. We all looked at one another, then Lucas said, "It's something dumb people do in dumb fucking movies."

I said to Rose, "Wagner must not remember the picture of him with the vest on during that speech, or he wouldn't have used it to frame Barde."

Rosa said, "Yes, I can see that: making a speech in front of a bunch of people, a man who lives on a mountain. I can see that. I can see him never reading the article."

Lucas had his arms folded, waiting for us to finish. I continued. "But you'd think he'd have a copy of the picture, a rare speech, or whatever."

"But obviously he didn't," Rosa answered, "or he wouldn't have used it to frame Barde. He's in the dark about his mistake. Let's do this story."

Lucas said, "He probably knows Barde came to visit Dan. So he must think Barde told Dan about the stranger's giving him the vest. Hell, Barde's lawyer told the newspapers about the gift-giver."

"So?" I reasoned. "I don't think Wilford Wagner is worried about it. More than that, I think he's up there on his mountain with no little thought of what's going on down here. I mean, he might not have even been framing Barde; maybe it was just a gift from one mountain man to another."

Lucas cautioned strongly, "No, I think this killer knows about all of his actions' reverberations. You two are nuts. Just take all this down to Richards."

Rosa said, "After tomorrow's interview."

I said enthusiastically, "I'll call Gabe for photos and video."

Rosa looked down at Lucas. "Don't worry. This is going to be fine. Hey, you're coming with us, aren't you?"

I spit out a quick, short laugh. Lucas frowned at Boise Girl. He said, "I go as far as my back porch."

Chapter Ten

The next morning I got on the horn to the local chapter of the NRA in Rand Point. They informed me that Wilford Wagner lived on top of Mine Mountain and had no phone. After some schmoozing about what a nice article we were going to write, positive publicity for the NRA, they gave me directions.

Rosa had insisted on driving all the way back to the hotel in Rand Point the night before. I assured her that she would be safe at my place, but she took off just the same. It got me to thinking that maybe she didn't trust herself alone with me. This particular type of egotism seldom came my way, so I let myself enjoy it. I had to admit that from my end, fantasies were being nurtured: a slow trip along a nylon leg, her soft mouth welcoming my lips and tongue—standard stuff.

She showed up with fruit and vegetables for the trip. I packed peanut butter and jelly sandwiches. Lucas' voice echoed in my head with warnings of danger and irresponsibility. The last thing he said as I opened his door to leave the night before was, "What price glory?"

The coast seemed to be clear this pre-noon hour. The town had returned to not concerning itself with me. Calls did come in from various media outlets, and Scoop TV booked a date for the story of the escaped convict barging into my home, resulting in a "shoot-out" with the police and FBI. Lord, they could end up bidding for my account with ten grand as the starting point. I said that I would have to call them tomorrow, and hinted that I might have a surprise for them. I felt very cool and important. After years—a lifetime—of obscurity, the world had come calling. "Tell us, Dan Holdsworth. Tell us the news."

The first few minutes of the ride offered sun and lovely, light-blue skies. All the rain had cleaned the skies into Heaven's reflection. Rosa and I kept a lid on our excitement. We smiled every now and again. When we picked up Gabe, we were all teeth. He seemed juiced as well. We did not talk at all about the glory ahead, or the danger. We approached it like another assignment. Did Gabe have all the film he needed? Did he have batteries? We could pick up more. Rosa asked if I had prepared some questions for the NRA spokesman. I had not, but she had. The one thing we did address was that under no circumstances would either of us bring up the vest. We wanted footage of him. We wanted it on record that we were casing him. We did not want to corner this rabid creature.

The fact remained that I knew enough to be scared, but had begun imagining what jobs I might be offered after busting this case wide open. And in the Bardes' home, pictures of me would hang prominently on the walls. That went a long way, too. What price glory: a drive up a mountain and an innocent interview about guns and the fall of society.

Then the clouds rolled out on cue, the wind crept out as a whisper, and then achieved howling status as we rose up Mine Mountain. We were all cracking up at a joke Gabe had heard from one of the sports guys when a logging truck appeared up around a bend. I had to swerve to make room. The road's dirt and pebbles whipped at us and we flinched and then froze in that flinch. When the truck had fully passed, I realized that I had come to a complete stop. We looked at one another and smiled and giggled again. But this was another joke entirely.

What price glory?

I found the sign that told us we had come to Wagner's road. It said, "Turn up this road in peace or war. We're ready either way."

Rosa said, "Yikes."

I said, "Man."

Gabe said, "Aw, that's sweet."

The road wound up and around for at least two miles until we arrived at a plateau. What appeared to be an electric fence greeted us—unless the "High Voltage" sign was a con; beware the dog I don't have, that kind of thing. My guess was that this guy had stocked up on generators of all sorts. An intercom was connected to a post. I pressed the button and we waited. After a bit I began to think we had come a long way for nothing. Rosa suggested that we have lunch, and then try buzzing again.

"Who goes there?" the intercom voice boomed militantly.

I tried to get to the point without arousing his suspicions.

"We are reporters hoping to do a follow-up story on the NRA rally."

"What do you need me for? It's a long drive just for that."

"In the article you talked about the preparations you have made to ensure your freedom and survival. Our editor thought we should write about the extent of those efforts. It's not a piece that will attack the process or lifestyle. There are a lot of people in this area and this country who are just now becoming aware of that option—you know: the original freedom."

"I ain't got time for this. Go away."

"Okay, Mister Wagner." I fumbled through my notes for a name. "But Jim Bashion at the NRA headquarters in Rand Point thought the piece would be good public relations, especially with the country's coming down on the NRA after all those school shootings. I forget how Mister Bashion said it. Oh, yeah: 'This is a chance to show what we are really about.'"

We waited.

The fence unhinged and opened inward.

There were two full structures, both three to four times larger than my old homestead. Added to that were sheds, a greenhouse, and a couple of garages. He stood on a porch cradling a rifle in his arms like one would hold an infant. He could have been anyone's father, uncle, or a young grandfather. He never took his eyes from us. He did not appear afraid, just on the job, the job of staying alive, of not trusting his survival to anyone but himself.

When we emptied from my Swinger he pointed for us to stay put. As he came down, he said, "Keep that camera off until we come to an understanding."

"Hi. My name is Dan Holdsworth." I offered my hand, which he did not take. "This is Rosa Baline and Gabe Teplitz."

"Teplitz. Is that Jewish?"

Gabe nodded. "Yes, it is."

Wagner frowned. He looked Rosa over and then spoke to me. "Do you have a list of the questions you want to ask me?"

Rosa replied, "Yes." She looked at her handbag. "They're in here." She waited for permission to reach into her bag, slowly. Wilford Wagner laughed.

"Go ahead, little miss. I ain't afraid of you getting the drop on me."

She handed the list over and he read it, periodically bringing his eyes up to us. Here and there it was evident he liked a certain question. Then he said "okay" and handed her list back. "First and foremost, I don't want to give away my softer spots of entry. So no wide shots from the video or camera unless I give the okay. Also, I don't want you telling what mountain I'm on. I don't want strangers coming up to see it after they read your article, and I don't want folks coming up here looking for food when things fall apart, and no one has manners anymore."

He welcomed us into the largest wooden structure. Most of the walls had some sort of weapons cabinet filled with rifles and pistols and ammo, or evidence of weapons—the head of an elk or bear. While there were separate rooms off to the sides, the bulk of the space was wide open, giving one the feel of an Aspen ski lodge retreat for the wealthy. Then I saw a picture of Jimmy Wagner standing next to his uncle, both holding rifles.

He had us sit in a living area with chairs and sofas forming a square around a homemade coffee table, a wide, tall, unlit fireplace ten yards away. Wagner promised to show us around the compound after the Q & A session. Rosa had just asked her first question—did Wagner really believe he would need all this security, or was he just giving himself all the breaks—when a woman appeared through a back entrance.

She was a slip of a thing, quietly shocked to see us, bearing a rifle and carrying a dead rabbit by its ears. She paused, choosing to slowly retreat from where she came, but Wilford waved her in.

"This is Marion," Uncle Wagner said.

She did not truly respond to our greetings, but looked to Wilford for permission to leave. He nodded. She grabbed a knife from the kitchen and went out back to skin the animal, I assumed.

Wilford looked us over with a smile and said, "Man does not live by bread alone, or even rabbit." He opened a box on the smaller table next to him that also held a lantern, and retrieved a cigar. He lit it without asking if it would bother the Lady Rosa or offering the other gentlemen one. He puffed it into smoky life and answered Rosa's question.

"True, I do believe that even if you do not think a bad thing has a good chance, or almost any chance of happening, you should prepare yourself for it all the same. I am a survivalist. I mean, there are enough hours in the day for such efforts. Having said that: There's no doubt in my mind that whether in my lifetime or not, this civilization we've known—however civil it actually ever was—will crumble like a badly built lean-to. And let me make myself clear: Hell doesn't break loose, it's always here; Heaven and Hell, always here. It's just that when the Big One—whatever form that takes—does hit, all these people who never learned to really provide for themselves, having been brought up on the government's tit, that government that did them no favors by coddling them, well, they'll be looking for any way they can to survive. All that morality they preached and lived by will not feed their bellies, thus they will take to the behavior that for so long horrified them. They will act like the animal Black Man, now as poor as he, now as desperate as he. And unlike their view of his desperation, they will feel themselves justified. All the while I will be here, a man who never changed from his set beliefs, but only because I saw the world for what it was, saw civilization for what it was: one man's trek through a jungle. Or maybe I should just say that civilization never existed. So when the civil ask for my gun after a school shooting, I say, 'You'll have to pry it from my dead hands.'"

He surveyed his guests' eyes with more than a hint of Mussolini behind his own peepers—though I know it's unfair to characterize him with that extreme ass-hole of a human. He asked, "So, does that answer your question?" But his and Benito's eyes had already seen that he had. What he said did have a definite logical path; it was easy for me to see separation from civilization; my parents had given that a try. But I knew this man was a murderer. I figured this all to be part of his psychosis.

Rosa moved on to the next question: "What do you think might be the best course of action concerning all these shootings at high schools, and of late at a couple of churches?"

His head bobbed up and down expectantly. "Yes, yes. There's only one answer to all that: Every teacher should, before they're given their teacher's certificate, be card-carrying handgun experts. Think about it! Some asshole is shooting up the place and he looks up to see five teachers lined up down the hall, locked and loaded. He'd drop his weapon in a second, or be killed as quickly."

Again his eyes checked ours for the light. I nodded pretentiously, not wanting to offend someone who owned as many guns as there were just in this one room. And one could not argue that it certainly made a little sense for overseers of children to be able to offer protection's extreme capacities. Still, the statistics showed that people who carry guns are more likely to get shot than those who don't. Live by the sword, die by the sword. And I wanted to quote the Robert Benton film, Nobody's Fool: "If you arm one idiot, you have to arm them all."

So many answers, so few actual solutions.

Maybe Lucas had the only true answer: never leave your home. Still, I've been out in the world my whole life and have never been shot at—well, until Reynolds killed my window. I think I am the average person; congratulations to the average, but extremes do happen, and crazy Uncle Wagner was prepared for all of them.

The questions and answers went on this way, with Gabe recording it all for prosperity, mostly on video, but with a few old-fashioned photos as well. Then Wagner led us around his fort. The greenhouse most impressed me. Apparently the brute had quite the green thumb, or shared green thumbs with the Missus. Tall tomato plants gave forth red spheres the size of Chicago softballs. And this entire reporting stance made it fairly easy to be around someone we were all sure was a serial killer. He liked that we were there; his pride was being caressed, his point of view heard. He was like a big, angry dog whose tail kept wagging as long as we kept feeding him large chunks of bloody meat in the form of compliments on his garden. We still should have been scared, but we weren't. We were doing our jobs, not flinging accusations at a cornered murderer—though I did notice that Rosa was staying close to my side as we moved from one area to another.

The other large wood home held more canned and pressure-cooked food than my mom had brought into being in her lifetime, would ever bring about in ten lifetimes. He also had a walk-in freezer in the basement filled with skinned animal carcasses hanging by those meat hangers: deer, elk, bear, and rabbits. A generator room filled up the rest of the basement area, except for the wood-burning broiler system that could provide enough heat for a steam-engine boat to sail across an ocean. The man needed never see another segment of society again. He convinced me that whether the government admitted it or not, he was his own state, and I had to admire that state's organization.

We ended up back at the main house chewing on some deer meat. Well, that was me and Wagner; Gabe and Rosa are vegetarians. My eyes were rolling up into my head with delight; the poor, dead animal tasted so damn good cooked with pepper. Rosa stared at me with great discomfort. It was then I sensed she was eager to make an exit. I told Wilford Wagner we were grateful for his time and that we would send a copy of the piece to him. He said to just leave it at the NRA local.

We were shaking hands at the door.

Wagner asked, "So, what does the Jew boy think of my home?"

My blood went cold. Rosa bowed her head, coming up with gritted teeth, saying, "We're all very impressed."

"I want to hear what the Israelite thought. Just curious what his type thinks of someone who minds his own business. See, Jew boy, how easy it is to make a nation without taking it away from someone else? What do you think?"

Gabe looked Wilford right in the eyes and wryly grinned as he formed his words. "Looking around this massive project of defense and preparation, there is only one thing to say: You have got to be the biggest fucking coward I have ever met."

Wagner's smile ran back into his face while Gabe's flourished into a mad, wide beam. Our host said, "Get him out of here before I beat that smile from his face!" I pulled Gabe out the door and down the stairs, Rosa helping me. As we reached the car I began celebrating in my head. We were done! We were out of here!

"Wait!" Wagner called out from his porch, then bounding down to our level. "What's that there?"

We all turned our heads, asking, "What where?"

"In your back pocket there," he answered, and came directly to me and pulled a piece of paper from my back pocket. I had no idea what it was; I'm always shoving notes and reminders in my pockets. "Oh," Wagner said. "It's just a picture of me at that rally. Sorry. I thought you might have made a sketch of my compound while I wasn't looking."

It was almost in my hand when he pulled it back. An expression of profound absorption creased his face as he inspected the photo, and then came a sad enlightenment. "That vest," he said softly. "That damn vest!" He pulled out a nine millimeter that had been shoved in his jeans behind his back. "I'm sorry," he said sincerely, "but I can't let you leave. This is terrible. This is just one of those happenings that you have no control over. I need to think," he said, desperately rubbing a red mark into his jaw.

"Don't kill us," Rosa pleaded. The sound of her quivering voice made my cold blood colder. I, too, began to shake, though I took her in my grasp.

Wagner shouted, "I don't want to! Damn it! You think I want to?" Then he shook his head as our motives materialized before him. "This is why you came up. You nosy townies! This is why you came up! You got yourselves into this. It's not my fault. You brought this all on yourselves. I thought this was all going to blow by, and it would have. You civil folk just don't know how to leave a person alone. You have to make me part of your world. Well, now you're part of mine, and it's none of my doing." He waved the pistol, ordering us to go with him.

I said, "Look, Wagner, you don't have to do this. I promise that we won't say a word. We'll let you live out here in your own world. We just wanted a story. We were idiots. We'll let you be."

He brought his face right up to mine and spit out his disgust: "Your type don't know how to leave anything be."

I trembled, but said it again. "We'll let you be. You'll never hear from us again."

Rosa was crying. Gabe stood perfectly still. Wagner fell deep into his options and the results thereof. I held out hope. Then he said, "No, you're going to have to come with me."

Chapter Eleven

Rosa was crying and my knees were shaking. Gabe had gone mute. We were at the top of a flight of stairs leading down to the basement of the main house. Between her breath-catching sobs, Rosa pleaded, and I joined in. Wagner just shouted for us to shut our traps and get down the stairs. My wobbly legs barely kept me upright; I leaned heavily on the handrail. When we got to the bottom of the stairs, Rosa threw up on the carpet, causing me to lose my balance and fall onto the pool table.

"God damn it!" Wagner screamed. "Damn! Damn! Damn!" He pointed his nine millimeter. My mouth and eyes widened in reflex. Gabe stepped away from the Boise reporter. I took Rosa in my arms. After a few moments Wagner lowered his gun and looked at me. "I'm going to get some towels and a bucket, and you're going to clean this up." Then he used his weapon to point Gabe over to me and Rosa. She was hanging on tightly to my midsection. I responded by squeezing back. We were sharing a nightmare. Tears never made it past my fear. My dry eyes saw clearly. My mind raced for an answer, for words, for action, for anything. Wagner told Gabe and Rosa to go through a door off in the far corner and for me to stay behind. She would not let go of me. "If you don't get her in there," Wagner warned me, "I'll kill you all right now." As I pulled her over to the door, something strange and hopeful occurred to me: This survivalist does not want to kill us—that, or he was being very careful. I got Rosa to the door and opened it, felt for the light switch inside the door, and there was nothing in there but a cement floor and a drain. I noticed the stains that led to the drain and a carcass hanger in mid-air. This was another skinning room. My hope vanished.

"Please," Rosa's voice vibrated in my ear. "Please don't leave me."

I pushed her off to Gabe, saying, "Do what he says, Rosa. It's going to be all right. It's going to be all right."

She stared into my eyes searching for knowledge, praying with the help of my steely glare that told her that she could believe. Gabe dragged her into the room, holding on to his equipment as well. Wagner slammed the door shut. He pushed me off to the side with the gun's barrel and then locked the door, keeping the key in the bunch on his belt.

He said, "Lay face-down on the floor with your hands behind your neck."

"What?" My whole body went into an uncontrollable convulsion.

He screamed and raised hand gun: "Do it now!"

I made it to my knees, then to my belly.

"Now don't move."

I heard him open the door in the other corner opposite the skinning room, and then heard the sounds of rummaging around—a metal clank, a curse, a broom falling. Annoyed feet stomped back into the room. For some reason it seemed very important that I controlled my bowels, the bowels that were so furious they rumbled and thrashed their contents toward an exit.

"Get up," he said with a human quality in his voice. Again a glimmer of hope formed in the back of my mind. He handed me a plastic bucket containing soapy water with a towel floating on top.

I cleaned up the mess, glad to be working for him. I rifled through my mind for an answer to the ultimate puzzle: how not to die. I kept telling myself to spring at him and grab the rifle. It seemed to me that I was going to die anyway; why not go down on the offensive? But I could only keep panicking. That was all I was good for at the moment.

There was no God, or at least no savior, only me to keep me from harm crossing streets, driving cars, swimming in deep waters. I gripped the wet rag with all my thoughts. Dan, help me. Come up with something. You're all I have. This moment, now that moment—they are your only tools. Help me, Dan. Help me. Stop panicking. Think, fool, think! I forced the cogs of my slithering mind into a slower motion, a softer gear.

Then it hit me like a thunderbolt. I came to my feet, turned to the man pointing death at me, almost smiling, and said, "I just remembered, Mister Wagner, that someone knows we came up here, and will know when we don't return tonight."

"Nice try."

And I was desperate again. "I'm not trying to trick you. It's the truth, the fact of the matter. He tried to talk me out of coming, said we should just go straight to the cops." I returned his gaze.

"You mean he knows about the vest?" he asked.

"Yes."

He stared deep into my eyes to seek out the bluff or the reality. I nodded. He felt around for the tall chair overlooking the pool table, his sight deep inward. It occurred to me that through our fear, Rosa, Gabe, and I had forgotten that Lucas was a lifeline, in that he was not here. Still, he might kill us anyway, the man who jammed a railroad speak through his nephew's chest. (I immediately wished I hadn't thought that.) I awaited his next words and actions more eagerly than a guy bluffing at a big-stakes card game. This was life or death, not little old money.

He muttered, "That damn, cursed vest. My act of kindness to a brother separate from society." He shook his head slowly. "That damn vest." He looked me squarely in the eyes. "You don't know what happened. And if I told you, you wouldn't believe me."

"I'm willing to believe anything that doesn't kill me and my two friends."

He turned his head toward the door behind which Rosa and Gabe waited. He seemed to have forgotten all about them, all about the door, the room, the house upstairs. He pushed himself from his chair, sleepwalking to the door, unlocking it and opening it wide for the prisoners. "Get out of here," he said. "Get in your car and get the hell out of here."

We hurried to the steps leading up, but I stopped, seeing this Marion woman at the top of the stairs holding tight to a rifle. I said, "Mister Wagner," and nodded my head upward. He came to me and saw his woman.

"Marion, open the fence for these good people."

She said, "But we—"

"Marion!" he shouted. After a pause, she removed herself from the doorway, and Wilford Wagner made his way back to the tall chair and stared blankly ahead. "Who would do this to me?" he asked.

Rose hurried up the stairs. I followed but halted, looking back down at Gabe. The red "record" light was on. He had the camera facing the muttering Wagner. "Damn it, Gabe! Let's go!" I yelled. He awoke from his camera-boy trance and followed me out.

My hands fumbled with the keys, our freedom just a moment away, the gate opening before me. Rosa chattered in my ears. "Let's go, let's go; hurry, hurry. Let's go!" Never stopping, she just kept saying this until we pulled through the opening to safety. I heard Gabe say something.

"What did you say?" I asked.

"I got it all."

Rosa asked, "Got all of what?"

"I got it all," and he held up his video camera, "from when he pulled the pistol out until he let us go—everything. I got Rosa hurling,

I got Wagner ranting. I got it all."

Rosa and I looked at one another. We did not smile. I brought my attention back to the road. It was straight to Sergeant Richards. I was off the case.

Chapter Twelve

"What the hell did you do?"

"Hey, Serge, are you looking at that photo?"

"Can't you do anything right? Maybe you really do belong in the back with the rest of the morons!"

A vein popped out from the left side of Sergeant Richards' forehead. His eyes ripped through me, bulging. He glanced over to Rosa, the poor thing still pale from the trauma. I should have dropped her at my place. Gabe sat across from Ellerth's desk just beaming. His eyes twinkled with an off kilter pleasure delectation. Richards stalked about the room, in between desks and chairs. He came back and leaned into my face.

"Don't even think of going up to Wagner's to report on the arrest. I don't want to see you for a while, Dan. Become the invisible man."

Gabe quipped, "Claude Rains or Ralph Ellison's young man?"

Richards leaped the ten feet to where Gabe sat and got right in his face. "What did you say?"

Gabe just continued to shed his light, a crooked grin not hiding itself. Richards' eyes widened, and I swore he thought of bringing Gabe and me around back for a beating.

"Get out!" he screamed. "Just please get out."

Sure, I guess we should have come straight over with the vest photo last night. Sure, I could see his point.

Ellerth rose from his desk dutifully to show he was there to lead the way. I took hold of Rosa and we made our exit, Gabe saying under his breath, "This really got interesting."

I dropped Gabe at the office, telling him to inform Rogers that I would be in. Gabe said that we were most definitely going to keep following the story. He figured Wagner was going to hole up at his fort, and Gabe planned on being there. I said that I had to take care of Rosa before doing anything. If the little fellow with camera would risk Richard's wrath one more time, I suppose I could.

Suddenly I thought: Perez and Reynolds are missing this, out combing the countryside for Barde.

I called Lucas from my place after setting up Rosa on my couch with a shawl. Lucas wanted to talk, but I told him I didn't have time just then, but that I would tell him later what had happened. Rosa looked a bit better, and had begun talking about writing her piece. I wanted a real drink, but pushed that option off to the corner. I sat across the coffee table from Rosa as we each slowly partook of our orange juice.

"I have to get back to my hotel room," she said. "My laptop is there."

I pointed off to my computer. "Use that."

"Dan..."

"Please don't go."

"I'm okay. I'm okay now."

"I want you to stay. I mean... please stay."

"Dan, I have to go to my hotel room to write my story. All my notes are there. How about a late dinner? I'll bring it back from Rand Point. What are you in the mood for?"

I could not speak. I wanted to, but feared a crying jag imminent. Tears welled in my eyes. So much was rushing at me at once. I could not say what the main force behind the tears was for sure, but it all came back to needing Rosa to be here with me. I spoke through fluid, my voice aching for safe harbor, fighting so hard not to break down. I felt so weak quite suddenly, like I had given everything I had in me to hold her in Wagner's basement. The emotional marathon finished, I collapsed.

"Promise you'll come back tonight. I don't care what you pick up for dinner." I could dam the river no longer. I was drowning as I fell onto the couch with her, with her then taking me lovingly in her arms as I inhaled the scent she had applied this tipsy morning. I sobbed while she whispered assurances of her return, and said what a strange few days it had been. I wanted to kiss her but my nose was running and my face felt swollen. I popped up from the couch, wiped the mess on my sleeve and strode to the door with pretend strength. Turning back, I said, "I'll see you whenever you make it back."

Back in my Swinger I said to Gabe, "Maybe we should check in with Rogers."

Gabe said, "That delusional newsman just going to holler for us to get up there fast, so let's get up there fast."

On the drive up I imagined how it could have gone today, me buried somewhere on Wilford Wagner's property, my mother and father holding out hope that I was safe in the world after not hearing from me for a long while; Lucas telling the police where we had gone, the police digging all over Wagner's property. I shivered for my own soul. Or did my soul shiver through this thoughtless body and mechanical mind? Or did the soul not give a damn, knowing itself infinite, and it was the human mind and body staring into the void, the great nothing. I felt bad about what I might have done to my parents. How foolish I would have felt beneath dirt, having walked into a lion's den; I could hear my mother crying.

The twilight gave birth to yet more creepy sensation as I pulled my Swinger over to the side of the road, a quarter mile down the road from the fence. The sky threw down cold rain. I could hear Richards on the megaphone.

"Wilford Wagner! Will you please answer me?" He called out as if he had asked the question more than a few times already. "I have contacted the FBI and the state militia! It won't be long before a helicopter is buzzing over your property! Let's make this easy!"

Gabe and I crept like Nez Perce tribe members: soft and slow, our prey just over the ridge. We became statues when we saw the two patrol cars. Ellerth and the new guy had their rifles aimed at the main house. Richards had just taken a breath, the megaphone at his waist, his head bowed a moment.

Gabe and I were close to each other on the ground, and I saw he had the drone ready for flight, the bird that captures footage—and then I saw Gabe had drawn a small eight-ball on the drone, off to the right on top. I guess he was self-aware.

"It won't be long now, Mister Wagner!" Richards called toward the compound. "Let's do this the easy way! No reason for anyone else to get hurt!"

Wagner appeared on the porch, a rifle in one hand, a megaphone of his own in the other. He spoke into it.

"Ain't you sheriff yet, Cole?"

Richards head bowed and turned and I could see him smile. He then answered. "You know the sheriff's office is in Rand Point."

"Why doesn't Reverend River have a sheriff?" Wagner called out.

"That's just the way it works in old Reverend River. I'm a sergeant and I answer to the sheriff in Rand Point. Wilford, let's you and me stop calling to one another over these damn megaphones."

"It seems to me, Cole, that a town should have its own sheriff."

"This ain't much of a town, Wilford."

Richards paused to think.

"Hey, Cole, remember the old geezer who used to make shine on this slab of rock? Old Mordaci Brown?"

I could tell by the way Richards' back rumbled that he was chuckling a bit, humor alive and well within the stress. "Yeah, Wilford, I remember old Mordaci Brown."

"You know what happened to him?"

After a pause: "No, I don't."

"They put him in the nut house in Rand Point! They got tired of him selling liquor! Got tired of not getting their tax on it! Got tired of his patience for sitting in your lock-up! Sheriff from Rand Point came down and took him away! You didn't know that?"

"No, Wilford, I didn't."

"Society does what it wants to, see? For some reason Reverend River has no captain or sheriff. It's just the way Rand Point wanted it! And they were strong enough to get what they wanted! They wanted Old Man Brown to know they were the bosses! Do you think he knows that now?"

"Wilford, why don't you come talk to me face-to-face?"

I could still see the scene without artificial light, but I wouldn't much longer. The day's curtain was falling.

"Because now society wants to string me up! And I know they will get their way, as is their way! But see, I lived my life by my rules and my beliefs! I'm not sitting hours on end in front of a judge listening to fools argue endlessly over simple facts. I'm not spending my final days in a nut house! Society might bring an end to me, but it ain't coming through my door! And it ain't making me a part of its justice!"

I turned to my right to say something to Gabe but he was gone. My eyes found him on the ground alongside of the squad car closes to the fence. He would shoot the moving pictures and then periodically take a still. He had the drone at his side if the moment presented itself, but if he sent it up now, it would just be a matter of who shot it down first, Richards or Wagner. The officers were too absorbed, too focused on Wagner to take notice of Gabe. I crouched lower and shook my head.

"Wilford, please, let's talk without these damn megaphones! Let's remove whatever's between us!"

"No, there is too much of that to whack away!"

The intensifying wind and rain knocked Richards' hat off and rippled his clothes, but he kept talking.

"We're two men! Let's talk like two men!"

"Remember when we first met, Cole?"

Richards shook his head. "I can't come up with that just right now, Wilford."

"It was at the town dance! Remember when we had town dances?"

Richards' head bobbed up and down. He momentarily let his arm holding the megaphone drop.

"Yeah, you remember, Cole! I was dancing with Nancy Perkins! You asked to cut in! Do you remember what I said?"

"No, Wilford, I do not."

"I said that I did not hold much for tradition! I said that you would just have to wait your turn! You don't remember, do you?"

"No. I surely don't."

"That was before you were a cop, Cole. You were less Society then! Remember? Just a boy jealous of another boy! Well, I want you to know that I'm still that boy! I never killed a person: only deer, elk, bear, squirrels, and rabbits! I didn't kill those boys! And for God's sake, how could I—" His voice broke. He paused. "How could I kill Jimmy? I loved him with all my heart."

"Then why are we doing this, Wilford? I believe you! I'll help you!"

The porch light kicked on automatically and back-lit Wagner, making him a talking shadow.

"You won't believe me for long! Society will kick in! The facts of the case will kick in! I don't know all of what's going on, but I know when I'm dead in the sights of someone's thirty-ought six! A picture is worth a thousand words, and the truth has nothing to do with words! Words aspire to truth, but they ain't the truth! They's just words! That's just a picture of me in a vest! It ain't the truth!"

"Wilford, we can work this out."

"I'm not sitting in jail waiting forever for a trial! That would be like a pillow over my face slowly taking my breath!"

"Wilford! Please let me do what's best for you!"

"Cole, you know what I been doing since those kids gone run down to town with their truth? Well, you're about to find out! And don't think I done kept Marion against her will; she don't want nothing to do with you all neither!"

Wilford Wagner walked into his home. I heard Richards say under his breath, "Oh no." He called for Wagner to come back and talk. About a minute passed. Then it was all sight and sound and fury. A flash like I had never seen before, even at the town's Fourth of July fireworks show. The sound attacked my ears and left me with a hum to hear the rest of the action over. First the other large home went up, then the sheds, one by one—then the greenhouse, and finally the home Wagner had just gone back into. It was amazing. I covered my ears, trying to keep my eyes from averting, yet wanting to take cover. I crouched, braced my eyes, then I looked again. Richards and his fellow officers did the same, ending up behind their vehicles, wood and other such particles falling all around them. Gabe never ceased shooting the video. He flinched when another structure blew up and took to flames, but he never moved from the ground, and flying elements were landing everywhere but where he sat up on one knee. The explosions gave birth to fire. I watched with a child's wonder. I wanted to laugh, and at the same time, the feeling that had overcome me back at my place, the one that had me searching for a mother's breasts, tried to return, but the sounds and sights were too much for tender emotions—it was a show. The fires raged. There were more explosions.

Wilford Wagner had brought an end to his state.

Chapter Thirteen

We continued to watch the compound burn, snap, crackle, and pop. The howling wind tossed the flames. The orange, yellow, and blue light stood out fiercely within the twilight. The houses were fiery hands and their outreaching flames the fingers. Richards stood transfixed, not leaving the moment. The rain that had come was now wind-swept mist. I caught Ellerth smiling, but then he muffled it. The new guy kept checking to see what the others might have to add to the show. He saw me and nodded the others my way. Richards was beyond disappointment and disgust. His eyes returned to the fire. Gabe had disappeared. Then I saw the drone flying over the compound, pausing here and there for a settled shot, then moving on to another part of the destruction. I think Gabe was out of sight so that Richards couldn't throw his remote to the ground and smash it.

"Shall I shoot down that drone?" the new guy asked.

Richards shook his head. "Let him make a record of this. Let him do his job." He meandered over and set up shop there at my side to resume his respectful wake. I kept my mouth shut.

"Well, Dan," Richards asked through a sigh, "do you think he killed those boys? His own nephew?"

I was afraid to speak. I took a breath.

"I don't know, Serge. He as much as told me he gave Barde that vest. He certainly was convinced he was going to be convicted in court."

"Dan, do you think he did it?"

I kept my smile at half-mast, my sight going from my feet to the fires. "Yeah, I do, Serge. The vest's having been to Wyoming, his nephew's being one of the victims. Then he kills himself. I don't care how much of a victim his own words made him out to be, I believe he wasn't the one to say; I think he was crazy. How could he kill himself, this survivalist? I would think he would have gone down fighting if he were innocent. And him saying he didn't kill his own nephew, well, I think that was for his brother's ears; he wanted those words to travel to his brother; he could not face his brother knowing."

Richards' wry grin held nothing but sadness. He looked at me easily, unafraid of eye contact. He said, "I can imagine him feeling the aspect of not being in control of his life the next few years in court, in limbo, others holding his fate; I can see how that would be a fate worse than death to him."

A delayed explosion gave the both of us a start. My eyes darted around for Gabe, finally locating him up the hill about forty yards, getting a nice overview shot of the happenings, aspiring to be a drone himself. The fire reached higher into the sky for a moment, then receded to its consistent eating of wood. Ellerth joined Richards and me.

"Un-fucking-believable!" was his comment. He chuckled until he inhaled Richards' solemnity. "Well, Serge, looks like the Barde guy was telling the truth. His description of the vest-giver matches Wilford Wagner perfectly."

"Yeah," Richards said, "he gave Barde the vest all right. I just wish we knew who gave it to him."

Ellerth and I furrowed our respective brows. Ellerth asked, "Whaddaya mean, Serge?"

"If he had known who gave him that vest, he would have told us.

He would have had something to go on. He would have had hope for returning to his mountain after being cleared." He turned his gaze to me again. "You see, Dan, I don't think he did it. Now I understand how you felt about Barde; there's no reason to think he's innocent, but I do."

"The sound in his voice?" I asked.

"The sound in his voice," Richards returned.

Ellerth said, "But Serge, he blew himself up. Not the actions of an innocent man, are they?"

Richards shrugged and walked off toward his patrol car, saying without turning around, "I called in to town for the fire folks to get out here to make sure this thing don't spread. They should be here soon."

Ellerth stayed by my side to express his view on all this: "Man! That was cool."

Richards had the rookie retrieve a bolt cutter from the trunk to get that gate open for the fire trucks. The rookie threw a rock at the fence to make sure the electric was off. I looked around and Gabe was gone again. I also didn't see the drone, but then it appeared from the other side of the compound, the great hawk photographer, dipping down just short of the flames, and then rising again.

. . .

Gabe went to his section of the workplace and I went to mine. I wrote everything from a trance: finding the picture of Wilford Wagner wearing the vest, going to his compound, being found out and held prisoner, going back and seeing the explosions. I was emotionally involved, but I still made use of my thesaurus. Somewhere in the article I said that while I believed this survivalist had killed his own nephew and those other boys, I would never know for sure. Even with a thorough trial, we would never know for sure.

Rogers slapped me on the back, and I knew that was appropriate, but I didn't remember why anymore. I had lost my grip on something.

I drove home misplaced, a mortal behind the wheel of a machine, knowing where to go, but not why, and thus feeling a bit of the machine myself. I had experienced this before, whether brought about by a large event—my dad's leaving my mother, for example—or just catching a glimpse of a shadow out of the corner of my eye... a shadow named Spooky Calm. I believed I was about to killed and then buried out on Wagner's compound, and that made me think of my mother crying, but now was the time for being ultra-present; all I really owned was this moment. That empowered me greatly, but left me immediately nostalgic for living in the three times—present, past and future—all at once. This too would pass.

Among the many messages there were three consecutive messages from Lucas, the last one being:

"Damn you!" Lucas screamed. "Will you call me and let me know what's going on, you thoughtless prick?"

I poured a glass of water and then called him back. I told him all about what had happened. He listened without interrupting, which was a grand trait that he possessed. I also told him all of it had me feeling lost, yet very alive. He said that he thought he understood; that when his mother had had a hysterectomy to remove cancerous cells he worried incessantly, but that he also noticed how that made him more aware of everything else. It was an emotional equation that made sense. A powerful negative experience ultimately wakes up all of you.

Then I heard a grunt and my old friend questioned me: "Do you mind my saying this? I think you're going to mind my saying this."

"What is it?" However, I knew. I don't know how I knew, but I knew.

"I don't think Jimmy Wagner's uncle did it."

I asked flatly, "Why?"

"He didn't have much use for anything that wasn't on his mountain. The more I think about this killer's carving out birds on dead boys' feet, the more I think of someone calling out to the world, wanting the world to hear him, and wanting to see the world's reaction. Wagner and Barde would never see our reactions from their mountains. This person is a boy himself—if this person is a male—with a magnifying glass, bringing the sun's heat down on an ant colony. That's what I was telling Rosa that got me and her going, when you came by with the picture of Wagner in the vest at the rally. I think I'm starting to understand this killer. The lunatic came upon the idea of framing someone so he could watch the trial. He wanted to have an effect on us. I don't think this Wagner guy would have come off his high place to watch a trial. Dan, I think I'm right about this."

Someone knocked at my door. I told Lucas I would call him tomorrow if I hadn't left for Los Angeles to work for the new TV show called "When Compounds Blow-up." I swung open the door and welcomed into my home a lovely journalist named Rosa. I told her about the suicide explosion, and she shook her head in disbelief, and made funny noises I equated with kinky sex. I did not tell her that Lucas and Richards thought this nut was innocent. What I did instead was take the back of her neck with my right hand and pull her mouth to mine. We kissed each other softly for a short while and then the passions held behind the dam were set free. Her pullover got pulled off, her black jeans unzipped. We made love for a bit, then we fucked; we kissed tenderly again, then we bit into each other's skin, leaving marks; we asked searchingly what the other wanted, then we ravaged each other rudely. I was already lost, so now I went missing further in her. She very much did the same. God, her soft skin! Her sweet smell! Lost, lost and lost again.

In the afterglow, after we had descended back to Earth, we held each other and she told me about the "sort of" boyfriend that she had back in Boise, and how any real relationships she got involved in had yet to survive her travels and her ambition. I said that if I hadn't been accused of raping Melissa's son, I would still be with her, I assumed. Eventually I asked her the question of the day:

"Do you think Wilford Wagner was our man?"

"God, yes! How can you even ask? He killed himself rather than go to jail. Lord, he's our Bird Man. He was going to kill us."

"Why didn't he kill us? I know, I told him someone knew we were up at his place, but why would that stop a psycho? And then he kills himself anyway. It doesn't make sense."

"He murdered little boys, Dan. In the light of day he just couldn't face it. He would never admit to it, never face his judgment. Dan! He was going to bury us up there! But then he realized it was all over, and he wilted like the crazy growth he was."

"Yeah, that makes sense."

"Shit!"

"What?"

"I have to get this explosion stuff off to my paper." She scuffled with the covers and began dressing.

"Relax. They've gone to print already."

"I know that, Dan, but I have to get the information to them. I have to write my article and email it in. And we have a web site updating 24/7, old man."

I said, "Please tell me your laptop is in the trunk so you can do it here."

She paused to grin my way. "It is." She was tying her shoes when a thought hit me.

"All your stuff is in the car, isn't it?"

She had made it halfway to the door, halted, and her shoulders fell. Sweet Rosa faced me as she said, "It's that time. At least it was that time. Now with this explosion I'll be here a couple more days." She paused. "Hey, we were never going to end up in the same city."

"I know. It's just that this is happening so soon after... the goodness."

"Dan, I've checked out of my hotel. Can I work out of here for the next day or two?"

I warmed again. "Please."

She smiled and then went to retrieve the tools of her trade. My plan was to catch a nap, let her start her article, and then see what she thought of another round.

I knew Wagner had killed himself. I didn't kill him. I could sleep and look myself in the mirror and everything else. I had only found a picture of him wearing a particular vest. I didn't bring about his demise. Still, I felt a weight. The spooky calm drifted away like smoke, the satisfaction of sexual release became a pleasant memory, and I was left with my psyche's gravitational pull. Then a thought: If Wagner did not kill his nephew and the other boys, the real Bird Man had planned to frame Wilford Wagner all along, not Mountain Man Barde, to whom Wagner had given the vest out of the goodness of his heart. The real Bird Man must have killed Wagner's nephew as a way of getting the frame structured, having already sent him the vest in the mail as a gift from an admirer. Why did that framing make sense to me? Barde was a good target, but I had to imagine that Wagner had angered more folks than Barde. Shit! Wagner did it! Wagner did it! Still, if Wagner was framed, I had been key in helping the killer play his or her game. Nonsense! Pure fucking nonsense! Still...

I fell asleep to the sound of Rosa's typing. I thought I had found calm in the eye of the storm, but the storm raged on; my dreams were hostile toward me. In the foggy mind unawake, Gabe and I were up at Barde's cabin. Apparently the animal man had been spotted there, and we now believed him to be the killer. When we busted into the home, the mother, looking more like Rosa, aimed her shotgun our way. Gabe leaped out the window, but I froze. She clopped over to me in her oversized work boots yelling obscenities, disgusted that I could ever think her sweet boy a murderer of children. I told her I was the one trying to save him, but in the dream I was lying. She made me get on my knees. As I complied, I felt a muddy, soft texture that I then understood to be bloody skin. She put the barrel to my head and told me to pray to God for forgiveness. I screamed.

"Dan, Dan! It's all right! You were having a bad dream."

I could see Rosa through dawn's slim light. She had a t-shirt on, having been asleep herself. I propped up for a few moments, rubbing my eyes and face. She in turn rubbed my back. I shuffled to the washroom and looked myself in the face. Who is he? I returned to my bed, shaky.

"God, sometimes a dream can really do it to you." I lay back on my pillow and she fell into my arms. She smelled of something wonderful, whatever it was.

"You okay now?"

"I'm fine. Jesus, do you feel heavenly in my arms."

"Yeah, I suppose I do. I have to get down to the police station for any updates, get some quotes. Come with me?"

"Oh, I don't know. No one loves me down there. Let me steal any worthwhile quotes from you, though."

"Come on, we'll go down together, then get some breakfast."

"You know what I have to do? I have to drive up to Barde's cabin to let his mom know her son is a free man. Well, he's kind of free already, but you know, in the eyes of society. I think that may be part of the dream I just had."

"Okay, we'll meet back here." She adjusted her sweet head to fit more comfortably on my chest.

"But you know what I'm going to do right now?" I asked.

And she began laughing, because she already knew.

. . .

I felt heroic driving up old Baldy Mountain. After all, I had found the picture of Wagner with the vest. I had proven Barde's innocence. God, I was swell. Yesterday's rain had the roads in slippery shape, but I and the Dodge managed just fine. I got lost once or twice, but eventually pulled up onto her property. She came out, and surprise, surprise, she wasn't bearing a rifle. Things were looking up. As I climbed out from behind the wheel, she called out: "What do you want? Don't come no further."

"I've come to give you some good news."

"I don't mind that. Give out with it."

"Well, first off, your son came to visit me after escaping from the authorities. He told me to tell you that he was off for Alaska, that he would write you when he got settled." She nodded that she understood, but I sensed no real gratitude. "And second, we proved your son's innocence." Her jaw dropped. That was more like it. "Yeah," I started, my time for bragging, "I found a piece of evidence that supported your son's claim that the vest was indeed given to him. In the same breath it revealed the real killer." (It was Gabe who said to look for articles that pricked my ear, but I did do the work.)

She didn't care who the real killer was. She just smiled and then began laughing. Then Mother Barde did the strangest damn thing: She began hooting like an owl, a very loud owl. She went on for close to a minute. I figured that's how these mountain folk celebrate. I was about to just offer a wave and make my way back to Boise Girl when a figure appeared from down a slope out of the thick brush. It was Barde. He walked dutifully toward his mother. When he saw me, he froze. Then recognizing me, he smiled and progressed toward me. The mother hurried over to him and reached up to his wide shoulders.

"They found the real killer, son. You're free! They found the real killer." They embraced. His wrists were handcuff-free.

Barde offered his hand and said, "I don't know why I knew, or why it was so, but I knew you were on my side. Thanks."

"Hey, it's all in a day's work." Then I spoke more like a person. "I'm glad it ended up right for you."

"Me too," he said. "I like going to town every once in a while. Now I can again."

KILLING THE BIRDS

They offered me food and moonshine, but I politely declined. The mother looked hurt, so I asked for a spot of the rocket fuel for the road. She gave me a big old jug of it. She really looked happy then. The wiry old mountain woman slapped me in the face lightly and said, "You ain't bad, for one of them."

. . .

A lot had taken place since I had had sex last night (and this morning, thank you). Gabe's footage was being shown across the country: the interviews with Wagner, the shots Gabe had sneaked while we were being held captive, and the explosion finale. I'm sure the viewing audience found it to be just what they had come to expect: the wacky world coming through their TV sets. To the inner circle of media workers, Gabe became a star overnight. Everyone wanted him, every major news organization. I had plenty of offers, too. I don't think John Rogers was ever going to get anything out of it but his own excitement.

I became the face of the story in that Gabe got a great shot of me holding Rosa to my side when she was scared out of her wits in Wagner's basement. For that one and only moment I looked brave, and that shot kept being shown and I kept looking brave until one might think I actually was brave, and that's just not the truth.

Since I was young I had had dreams and ego fantasies about going back to Chicago and becoming a famous writer, but I had come to accept that I was never going to be anyone. Here I was on the phone fielding various offers for jobs and interviews, my favorite being a book deal.

Rosa wasn't back yet, so I drove over to Lucas' place. He was drunk and unhappy. I told him that I hoped he would eventually be happy for my success. I waved the jug of moonshine before him.

He said, "I am happy. Why, don't I look happy?"

"Yeah, yeah, you look fine... little pale maybe."

Lucas shook me off and said, "You're pale, pal."

His eyes were red and his words slurred... nothing I hadn't seen before, but sometimes, times like this, his unhappiness shone dark. The last thing he needed was another drink, and that was all I could think to offer.

"Barde's mother gave me this big jug of shine—kind of a 'thank you' for bringing out her son's innocence."

"You're quite the guy."

Ouch. He wasn't even a little happy with me.

"Should I pour you a drink?" I asked.

"Sure, pour us a drink."

Then he leaned forward, as forward as his extraordinary stomach would allow, and vomited on the carpet.

Chapter Fourteen

I cleaned up the mess, however reluctantly. In the end, though, there is never a choice. Lucas and I have been partners for so long that certain responsibilities go unquestioned. He mumbled, shouted, and punched my shoulder when I wiped his face with a wet rag. He was smashed… useless. I listened to him rant from the couch—this after trying to converse with him in vain.

"You just forgot about old Lucas… old, fat, doesn't-leave-the-house Lucas," he said, then muttering down at his belly incoherently. His head shot up and glowered at me: "I thought you were dead! Running up some mountain to ask a murderer some dumbass questions," he scoffed. I thought my apology to him over the phone had been enough, but the liquor brought his unresolved anger back up from his gullet. Under his breath, he said, "I thought you might get killed; now I don't think he did it." Then very loudly, "But I'm just sitting here worrying! And what about me! What am I going to do if you're gone? It'll just be my fellow losers on the Internet and Wells dropping in twice a month." His head wobbled and that had me thinking he would pass out. Then he was back to mumbling. "I guess that's coming to be now; your turn to fly the coop. Stop by Reno on your way out and say 'howdy' to my slut mother. Just watch your zipper. Watch your zipper close, unless you want a blowjob from an old bag. At least have her take her teeth out."

That hit his funny bone and he laughed on and off for a minute.

I was on the floor now scrubbing the carpet. He frowned down at me as I looked up to see his brown eyes swimming in bloodshot red, unfocused. "I really blew it," he said. "I really blew it; never had a woman." He inhaled deeply to bring about a full resounding shout. "And I really like women! You have no idea what that is like: to want something, something that everyone else has had, and not to have it yourself!" He fingered the chair's arm and came up thoughtful. "I can't even get myself to call a whore; I'm so damn embarrassed by my body." He coughed and looked around his homestead. "Well, at least I'm not homeless." He muttered inaudibly for a minute or two and then did pass out.

. . .

The brisk northern air actually hugged me as I paced around my car, not sure if I should leave Lucas. The night had come suddenly, and though I wanted to hurry home and apologize to Rosa for making her wait, I ceased my pacing and looked on the home I spent my life in from my teenage years on. The structure could never claim to be a barrier between a small-town writer and the Chicago Tribune; still it held a crippled brother who had come to be the one person in this world who had come to depend on me. I drove home not wondering why life was such a procession of tug-of-war, but feeling the various grips pulling me this way and that.

Hell, this could be the new beginning I had always wanted, and yet part of me yearned to retire. I could move back in with my mother, write novels, and help her keep up the place. Maybe find a hard-headed woman to join me in my conversion with the land. I'd have quiet time writing, meditating over all my experiences, but wouldn't create any more complicated experiences—just the simple, brawny ones: working the land, pressure-cooking fruit and vegetables.

It could never be that simple, not for me... my Dad maybe—and I do think life was simple for my mom. Ah, everything's relative; what's more complicated, more traumatic than raising kids.

My dark single-floor dwelling spoke volumes, or at least told a story. I knew my answering machine held a goodbye from Rosa. I braced myself with a deep breath and hit the button.

"Dan, it's Rosa; I had to go; the car was packed, I had to..." I heard her hunting for words. Suddenly she blurted out frantically, "I have a cat at a friend's, a friend who is cursing my name. I had to get back. I left my card; call me if you're in Boise." Her voice vanished and I assumed that she hung up, although I didn't hear a click. Then: "Hey, here's a word you wouldn't call English: inamorata. Ask Lucas what it means, or just look it up. I really don't know what to say. For all the unknowns and limited time in a couple of days, I still feel I'm inamorata; still I have to get back to my life. Take care."

I lifted my old copy of Webster's Dictionary from the shelf and plopped down on my ancient couch. I skipped the origins and went straight to the meat. Inamorata: A woman loved; one's sweetheart or mistress.

Under that listing I took note of a very similar word. Inamorato: A man loved; a woman's lover.

I began rummaging through my box of old writings: two novels, a screenplay, a play, and a bunch of short stories. But what kind of writer was I, not knowing off-hand what inamorata meant? Still, a New York publisher had called. All the queries and outlines I had sent out to New York, Chicago, Los Angeles—all deep expressions from my soul—all turned down with form letters or ignored completely. Now I stumble upon a killer and I have a story worth telling. The business of business is business, and everyone prefers their gossip juicy.

I woke up in my chair, a manuscript in my lap, my dad sitting off in the kitchen reading, as was his way when he wasn't working or fishing. I cleared my throat and he looked my way. My neck creaked as I moved it, so from there on I took everything slowly, pushing myself from the chair like an elderly man. I made it to the washroom and managed to shower, and felt surprisingly good, as if something had clicked inside my head. Survival and sleep do that to you, I think. I entered the kitchen, bid my dad 'good morning' and poured us each a glass of juice.

"Your mom was worried. I'm here to see you're all right and report back her."

"Where does she get her information, living out there along the Sticks?"

"The CB, I'd guess. We all love gossip."

"Everyone loves gossip except you, Dad."

"Well, everyone likes it more than me. I'm still human."

"Do tell."

He smiled and said, "Or maybe that widow neighbor brought the story to her."

"You know about that?"

"I have a CB, too."

I smirked. We each let the decent moment have its wordless say, but I can only go so long without talking or writing.

"Tell Mom I'm fine and I'll be up to see her."

"Just call her; I was just being folksy about reporting back to her."

I nodded.

"Okay, Pop. But hey, ya got a couple of hours for some late-season fishing?"

"Check the calendar, Son; it's a work day; I have to go."

I saw the title of the book as he rose: All the Pretty Horse. As he opened my front door I spoke: "If you're human, and you do suffer some gossip, don't you want to hear any of this? It's been a wild few days and I know you don't have a TV. I proved a man's innocence!" I felt hurt feelings rise in me. I tried to push them down. "Did you hear about that?"

"You know, I was so impressed with the man blowing himself up, I forgot all about the other fellow. What's his name?"

"Barde."

"Well, Barde is certainly in your debt. Oh yeah, everyone is telling their Wilford Wagner stories down at the mill, arguing if he did it. But Dan, I found out all I wanted to know when I heard you snoring; you know, breathing." He smiled widely. I had no choice but to do the same.

"We're different, aren't we, Dad?"

He interrupted his departure: "I suppose, but not as different as we might think. Hey: what about the weekend for some fishing? I'll pick you up." After stepping out the door, he leaned back in. "After we catch dinner, maybe you and I can eat it with my new lady friend."

I recovered as quickly as I could manage. "Sure, that sounds nice."

"Call your mother," and he was gone.

It should not have shocked me that Dad had a new woman. He has had a few since the break-up all those years ago. I guess it's just the thought that I have to meet the new one. I even kind of hope this is the one. He's so picky. But to be fair, he just doesn't like trouble or mixing in town gatherings, but most women do—at least the ones who have chased after him do. He needs a mountain woman that just wants to be still and smell the four seasons, and let him read. She won't have to fish, but she would have to be proud of his ability to catch them, and maybe take to cooking them in new and elaborate ways. This is a man who wakes at five every morning and gets in bed at night around nine. That's Saturdays and Sundays, too. But he wasn't apathetic by a long shot. He just lived within himself and let the world do the same.

We were different.

. . .

Mom was fit to be tied. She got on me from the get-go... said I broke my promise not to get into this kind of stuff any deeper. She paced, scolded, and even got choked-up. I finally shouted at her to sit down and listen to me for a minute. I then had a seat myself.

"You're just going to have to let me live my life and try not to worry. I'm going to do what I'm going to do. You have a girl in Nashville, another boy in Chicago, and grandkids to boot; you're going to die of worry."

She tried to compose herself. "But I don't worry about them, Dan. Oh sure, I pray for them every morning and every night before bed, but I've been around, kid; I know the world's a dangerous place, either on this mountain I live on or in Chicago—but you, Dan, you up the odds with your... ways."

I thought she was going to say "antics."

"I don't know what to say, Mom. It seems to me there's nothing for you to do but pray. You can't stop me from being me. I can tell you this type of thing will never happen again, or I can say I'm going to be an investigative reporter in Chicago. Either way, I will always be an alcoholic. I'll always mix it up with the other townies. Peace is not my path. I'd like some of that sweet pap flowing through my mind, but I'm too interested in this stupid planet to save myself from it—obsessed with it, really. And yea, I want the people of the town and the world to know and love me. You're just going to have to like that about me. We can't keep having this same conversation."

She nodded and said, "We do keep having the same conversation over and over again, don't we, you and I, everybody; the same conversations, the same wars, the same struggle to control the other, like others are a part of your body—a misbehaving part of the body. She got up and started frying some zucchini.

KILLING THE BIRDS

Chapter Fifteen

The next week started out fantastic enough:

I told the Chi-town Tribune and a couple of Hollywood rags that I would indeed like to work for their particular organizations, not telling each about the others, but just send along the structure of their proposal so that my agent/manager could look it over. (Bullshitting was so easy for me sometimes.) I also got the book deal started. They wanted a fairly detailed account of the Bird-Man case along with my emotional response—basically a novel, a mystery, but bare-bones true. I said, "Sure, but I want you to read some other pieces of mine. You know, we'll be friendly." They agreed to survey my catalogue, see what they thought, now that I was technically famous. They said to look for the first draft of the contract in the mail.

In between all of this and the TV interview offers, I went fishing with Dad and had met his lovely, plump roommate—it had gone that far. Her name was Brenda and she hovered over him like a cherub. He, in return, treated her poetically and yet directly. He also patiently listened to her tales of ghosts in a cabin in which she had once resided. She wasn't as verbose as me or as know-it-all as Dad. She was a more pleasant person than either of us two males, and strong like my mom. I liked her and I decided that I very much wanted them to make it. This world can be so much friendly with a thoughtful bedmate. Now my mom had hers and Dad had his, for these were the days that Time had promised: healed wounds, a wider perspective.

I went to the internet to check the Boise Tribune, to read my sweet Rosa's writings. I was floored. Her name did not appear in anywhere in the paper. There was a fellow with a byline and a picture telling all about the happenings in Reverend River. He called us Rand Point's hick cousins. This chap did not tell it as he had been here, but more like a gossip columnist. He did mention his tireless assistant once; poor Rosa, the mystery researcher. The even sadder thing was that the articles were quite effective. I found myself caught up in the film-noir mood done mountain style. Though I don't know why I felt sorry for her; a job is a job; we can't all be famous.

I could not get myself to call her.

I made Lucas my agent/manager. He immediately began shooting out information on the subject of representation. We talked about a system in which, wherever I ended up, I'd submit all my choices through him via the computer. Also, we agreed that any deal would provide me with a couple of months a year back here in my Reverend River; time for family, friends, and my old writing room.

Then the offer arrived: Later Reno's Late Night Show—a rare invite on their part. Most late-night TV shows had given up on book authors and serious reality segments; there was a whole industry of that; they mostly had celebrities shopping their projects, the latest pop wonder, kids with science projects and pet tricks. Still, there is that oddball, the Nobody who mixes it up with a Somebody and has the big light shone on him. I had crossed paths with a serial killer, had beaten the cops to the truth, and had saved an innocent man. Every now and again they throw a hero a bone. I did not know all the rules—just that I had been able to keep my new deal with Scoop TV for twenty grand and still was allowed to do the Reno show. And it was all because of Gabe's footage.

It must have occurred to me that this would be a good time to have an anxiety attack, because a powerful one took hold. I holed up for a day and turned the phones off. I felt some control again.

Out in the social scene, my back got slapped at every turn. "Way to get that sick animal, Dan," Doc Paulsen had called out in that reedy tone of his. At the post office, the friendly black lady Lowesa pulled my face to hers and kissed me. She had a bit of the old revelation, saying, "The Lord sent you down here just to do that, Dan Holdsworth. You are one of the few free men here now. You did your thing. You stopped that man from killing any more of our boys. Thank God and thank you!"

Wow!

For a few days there, my money was no good at the café. Fat Sara made me take cake when I wasn't hungry. Her daughter Little Sara—only two pounds lighter than the original—kept stealing long, involved stares into my face. It was as if she didn't recognize me. Hell, I had baby-sat for her and her brothers more than once in the old days. Now I was a star, Reverend River's prince, and a guest on Later Reno's.

I celebrated in a grand fashion. I called Lucas from the Athens Bar. I informed him that I had a couple of cases in the trunk, some weed as a gift from Wells, who was holding court so loud that I had to shout that I would be over at Lucas' in about an hour, after the boys had bought me a few more rounds. He laughed and told me to be careful.

Things got going quick, or maybe I got drunk fast, because after telling the great story a time or two more, I was on a wobbly table doing my victory dance for all to see. Max took to throwing pennies and nickels at me. Then the sky broke wide open and a cold November rain poured down in buckets. I had to go dance in the angels' joyful tears. Wells' younger cousin joined me, and the rest watched from the doorway and through the window. The pool hall across the street took a break from their games to take in the dancing fool. I believe it was at that point I was screaming over and over, "Man, I could have been killed! That crazy Wagner fuck was going to kill us! But I'm alive! I'm alive! I am so fucking alive!"

Athens' owner, a trucker named Grolsch, whose wife cheated on him at every turn, braved the rain to say that it was time that I went on home. He said he was not going to let me drive. Someone would have to volunteer. And there were plenty who did offer their services to the reigning king of R & R. But I dashed up the road, calling back: "I'm going to run in the rain!" The approving cheers barely cut through the downpour to reach my drowning ears.

I made it as far as the big bar on Main Street. They didn't know me at first, but then a guy purposefully placed himself on the stool next to me and roared over the music, "You're the guy who took down old Wilford Wagner, aintchya?"

I nodded and smiled proudly, happy to be out of the rain, drinking a beer and nipping at a double-bourbon, all of which I had paid for myself, thank you. After a deliberate pause in which the man seemed to be contemplating whether he should continue his exchange with me, he asked, "You know anything about him, this Wilford Wagner, other than he wore that vest and lived in his own state?"

"Well, I did interview him before the arrest. He did show us around his compound before freaking out and taking us down in his cellar to die." And I just broke out laughing. The thought that this all had really happened, at a safe distance now, yet still real, was funny to me.

"Hey, Ass-Hole!" the man roared. "Wilford was my brother! And he ain't killed no-one!" He remained snarled, eyes ablaze, but then took a breath. "Maybe it ain't your fault," he said with only a little less hostility in his voice, his teeth clenched, "but I'd appreciate you not bragging on being alive while a real good man is DEAD!" He stood up straight and walked away, out of the tavern. A man followed him directly. A few people who could hear us over the music looked me over curiously, as if I were a three-legged dog. I finally remembered the guy's face from the soggy funeral. Indeed he was Wilford's brother...

Jimmy's father. I downed my drinks, shook my wet head, flung a tip for the bartender and stumbled out into the unrelenting rain.

It was hard to say for sure, looking across the lot, but I thought I saw Wilford's brother getting into the passenger side of a Pathfinder. The other fellow about to get behind the wheel of that car was looking over my way. He shifted right into mid-stride toward me. I tried to smile. I couldn't see his facial expression from under his cowboy hat and through the rain. So suddenly and unexpectedly, his fist crashed into my face, my jaw specifically. I fell back into the tavern's side door and down onto the wet cement. I saw my own blood poison a puddle. I abruptly lost my breath as his boot launched into my soft belly. He kicked me in the head, a glancing blow but still brutal enough to close my eyes, dots swirling on the insides of my eyelids. Everything was a blur for the next minute. My eyes thought they saw—from the ground and the haze—Wilford's brother pulling the other away, telling him to get hold of himself. There were witnesses, mostly the same folks who thought I was a three-legged dog. A hand reached down to take my arm. I resisted, so the voice belonging to the hand said, "I'm going to help you up."

Vertical life brought shocking sparks of light, and I was a boat out in rough waters—a storm, a carnival ride. I felt the hard cement slap the left side of my body, my head taking a scary knock. The voice said, "I'm sorry. I didn't see you tilt." I think I began to giggle for a moment. The voice said: "You ready to try again?"

This time the vertical world was not quite so abstract. A few sparks, a wave or two, and then we were walking around to the front of the tavern. In that strong light, with a little less rain, I saw my helper to be the teenaged Indian who had shared a cell with me and talked to his grandfathers.

"Hey, it's you! Thanks for the hand." I wavered in front of the club, letting the words float before me. "Were you in the club?"

"No, they don't let me beg for drinks there, no matter how casual I do it." His eyes barely caught my face. They were mostly beyond me or focused on the ground. I was good and smashed, and beat up to boot, so I lazily looked him in the face.

"So you were looking for some friends, and you saw your old prisoner buddy and decided to come to his aid?"

"Something like that."

I felt that I should move on, but had a more potent urge to just stand there leisurely, letting the night drift, allowing redemption or guilt, whichever this particular night willed now that it had done its worst.

I said, "I guess ya get beat on every now and again whether you earned it or not."

He spat back quickly, "Sometimes you have it coming for other stuff that you got away with."

I smiled, teetering. "Is that a quote from your grandfathers?"

He inhaled his smile and said, "No, that's one of mine, or whoever wrote the whole Karma thing."

"Whatever," I quipped out of the side of my mouth, then sauntered out into the middle of the street and took in the club and the teenager from a distance. I owned this town, lest anyone forget that. Then the rain came down hard again as if the love of the sky's life had died. Strong, howling gusts came in behind that rain. I howled. There was nothing else to do. The Indian backed into the tavern's doorway just to get knocked aside by a couple leaving. I laughed hysterically.

My protégé shouted, "I want to get the hell out of this flood!"

"You got nowhere to go?" I called out over Nature's tantrum.

"Not within walking distance!"

I thought but a moment. "Follow me!" I sprinted north and hung a right at the first intersection. I looked back to see if he was with me. He kept an easy pace at my heels. He could have been a quarter mile ahead of me at my fastest clip. I wasn't sure what time it was, but I thought the Methodist church basement might still be having a meeting. We could get out of the elements, get a cup of coffee, and maybe even catch a ride home. Actually, Lucas was only a mile away but I didn't want to take the kid there; Lucas had had his fill of surprise guests for a while.

All the running had me a wheezing, beaten, a drunken scene when I bounced the church's swing-open doors against their respective walls. The gang was startled, jolting from their clean-up responsibilities after the meeting. John, usually the meeting's leader, was the first to speak out. "Damn it, Dan! You know the rules about coming here drunk! It's just damn thoughtless!"

"Hey, relax. I got caught in the rain. This is my friend..." I struggled for his name.

He said, "They call me Raven." He pointed to his hair.

Nora Morse stepped up, took one of my arms, and peered into my face. "He's been beaten," she said placidly. "Sally, get a wet rag, warm; Stan, bring a chair before he collapses; Tom, bring the wet boys some coffee." Each in turn followed her calmly spoken directions. It wasn't long before I was halfway through a cup.

Stan hovered over me. "You boys need a ride home?"

"I suppose we do, Stan. Thanks."

Nora dabbed at my face with the warm, slightly soapy rag. I flinched periodically.

Stan continued, "We ain't seen you in a while, Dan. Though, with all the hoopla, we thought you might have turned this way again. You've been through some stuff."

I smiled and said, "And it's hard not to celebrate celebrity."

Stan said, "Yes, we drunks have to learn new ways to celebrate."

I said, "Oh, take the fucking serious look off your face. Wait, that's the same sad fucking expression that represents your sober happiness." I'm not sure where that came from.

Nora, the woman who worked behind the drugstore counter, took Stan's arm, seeing he was about to get riled, and said all the more easily,

"This isn't the time, is it, Stan?" She turned her head: "Tom, you drive them." She turned back to my scowling mug. "Go on home now and get some sleep, Dan. Call me if you like. You know where we all are."

I nodded my head, letting the righteous rage recede. I shouldn't have come here, of course, but drunks running in the rain are on a journey to annoy in search of attention. I wanted to tell them my higher power was still just me and always would be. What they offered me was coffee and a ride home. So I bit my obnoxious tongue and had Tom drop me and my young buddy off at my shack.

I phoned Lucas, who was pissed at me again, but resigned to my freedom and popularity. When I told him I had left the beer in the trunk by Athens, he did declare his sufferance in no uncertain terms. I was still thirsty, so I told him I was out the door to walk the three miles into town, get the beer and drive back to his place; I got a ride home just to walk back into town—classic drunk. Still, Lucas did not try to dissuade me. I belched and said, "Come, Tonto, it's a walk to town to fetch my car and beer."

"I have a good sense of humor, but we're not close enough for you to call me Tonto."

"Okay, Raven. Let's fly."

The walk brought blustery revelations from me, small quotes from Raven's grandfathers, and silent memories of the countless times I had taken long walks into town. Every now and then Raven talked to himself, and I accepted my comrade as he was. Somewhere in between his conversations with himself and his grandfathers, he and I started talking to each other again.

"White man, you know why I was there in the parking lot and saw you getting your lights turned off?"

"Do tell."

"I watch people pull up into the lot, get out of their cars and go into the tavern, and then I get into the ones that aren't locked—there's plenty of them—and I get warm and smoke the butts in their ashtrays.

You'd be surprised what they leave in the glove box or under a seat. I've sat in their cars and smoked their pot and drank their primer beers and kept nice and warm and dry. I like the couples the best. A girl goes into a club, she's going to be in there with her friends a while. A guy might check out the scene with a beer and then he's back on the road. I've had some close calls and I've been caught."

"Someone turn your lights out?"

"I quickly tell them I'm just trying to get warm. They see nothing is gone except a cigarette smoked from a pack they left behind. They just smack me and warn me that if they ever catch me again in their car, it's a death sentence. I don't go in their car again. I make sure to remember their car."

The storm had passed. A calm, wet world took us in, and we remembered the fury fondly. We were grateful to have survived its wrath.

"You don't have a home?" I asked.

"I have a cabin on the mountain. I have family further north, right on the Canadian border and across it, but this is where my grandfathers want me to be, so I'm here mostly. I scrounge around town and then take to the hills and my shack for some peace. I'll fish, hunt... starve. But my grandfathers know survival tricks, so we get by."

"Well, I'll be straight with you, Raven: After what I've been through, here in Reverend and out in Rand Point, I take friendship and cohabitation seriously. No chances with people I'm just getting to know. So I'm going over to my friend Lucas' place. Where can I drop you off—the mountain shack?" He and I both knew I was in no shape for mountain roads that they were in no shape for me.

He entered himself for the answer, muttering, maybe consulting his grandfathers. He finally said, "The abandoned switchman's shed. You know, a few miles before the yard?"

"Yeah, I know of it. I threw rocks at it when it was still in use. Ya sure you want to go there?"

"Yeah; the old lady that lived there died. They found her a mile off by the stream. She must have been thirsty. Maybe you can wait while I scout it. Someone may have made a claim on it."

On the drive to his flop for the night he asked if I could spare a beer or three. I said that I could spare beer to anyone who picked me off the ground after I'd been trounced upon.

He said, "We lone rangers have to stick together."

I said, "You speak the truth, my faithful Indian companion."

I looked over to him to see if I had gone too far, that I didn't know him well enough for such irreverence.

He smiled and said, "You're all right for a white man."

Chapter Sixteen

We each had our own smoke, me slouching in the sleepy arms of the couch, cradling a beer in my lap, Lucas at the computer, puffing and talking away. He had to get out that oral exchange bug while someone was actually in the room with him.

"So I'm capable of buying something in theory, then selling it for a profit, you know, in the real world."

"Wow," I said unconvincingly. "That's cool."

"I'm thinking of doing some renovations around here. Maybe knock down a wall, give myself more room to roll around in here."

I nodded.

"Hell, I was even thinking of having that operation, finally get my act together."

"Operation?"

"You know, gastric bypass. They make your stomach smaller, or whatever. You literally can't eat too much. It's a shot at sanity; it's a shot at a real life."

"You got a real life."

"A real crappy life."

"Anyway, the operation sounds scary."

"Right," and he chortled, "but interviewing a man you consider to be a serial killer out on his own property, that's not creepy."

"I know, I know."

"What price glory, pal."

"I know, I know."

One of Lucas' internet pals buzzed into his system. The communication came from Ireland. I fell asleep on the couch between sips of beer, the joint snuffed out and on the side table. I came to every once in a while, once from the shock of spilling the beer in my lap. That was always startling. It entertained Lucas, though. I placed the beer next to the joint and laid myself down properly.

I awakened to the smell of eggs and bacon. Lucas rolled over and placed a plate on my lap. He said, "Don't spill it." I began eating, took a break to relieve myself, and I was back on the couch munching when Lucas brought me juice. "I need you to shop for me today," he told me.

"Okay, Luke. Then tomorrow I have another interview with Scoop."

"You'll bring them up to the compound wreckage, while some hairdo with a microphone will ask in-depth questions about the horrifying experience and your determination to discover the truth."

"And they'll pay me twenty grand."

"You're a star."

"I'm a star; I'm the last paper boy."

. . .

The next day I, along with a Scoop camera person called Aubrey—a pretty woman who most likely could kick my ass—and the handsome Ty Riggs, did just what Lucas said: We hit the places of interest, finding cool spots to set up and shoot little Q & A sessions. When the camera was off, Ty told the recent Bird-Man jokes, such as: "This Bird-Man guy ain't so bad; he just has a foot fetish." And, "That Bird Man blowed-up real good." But the second that camera's red light blinked on, Riggs spoke like a psychologist with a hint of village wise man. "Has any of this really sunk in yet, Dan?"

"No, but I still get the twenty grand, right?"

Ty Riggs shook his head and asked the question again. Quips like that usually got cut, because they undercut the drama, which is what Scoop was selling on this occasion.

Which brings me to my behavior: The simple rural man meets Dick Tracy. I knew after each portion that was shot that I was not going to relish watching it over at Lucas' place. However, I did try to slip in an amount of honest-to-goodness humility about the whole thing, and also to express that this type of tragedy doesn't compute—and if it does, it ends up an odd number. Riggs reminded me before a subsequent take to mention my condolences to all the boys' families, and that hopefully there has been a closure provided them at least. Well, I did express my condolences thanks to the prep from the old TV news pro, but I did not say a further word to the mothers, fathers, brothers, sisters, aunts, and uncles. I offered no philosophy. I just said that I was sorry and what a terrible tragedy to have to endure, and indeed, there was a type of closure.

That is when I knew I had completely crossed a line—for I was half-sure Wagner did not do it, whatever "half-sure" means, whatever "sure" means. I spoke of closure over the airwaves to the world and those parents because it worked better on TV than the truth of my mind, and I could still go on the Later Reno show a hero. I crossed the line from newsman to entertainer, from journalism over to show biz.

With the piece completed, Riggs asked if there was a nice spot where we could drop in for a beverage while waiting for their arranged rendezvous with a helicopter. I hemmed and hawed a bit, not really hankering for an appearance at the two watering holes in town after my performance the other night. I decided to play the role of host according to what makes Reverend River, Reverend River—which was, say it along with me—Reverend River.

"Let's get in that van you rented and I'll tell you where to go."

I directed them to the liquor store. I hopped out, telling them to wait, ignoring their follow-up questions. I returned with a fifth of Wild Turkey and three plastic bottles of water. I directed them down the riverside road a ways, and called for a turn where there was a roof with park benches. I crawled out from the back area of the van and they followed hesitantly. Aubrey took to smirking.

I said as I watched the water ripple on what had become a sunny and windy day, "This is about fifteen minutes from your copter meet." I cracked the bottle's wrappings and pulled off the infamous cork top. I tilted it toward my guests and had a northern swig: a one-bubble reaction at least. I winced and offered it to Riggs, who was standing closer to me than Aubrey.

"No cups?" he asked.

"No cups," I confirmed.

He looked at my extended hand curiously, as if the bottle were a question he couldn't answer. I said, "I have no disease, I don't think." Again he just looked on, unable to answer his own question, squinting now, making it clear to this country reporter that he was trying to make me out. I offered it then to the muscular, tall, and surely capable Aubrey. She had taken to hiding behind her long, brown hair, so I had to grunt to complete the overture. She seemed to truly contemplate whether she desired an alcoholic kick or not. I don't think her pause reflected my mouth's cooties. She did take it then, the smirk returning. She handed it back to me and I did not hesitate to tilt the potion again. After a wince from the slug, I passed out the bottled water and meditated on the sunlit river.

"It's a river if ever there was a river," I said.

"That it is," Riggs concurred. "That it is."

The camera operator smiled and motioned for another slug of the potent turkey. She had two drinks with space in between and handed it back.

There were so many textures before our eyes: the blue sky, the surrounding mountains, and the dark, moving water.

I said, "No one takes this river to court when it takes one of us." I had another swig. I held the bottle out again to Riggs, who once again declined, but did sip from the water I had given him. Aubrey accepted the Turkey and then it was my turn all over again.

"Aubrey!" Riggs' resonant voice suddenly boomed. "Let's get a shot of the river with the sunlight on it. That'll make a nice set-up of a small, friendly town; then we hit them with the story's darkness."

She hurried to the van, returning as swiftly, trying to catch the light, with a question on her lips: "Do you want me to do some improvisational copy, or dub some later?"

"I'll do it later. Just get some good shots now."

I had another healthy swallow. It was a pretty day.

"Dan," Riggs began reverently, as Aubrey bobbed and weaved with her video camera and then became still around us, "God made this river and He made us. That means He made this lunatic Wagner. I can't say whether Wagner's blame is any more sophisticated as blame on this river when it takes one of us down. What I do is bring the evidence of happenings to my viewers, my followers, if you will.

"When I said drinks, Dan, you immediately thought booze. I just wanted to have a cup of coffee with you. But I'm glad you brought us out here. This sun on the water is evidence, too."

He stopped, finished his water and then smiled at me. Now I knew a bit more about this Ty Riggs.

. . .

My dad drove me into Spokane. There, Reno's show provided a small aircraft to carry me away to La La Land. Dad couldn't help smiling; his boy was off to talk-show world. Something about it tickled him, which I did not expect. For my dad, such titillations usually came from carpet-crawling children and books about the sea. To him, media adventures were clothesline chatter propped up to look like valuable information. But now his son would be on the other side of the screen, and he was going to giggle watching it.

Again, my appearance on the late show was an exception; the format does not aim to depress. The hard-hitting news, sorrow, terror, and annoying arguments fell to news magazines and Nightline and Dateline, and all the other lines, but Reno risked the code against the story's interest of the viewing public. This was a big, popular story. One of Gabe's best and most used shots captured me and Ellerth watching the fire. The night was my dark backdrop, the burning compound lighting me, its dancing flames creating a surreal reality. I had recovered from the initial shock of it all by then; I didn't have a goofy look on my face, fortunately. In fact, as Gabe close-upped on me during the shot, leaving Ellerth out of frame, my face expressed determination. I think it was more that I was trying to survive in the same space as a disturbed Sergeant Richards, but it came out looking pretty brawny—which is just not the whole truth of the story, is it? In fact, Gabe had footage of me stumbling and bumbling, but either he didn't sell that footage or the folks he sold it to didn't use it. I believe the former.

Dad waved as I climbed into the single-engine plane. It was just me and the pilot. "Strap in good," he said good-naturedly.

The take-off felt like nothing I had ever experienced. I was at once frightened and thrilled. I wanted my pilot's license and I wanted it now! The runaway speed, the anticipation of lift-off, the inevitable moment of doubt, of being pushed back against my seat, then up, up, and away in my beautiful... balloon.

After a while in the sky I became bored; just another bus to Palooka.

From above, Los Angeles looked like a few separate cities. Once on Earth with the rest of the ants, everything moved along much more rapidly than I was accustomed to. Every time I visited my brother in

Chicago, this panicky inadequacy regarding the pace overwhelmed me. To a lesser extent, my sister's Nashville. This day I searched through the masses in motion for a sign that read my name. I waved and he finally noticed me.

"You Dan Holdsworth?" he asked with what might have been a Brooklyn accent.

"That's me."

"Show tapes in an hour and a half; gotta get you to make-up."

The limo was a nice touch. I have always been attracted to style and luxury. No, I wasn't ever going to spend a half million on a Ferrari, but I liked the back of a limo. I appreciated the trouble women went through in the name of clothing. I enjoyed Wild Turkey bourbon much more than rot gut. And every now and then something like a limo comes along.

This was my fifteen minutes. No doubt about it.

The backstage area moved faster than the airport. There wasn't a room, a hallway, a washroom, where someone wasn't charging in, blurting out something as a town crier, then hurrying out. Beth Warren—the woman with whom I had communicated by phone—brought me to her office to go over the questions for my segment.

"We went over these on the phone. I just wanted to refresh you."

"I like being refreshed," I quipped, feeling like an idiot.

She smiled politely and brought her attention down to the list as I eye-groped her breasts wrapped in a tight pullover shirt. She may have been all of forty, but at the moment she had my vote for Miss America. These bolts happen from time to time for us men, and I assume for the ladies as well. She had on thick black glasses and was just too smart-looking for words. I was enraptured by this woman's look and presence. This lady surely had a boyfriend or husband or girlfriend, and they were all one lucky buck.

"He'll introduce you big, so don't get overwhelmed; you'll be coming out; there's a step before the desk set; don't trip; just try to relax. Have fun with it. He'll ask you how you are doing. You'll say you're fine. He'll take note of the audience's approval of you and make a comment in that direction. This will all lead to the question, "What does it feel like to have solved the big case?" You have your response. Then he'll set you up to tell the whole story, the whole case. He knows all of it, so he'll chime in here and there, improv a joke. Enjoy the mirth but keep your train of thought; he'll be coming right back at you for the rest of the tale."

I kept nodding my head and smiling and frowning as she went on about the planned presentation. She remembered getting an anecdote out of me on the phone about pressure-cooking fruit with my mom for those long, cold winters when access in northern areas can be a shut-down situation.

She said, "He'll probably bring this up at the ending. You won't have much time at that point, so draw a quick picture of Americana Northwest. The good folks at home and here in the audience always enjoy a slice of life from a person they're interested in. Or Mister Reno will go a whole other way, because he's an ass, and you'll do best to hang on to your story—that's what the people want."

She did not hesitate. There was no conflict about her. Assignment: Entertain the viewer. She did not once try to sell me anything except the routine and the dynamics of the medium. I watched and listened in awe. I did not think that she could help me find the answers, but she had her answers down, her ducks in a row, and I sailed on her wind. She led me to make-up, made sure I was comfy, and then vanished into the hall vacuum that pulled and pushed the rest of them up and down, in and out, room to room. I missed her immediately.

The make-up guy was a sweet-sounding man named Roberto who did what he could to make this mug presentable to America. He didn't mind offering what he could to help me relax, such as a dirty story about one of last night's leading ladies. He had me smiling, but the nearing show time brought about my gut to wrench.

Actor Nathaniel Avenue walked into the room and addressed the make-up artist. "I'm almost on my way out there. Bobby baby: how do I look?"

Roberto surveyed him prudently. "You're good to go."

"Yes, but to go where, back to your place. I know your type." Mister Avenue then brought his incredulous eyes down upon me and asked, "Do I know you?"

I said, "You might know of me."

Roberto said, "He's the guy who caught the Bird Man person."

Nathaniel Avenue became still, impressed, his right hand then coming to his chest. He said sincerely, "You did a good thing." He offered me his hand, which I took.

On the way out he swayed back in the doorway and asked, "Pal, is this your first tango with Hollywood?"

"Yes, sir, it is."

"Watch your step; she's got big feet."

I heard the band kick in and the show's announcer calling all to gather. The big program had commenced. I felt I might throw up.

CHRISTOPHER SMITH

Chapter Seventeen

I stood behind a curtain, the prize in a box. I thought I could not be more petrified until Later began what I knew to be my introduction; I got more petrified. I very nearly ran away.

"Ladies and gentlemen, my next guest is a true American hero. He's a reporter from Reverend River, Idaho—that's way up north near the Canadian border; of course you all know that by now—he's the reporter that caught the real Bird Man, thus clearing a wrongfully accused man of all charges." Applause like I'd never heard before. "Please give him the welcome he deserves! Dan Holdsworth!"

Now I knew why the lights throughout the back stage areas were so bright: they were preparation for the stage lights' brilliance. How did all those celebrities saunter out so smoothly without bracing their eyes? I saw—just in time—the little single step up to the interview pad. Later Reno grasped my hand, and that felt good; I knew I wouldn't trip and fall at that moment. He leaned over and said into my left ear, "Relax and have a good time. We're just people here." I looked into his eyes after we released hands, grateful for those words, that knowledge. I then shook Nathaniel Avenue's hand again. My rear found its chair and I took a deep breath.

"Let me ask you, Dan: it must be a strange transformation your life has taken since you first met the (into a low comic voice) Mountain

Man Barde (audience chuckle, then Later goes back to normal voice) in that prison cell. It seemed to me as I look back on the unfolding story that you kind of got pulled right into it."

"That's very true, Mister Reno—"

Some of the audience laughed heartily, I could not say why..

Later said, "Call me Later." (audience chuckle)

"Thanks. Sorry."

"No, you've only been brought up right. However, I am only a couple of years older than you, pal."

I chuckled more gregariously than I meant to.

"But it's true. I'm glad you said what you said. I did just get pulled into it. So it's hard to listen to that hero talk. I feel like it was just a happening; an extreme happening, but a happening all the same."

"Yeah, but Dan, it's one thing to be exposed to a bad situation, then forced to be involved further, it's another to act properly under that pressure, to act bravely."

(More audience applause.)

"Sometimes I thought I was brave there, other times I think maybe I was just a might reckless."

Later looked at me knowingly, and said, "Yes, I think I know what you mean. You and your camera man and another reporter—Rosa Baline—went up to get that interview from the notorious Wilford Wagner (A few audience members booed the Wagner name), "before notifying the police about the evidence you had found that incriminated this Wagner nut. Why would you do that?"

Now I had to lay down the bull. You're not under oath on a talk show.

"Well, Later, it wasn't like we knew for sure he had committed these heinous crimes. We used the interview as a cover, a follow-up to a story in the paper of Wilford Wagner speaking at an NRA rally; we used that as a way of having a look-see around his place." (audience chuckle for the word look-see).

Actually, Later old fart, we just figured the footage would be neat to have when the story broke, a cheaters start against the rest of the runners. See, first footage and then call the police.

"So you're snooping around like amateur detectives on a bad TV show." He made some arm movements meant to represent snooping. The crowd loved it! We waited for the hysteria to die down. Then old Later spoke solemnly, like the lounge singer saying between songs, I'm going to bring the room down a moment.

"But it wasn't a TV show," he said. "And it got scary, fast. I advise the more sensitive viewers not to watch this footage we have. Some of you have seen it before, so you know what it is. Wilford Wagner has found them out, knows they've busted him, so he's taking them down into the bowels of his military compound to keep his horrible secret hidden. Go ahead, Larry."

Beth Warren hadn't mentioned this video when preparing me for the show, and I don't think that was by accident. It was a downward shot of Rosa trembling as she made her way down the stairs to Wilford Wagner's basement. Gabe must have been right behind her. When we got to the bottom, Rosa threw up. I couldn't believe they were showing this. I have to say Gabe got a really good shot. Most of the crowd burst out with a nervous laugh. Some were stunned, and shifted into a building groan. Then we were back.

I was shaking my head as Later said profoundly, "That's how scary it is when you truly think you're about to be killed by a psycho." He looked for me to respond, but I had left the building, thinking about poor Rosa. I barely managed to get my eyes as high as his.

Mister Later said to Mister Avenue, "It was kind of like that Blair Witch movie. Remember that one?"

Nathaniel said, "Yeah, but Witch was ninety minutes of hand-held camera movements that made the viewer throw up." After the laughter, he continued, "But they probably cost the same amount of money to shoot."

Later cackled, then stopped dead and adjusted his tie. The audience had exploded into an approving applause for Mister Avenue's wit.

Later shifted gears: "This must be something, Dan, being in the big city under the bright lights. I gather Reverend River is a sleepy little town, very small."

"It is: couple of wood mills and one main street—other than that, mountains and mountains."

"Like you're back in Mayberry or something," Later said. "Though I suppose even Reverend River is with the times, everyone taking pictures of mountain streams with their phones."

"You're right," I said, "it's in between times; sort of out of time as well."

"How do you mean?"

"How do I put it? Well, folks will follow twitter and such, and even do some tweeting themselves, but never admit to it in public."

I got a nice laugh and that felt great.

Later said, "Come on, you wrote that joke backstage."

I just shook my head.

"Hey," Later said suddenly, "did you ever see that Barde guy again, and get a thank you for discovering his innocence, because his goose looked to be cooked?"

"I did, I went up to his and his mother's cabin and he was grateful. His mother gave me a jug of moonshine."

Nice laughter for moonshine and Later turned that applause by saying, "Coming up next, Sherry Raven is going to sing us a song!"

Wow! Sherry Raven was backstage? I didn't know that.

Later said to me cheerfully, "Dan, great job. Take whatever opportunities the people will give a hero and run with them."

Nathaniel Avenue said, "All of this attention is why you went up there in the first place. Don't kid a kidder."

Busted.

The stage director announced, "We're back in five, four, three, two..." After the silent "one" count, the red light appeared above the closest camera.

Later emoted for all to hear: "We are back! My next guest..."

I watched the graceful, lovely and talented Miss Raven from an odd place. It was so nice to see her playing her guitar and singing, expressing herself to the audience's delight. I liked her a lot. Her name being Raven, I thought about my Indian friend and his grandfathers. God, Sherry Raven was pretty, but something else occupied the same space I shared with her, a disruptive something that I couldn't put my finger on. Sure, Rosa's spewing due to fear had started it, but it had other teeth and other surprises. Let's face it: I was spiritually and physically somewhere I had never been before. I heard Avenue's words: watch your step; she's got big feet.

Ultimately, I did get lost in Miss Raven's face and song.

. . .

"Hi, Miss Raven, I hope I'm not bothering you."

She moved backward and offered me entrance into the room.

"I'm a really big fan!" I exclaimed. "Great song tonight!"

"Thanks."

I stood dumbfounded. What else could I say?

I finally said, "I just had to come back here so I could tell my friends that I had met you."

"Yes, that's quite a story," she said with a sweet sarcasm.

"Well, I'll let you get back to whatever."

The backup vocalist said, "Hey, you're the guy who stopped the Bird Man!"

I smiled just way too widely.

Sherry Raven said, "Yeah, good job, guy."

"Well, all in a day's work for a small-town reporter."

That was all I could think to say.

Miss Raven smiled and said, "My friend Tyler says the best shot of you is the one where you're watching the fire, all determined-like, but I say it's the one where you're holding the woman close, after she barfed; your face was full of fear and disgust, but as her head hits your chest, as you hold her close, your expression changes in an instant. It's just pure resolve." She turned to her vocalist. "They freeze it right there, her clinging to him, and he's all resolved."

A surge of power jolted through my body. I pulsed, hoping no one noticed. Later Reno popped his head in, a big cigar in his mouth, glasses on now.

"Sherry, you were great!"

"Thanks, Later. We didn't get to talk tonight."

He said," Next time we'll get ya in that chair!" Then he smiled intensely.

She asked, "You staying for the after-gathering, Later dear?"

He said, "Gotta go." And off he went.

The back-up vocalist and I wandered off to get some food and drinks spread out on a table immediately backstage behind the curtain. Miss Raven dropped into a conversation with Nathaniel Avenue and the stage director. I poured myself a glass of Stoli and it burned going down. Without a real retreat I absorbed more of the courage fluid. I then took to looking around the room. Beth Warren wasn't running around non-stop, a slave to every concern—all chores were dispatched now, the show in the can. I bet Beth Warren vibrated her intensity from the second she bounced out of bed until the post-show party commenced, where she now lazily wafted over the cheese plate. I wanted to approach her, but chose instead to toss the rest of my drink down and fill another.

Avenue, now at my side, said, "Hey, leave some of that Stoli for me. You think you're the only one with problems?" He grabbed the bottle from me in mock drama, and with trembling hands managed to fill his glass. I was not the only one laughing, not the only one charmed; anyone within ear distance of Avenue didn't have a chance at dodging his personality.

He said, "Sorry," in a defeated tone. His apology was as manufactured as his desperation. I laughed. "I don't have time to explain it all to you," he said, "but suffice it to say that there are dragons in the wine cellar." Then he winked at me. "There are chocolate demons playing chess in the den with Mother." He raised his eyebrows as he looked to make sure no one was listening, and he ignored the fact the Lady Raven had joined us. He said, "The fat man walks dark streets in daylight."

I said, "The flagon with the dragon holds the brew that is true." Avenue guffawed happily for my Danny Kaye reference. After he recovered, he opened his arms and sang the whole confusing song. He remembered every word. Then I, Avenue, Sherry Raven, and the hardworking Beth Warren whose day had just ended, whose limber shoulders and fit legs had welcomed me to the backstage life, well, we all drank to excess and went clubbing. The last thing I remembered was absolutely owning this nightclub, one of the mellower ones. Avenue sang sitting on a piano—he was quite good. Miss Raven tinkled those very same ivories expertly and sang a bluesy tune. Eventually we all hit the dance floor, four grown adults high on Stoli, good vibes, and celebrity. Fame fell from our hair, paparazzi flashing their image-stealing, image-making bulbs. It was a living dream. We waded in the pool of limitlessness. How the eventide ended I could not recall, my consciousness having fallen overboard into an ocean of booze.

I woke up next to the hardworking woman named Beth as she dressed. I lay there praying I could remember the good time. Please don't let me have done this with no real knowledge, this thing which is all about conscious hunger. There! I could see her red bra in my mind! I was remembering, I was remembering. And lord, what a memory! It existed! It was alive!

"We won't ever see each other again," she said.

"I wasn't that bad, was I?"

She twisted her heavenly hips to show me her smile. "No, that has nothing to do with it." She went to the hotel room door and opened it. Her back to me now, she said, "That was a fun night." Then she disappeared into the world on the other side of the door, no longer in view, no longer my Blue Reality. A life lived in twenty-four hours. Who was I now?

God, she left quickly.

CHRISTOPHER SMITH

Chapter Eighteen

I had planned on spending a day sightseeing, maybe watching a sitcom being shot, going to Disney World, or whichever one is located here and not in Florida, but first, business: checking in with one of the magazines that had offered me work. However, after taking a shower I experienced another one of those recent anxiety attacks. I shivered, feeling afraid. It could have been the alcohol. I took deep breaths and ultimately got up the nerve to check my messages down at the front desk.

Holy Mother of Pearl!

Twenty messages in the order in which they arrived. They were mostly from agents wanting to set up meetings. I knew my fifteen minutes of fame were speeding toward their fate, but sometimes these life events had a life of their own. The same set of circumstances could have happened to me some other time and nothing would have come of it but my articles and a little buzz from neighboring periodicals. Of course, I think Reverend River still would have patted me on the back. But this whole Los Angeles deal could have easily not occurred. This Bird-Man hurricane that tossed everything in its path had landed me on the Later Reno Late Show. That's not how it had to go, though—and it still wanted to keep going.

Near the bottom of the pile I came upon a message from Gabe

saying that he had just gotten into town and wanted to get together with me. He left a number for another hotel. At the very bottom of the pile was a very short message: Rosa said "hi." No number. No congratulations. Just "hi": a distant wave from someone's Girl Friday written down by a hotel desk clerk. Maybe "comrade" was a better word for us than "friends." Wars demand a loftier expression than "friends." Foxhole buddies: that told more of the story. We hadn't really known each other long enough to boast any true friendship. For now, we had a type of bond that would release with time. Who was she, really? Had she hidden her position as a researcher, or had I simply never asked? All I knew was that I felt very close to her as I read her short message over and over: Rosa says "hi."

Gabe was not in. I left a message saying I had set up a meeting with one of the many agents that had called me, talking about a Bird Man script and helping me get the most money out of the right studio. I gave Gabe the agent's address if he thought he'd be in the area, saying that I would call back either way.

I felt quite mature riding in the back of a taxi. Not something I did in my first 10 years of life as a Chicago resident, not something I had done living out in the Sticks. Taxis were in movies where the folks have the money for that type of convenience. I remember taking the bus as a third-grader with my mom, going to get my "good" shoes for school.

I tipped the cabbie 10 percent and said, "I'm probably going to be around here a half hour to an hour. If you want another fare in this area, shoot back around."

He handed me a card and drove off.

. . .

I sat across the desk from a man dressed head-to-toe in black and his hair cut short, his eyeglasses very sharp looking. I thought maybe he was 30. Ended up he was 24. During our introduction and getting-acquainted period, he took four phone calls, read two texts, and leafed through a script he said was going to be perfect for George Clooney.

"Dan, I'm the real thing. I'm the mouthpiece for some real stars. I won't give you the list; that's proprietary. But I can tell you that when I saw your segment last night I put two and two together and came up with a lot more than four."

"What number did you get?" I asked with a shy smirk.

"It's not a number, Dan; it's possibilities—though the number will be big for a first-time script-writer. It's your story; it's real. And it isn't the numbers two and two being plopped on top of one another; it's the heat being turned into energy being turned into action turning into a hit film."

I said, "Tell me the truth: Was I really all right on the show last night? I mean, if I wasn't, please don't let me ever get in front of a camera again."

"That's what I'm saying, Dan: You've got the good stuff." He began slipping a pen nimbly in and out of his long fingers. "You're very loose." Before I could jump in, he had figured what I was going to say and cut me off. "Sure, you're nervous inside, the butterflies and all, but you are releasing a relaxed, Midwest quality that the people like. I know you're from up north, but you get my drift—folks tweet but don't admit to it in public... hilarious. With the story you have to tell and your rugged good looks, I think we can make you more than a good living. I'm talking more than adequate cash."

"Well," I managed. "This has been quite a couple of days." By the time I arrived at the end of my sentence he had taken another phone call and had been handed a contract by his assistant to look over. He pointed a finger in the air for me to hold my thought.

I could not live like he did. Maybe in time I could be trained to juggle phone calls, texts, and meetings, but I think I'd get lost in the details. Also, I thought: I'm not the kind of priority that he holds calls for. But that was fine.

"Okay," he said and sighed a small heart attack. "I'm back. You were saying what a couple of days it has been. You were going to say that you would need time to consider my offer, consult with someone, perhaps."

I nodded dizzily at the master's feet.

"Tracy will give you a copy of the basic deal we have here. You can look it over, take it with you, Dan. I know you received more than one message last night, but you came to the best one first. I can assure you of that. I'm not desperate for clientele, but I think you are—excuse the expression—a commodity that I can turn into big numbers. And that's my game."

He shook my hand, dragged me out into the assistant's welcoming area, told Tracy to set me up with a sample contract, and then rushed out the door and into his Jaguar—gone! I accepted the papers from her gently and thanked her as my mother had taught me to do.

She smiled and said, "I'm not involved in pitches or sales or anything. I'm just his sister's best friend who needed a job." I nodded my understanding. "But I can tell you, since I've been here, this guy gets things done, and he gets things done fast. By the way, you were great on Later Reno last night."

"Thanks." I paused awkwardly for a moment. "So you really think Denny Harris can make it happen for me?"

"Well, Dan, you made it happen, but he's got everybody's number in this town. He's 24, but his dad was in the business big time; Denny knows everyone."

I smiled that I was impressed and thanked her for her time and consideration. I stepped out into the perfect weather, the sun now a factor with the smog having burned away, and realized I hadn't called a cab. Just then a car pulled up and a smiling Gabe waved from behind the wheel. He said, "Talk about timing."

It was rare to see Gabe smile that widely, that normally. It had to be our meeting in this new world, partners in the craziness that had brought us here. He found us a burger shed where we ate on the outside benches.

"Well, it looks like the Night News," he said suddenly.

"No kidding."

"Yeah, they threw a big package at me. The papers are all but signed. I should be off for South Korea next week."

"Jesus. What's it all about? And hey, what kind of money are we talkin'?"

"More than I've ever come close to making before; a whole new level. I just couldn't pass it up, though it sounds like a lot of traveling and hard work."

"Well, Gabe, from my view, you've never shrunk from hard work. All this fame I'm getting would never have happened without the images you captured. You deserve whatever you get, Gabe."

He didn't thank me for my sweet comments, and I remembered then that he had never said "thank you" to anyone in my presence. He was when I first met him, and still was this day, an enigma to me.

He asked, "How about you, Dan? The Reno show—now what?"

"I tell ya, it's overwhelming. This Denny Harris guy is talking a Hollywood movie. I write, so I'll write one."

"Sure," Gabe confirmed, chewing on his fries. "I can see that. Getting in the door is the hard part. I can see you in front of the camera."

"Agent Harris did comment on my rugged good looks."

"I guess that footage I shot of you was your screen test."

I laughed and went back to my sandwich.

Then I said, "Maybe I'll end up working the boat shows."

"A famous sea lion on display."

"Right."

"Well, Dan, take the money and run."

Gabe said he had a meeting and then was off to New York, or we would hang LA style. He pulled up in front of my hotel saying that he wondered when we'd see each other again. I thanked him for all his brave camera work, and he didn't even nod. I opened the passenger door, but then paused.

"Gabe, I still don't know you. I mean, I know you're a great reporter. I know you don't seem to be afraid like the rest of us."

"Don't let my bravado fool you. When I was locked up in Wagner's skinning room, I almost soiled myself."

"No kidding. Well, it's hard to tell with you. I guess I want to know at least one thing from your past. Every time I've asked, you've given me some strange story: you killed your brother in a love triangle back in New York, or some such lunacy. I'm guessing you're from New York, but we never really even established that. And what else: Did you go to college? Did you ever want to have kids? I never think much about kids, myself."

He grinned, if that's what you could call it—it was so slight. He glanced over to me and then looked straight out the front windshield. "Dan, I never thought much about having kids. I am from New York. I graduated from Penn State with a degree in film and liberal arts. I did kill my brother Stan in a fit of anger. I didn't mean to, but I did. It's easier to kill a person than you might think. We are at once very sturdy and very fragile. Now, with my having told you this, do you think it helps you to know me better?"

"You're serious."

"I have to go. Give my best to Reverend River, if you ever see it again."

"I was going to head back in a day or two, but I don't know now."

"I'll see you, Dan. I have an appointment."

"Why aren't you in jail for killing your brother?"

"It was an accident. Look, Dan, do you want to come to this meeting with me, because I am leaving."

I pushed myself from the seat, then pulled myself up using the roof, and shut the door without peeking in for a touching wave goodbye. I watched as Gabe drove out of my life, a stranger, a partner in news, a fellow nut job.

Gabe's claim of having killed his brother hung over me heavily. I had made it just inside my sixth-floor room when I decided that I would take my usual recourse when faced with life's troublesome notions: alcohol. How had I made it that year without it? My body had been falling apart, but even then I couldn't dam the rushing, habitual river—suddenly, out of nowhere, abstinence. God, those were rewarding, strong times, but they were gone, and I had a fight ahead of me to get them back. For the moment I would take the elevator down to the bar, where however expensive the drinks, I was going to have quite a few. I had Scoop TV money; those are hooker wages.

Around my fifth double vodka, chased by a couple of imports, I knew for certain that Lucas was never going to be my manager or agent. This Denny Harris who promised me the moon would have that honor. After all, it was his job. Whatever Lucas did in front of that computer screen all day did not come close to preparing him for what a famous guy like me needed. Denny had all the numbers and knew all the people. The 24-year-old child with the Jaguar was definitely my man. Lucas would have to settle for being the best friend I ever had. I felt weird about having to tell Lucas, but I bet even he had been having second thoughts about it all anyway.

Pulsing in between all my thoughts and feelings was Gabe's killing his brother. I had shouted at my brother at the top of my lungs when we were drinking one night up the incline, our parents and sister having gone off to the market. I cannot tell you what our argument was about, but I remember clenching my fists in great anger. I wanted to hit him, and hit him hard. We ended up clumsily tangling, our graces wiped out by emotions and the fact that we did not want to hurt each other. We tumbled down the rocky surface and I smashed my forehead pretty good. When my brother saw the blood, he went picket-fence white. He was calling out about the hospital and he was sorry and let's go to the hospital and wow was he sorry. I remember pushing myself up to a sitting position and laughing good and hard. But it wasn't so funny, just another lesson in dealing with the deep well of our many impulses, and the momentary misconception that we were each the one and true God. We were novices attempting to become craftsmen. I realize now that we were both lucky to have survived our many life lessons. While it's wonderful to be young, I am happy to not be so rash anymore.

I'm trying to catch liquid and sculpt it into a figure I can put a name to, an unchallenged truth on which to hang my winter coat. Still, it ends up to be concrete physics leading to no ultimate answer; the facts are there but the truth is in doubt.

Did Wilford Wagner kill his nephew and those other poor boys? Was I a hopeless alcoholic doomed to repeat my damning habit, no matter how large the space between binges? Would Denny Harris make my life a wonder of famous friends and bright, loving lights? Join us next week on Soap.

I had that break-up feeling, like Reverend River and I had separated. I said out loud to the bartender, "I don't want to go back to Reverend River."

Chapter Nineteen

I wrestled with my covers until I became too tired to fight on in search of slumber's true arms. Among the poisoned dreams, the unrest, and the many trips to the bathroom, I knew I had arrived home to alcoholism. They say it's a progressive disease. I knew this even more clearly by my desire to drink right then with the morning sun's rays knocking politely at my closed blinds. I had always been smart enough to eat first, and would nourish myself now, but how long I kept on this day's wagon was anyone's guess. Was it my will? A.A.'s disease? Or so micro-elemental it couldn't even be seen, but still full of reason? And the side pain had returned. When I quit a year ago, it took me two months to rid myself of that all-too immediate comment by my liver as to its disposition. Now it bellowed from the ship's bowels: "I can't take in this deluge! I'm trying, Captain. But I don't think I can keep it together much longer!"

Still the Captain wanted his bottle.

I lasted the standing time in the shower and then sat heavily on the couch with a glass of water in my hand, a complimentary apple waiting at my side. I seem to remember deciding to stay in L.A. from now on, meet the folks in Nashville for Christmas; a new career, a new life. I would miss the old realm, but all good things must come to an end; if you don't move, stagnation sets in. There are other sound sayings to justify my reasoning—plenty o' wise words.

Suddenly I had a pang for home.

Where the hell did that come from?

I sank to the lobby in search of new messages, more admiration and more possibilities. Again, I sorted through a pile. Most of these were from the various TV tabloid shows, one specifically from Ty Riggs. I leaned on the counter, rummaging through the messages a second time to settle my priorities. I swore the clerk stole nasty looks at me. I asked him if I could borrow a pen. He sneered, I swear by all that's decent: he sneered at me and gave no answer.

I said, "Hey, pal, I'm friendly country folk, but take that bad-ass look off your face or I will lose that affability."

Yes, I said that. He was really giving me dirty looks. I did not shout it though; just laid the groundwork in no uncertain terms.

He said, "I have other concerns." He was very dignified, don't you know.

I walked directly out of the hotel feeling for the Denny Harris' contract sample I had looked over feebly. I hailed another cab and directed the driver to my new agent's workplace. I would just say to Denny that everything looked in order, and I wasn't one to beat about; let's do it; I'm in your hands.

I smiled brightly at Denny's assistant Tracy. I suddenly felt healthy and happy, at ease to boot, glad to be out of the hotel. "How are you today? May I call you Tracy?"

She had a surprised look on her face.

"Oh, I'm sorry," I said. "I didn't call for an appointment. After looking the papers over I figured I'd just drop by, you know, while I was out and about, to see if Denny had just a moment."

She still appeared taken aback, stilted as well, and I thought I had brought out that explanation of mine rather smoothly. I didn't know what else I could say as she looked from me to her boss' closed door and back to me.

She managed this: "I don't think he's in."

"Oh." I smiled stiffly and then scanned the room with no purpose. "Okay, well, tell him I just dropped by, and I liked the look of the sample contract. I'm at the same place."

She nodded with a pantomime quality, staying away from words. Then Denny burst into the welcoming room in mid-sentence. "Tracy, get these numbers updated; call Billings in New York." He saw me, remained a statue for a full ten seconds, finally saying "Hey, Dan: great to see you." He took one of my hands and had his way with it. "Boy, you couldn't have come at a worse time. I have to run."

"Well, just give me a buzz at my hotel. I was telling Tracy here—"

"I really have to go." And he did go, very urgently out the door and into his Jaguar.

I turned to Tracy. "He really is the busy one."

Again she just stared at me as if I were a talking potato. I said that I looked forward to seeing her again and awkwardly made my exit, having a go at the doorknob three times.

I walked a while. My mood dipped to a sullen mope. I'm brushed off by my to-be agent, hotel clerks are giving me dirty looks, and the once-friendly Tracy thinks I'm an mumbling spud. I tried to shake it off. A drink! Have a drink! My, what a good idea! Who came up with that one? A richly deserved raise for such an employee.

I came upon a busy street where I found a cab. This trip was getting expensive. I either had to become a success in a certain amount of time or run back to my shack in R & R. Or maybe that New York book publisher would throw an advance my way. Let Denny eventually get around to me. I had many irons in the fire. I told the cabbie to drive me to a bar within walking distance of the Paramount lot. I had always been a movie buff, and Paramount was the paramount. I didn't know what I was going to do, but I had Hollywood at my disposal now. I was alive today; let's see behind the curtain; another story for the folks back home to go along with getting drunk with Nathaniel

Avenue and Miss Sherry Raven.

Man! I got drunk with Nathaniel Avenue and Sherry Raven! Why so glum? The palm trees wafted high above me, the ocean out there somewhere. Why not take a day?

I paid the most recent in a list of cabbies and stepped my tourist's feet into a lounge a mile from the Paramount lot. I immediately fell into an interesting conversation with the old tender who greeted me, I believed, as he had greeted so many in his time, taverns before and this large, two-room, velvety-swank Hollywood watering hole: with this stanza from a poem:

We make ourselves a place a part
Behind light words that tease and flout
But, oh, the agitated heart
Until someone finds us really out.

I said, "Nice."

He returned, "Bobby Frost."

"What does it mean?" I asked, mounting the stool.

"It means what'll ya have?"

"I see: 'Till someone finds us really out.' I'll have quality bourbon, a double, and a Heineken."

By my second drink I had heard of his time in the Marines and the particular war in which he fought.

"We all thought this was the last war we were fighting, that it would be the end of such things, and that's why we offered ourselves up, as men." His Irish accent remained after all his years as an American. His trembling hand finally worked the lighter into a flame and he puffed the cigarette as an old friend. His thin white hair was slicked back and he scratched his skull with the same hand that held the cigarette. "We had to do it then. No question. But why do we have to keep on doing it?" He shook his head at the mystery. "Yet it is no mystery, not like I make it out; it's not a poet's query. We are made of wars, as we are made of sun and water. Still, that's just the fourth drink talking."

He said, "Most of these young stars and hanging-on has-beens, they don't want to think their struggle isn't original. They come in and out of here, these movie stars, writers, lovely actresses and trampy starlets—ain't none of them accept that it's all been done before. It's all right they keep doing it, mind you. Wake up from your dream, don't wake up, it's I'll be here." He tugged from his smoke and the fog floated from his mouth as he talked on: "Trances. Everyone is in a trance. Normal people like you and me know that. It's harder for the suffering artists to get that through their skulls, that there is nothing new to say. I mean, relax, for Christ's sake. There's a couple of good wars, the rest are shat."

The son reprimanded his father as he tied a red apron around his hips: "Dad, you're not supposed to drink this early." He was taking over for the old man and he asked me if I wanted another and I nodded that I did. He was a younger and healthier looking version of the good fellow that had been entertaining me.

"Hey!" the son blurted out at me, causing the father to jolt. "You're that guy who caught the Bird Man!"

I smiled bashfully, though I was growing used to it.

"Yeah, that's me."

I felt a little sorry the old man had to hear that I was one of the famous, but at least I wasn't an artist, really.

"Your drinks are on the house," the son said to me.

The old man laid it on thick, saying, "Saints preserve us!"

The old man, who had been getting ready to leave, pulling off his apron, sat back down and insisted I tell some of my war stories. Then he insisted on another drink for the occasion and the son did pour him a double of Irish whiskey. And I said, "When in Rome," and ordered myself an Irish whiskey.

I told my tale honestly, like I have not told it to a person other than Lucas. I did not lay it on thick, I laid it down. They smiled, they furrowed their brows parentally at me, and they laughed. It was one of the best times I ever had. They had good ears, and that's a writer's dream, and a person's profoundest sanctuary.

Someone who had been listening called out, "Turn up the TV; he's on; he's on." It was me on Later Reno, and then clips from the compound fire. By the time the audio got turned up, the anchor person said, "And now we find that Dan Holdsworth had been accused by his girlfriend's brother of molesting his sister's six-year-old boy. No charges were ever made, and none are pending."

The son of the old war hero said to me, "You better go."

"What?"

He said again, "You better go."

I said, "I could never do that, I could never..." I looked to the old man. "I could never hurt anyone like that."

"Then you have that going for you. And if you're lying, then you don't. But whatever it is you have, it's yours, so take it somewhere until the war is over."

Someone in the bar called out, "Fucking pervert!"

I backed off the stool and got out quick.

I thought about myself like any animal who wanted to survive would: I kept moving; pack your bags, my boy, and get the hell out of Dodge. Then I fell upon this thought, a feeling for someone else: How could Pat do this to Colin? What a confusing account for a 12-year-old to hear from his uncle. Colin probably wondered if he had blacked it out; I wanted to call to him telepathically that there was not a real memory of being molested to be blacked out. And whatever he remembered, now people would be looking at him: "That's the boy, the one from the story. The one who is unlike us because of what happened to him." I wanted to tell Colin, even though he was never molested, "You are more important than what happens to you." Then I remembered the bad vibes this morning; the clerk not giving me a pen; Denny's assistant Tracy treating me like I had a ticking bomb in my hands; Denny, apparently, dropping me as a client. It was the Rand Point curse; it was the Wrigley Field foul ball. I couldn't pack my bags fast enough. It was a nightmare in which I had to get moving, but I was in slow motion. No one could move fast enough for me: not the cabbie, not the Greyhound ticket agent, not the driver who had yet to get on the bus. I wanted to be no one again. Lord, let me be no one again.

Back when it happened in Rand Point, out of nowhere everyone had begun treating me strangely, both Melissa and her best friend and her mother—looks I could not account for. I never traced it back to an innocent morning of being awakened by Colin the way he had awakened me so many times before. Melissa was suddenly cold to me, and we weren't having sex. Things had been going so well before, so I got to thinking that maybe this girl wasn't the one. Then one morning, Pat's friend Walt dropped by to ask if I wanted to go hunting. I turned him down. Then he said he wouldn't be long, and that he had pot ready for smoking and cold beers in the back of the pick-up. "Oh, hunting! Sure. Let's go." Up in the mountain realm the planet sighed serenely. The sky high and so was I. Walt handed me a rifle and asked if I would do some brush work: walk around to the other side of a thick area in hopes of chasing a creature out to where Walt would be waiting. Actually, Walt was waiting for me to appear on the other side of my circle. He was Colin's father's closest friend. Pat had told him I had molested Colin. Walt was going to kill me and say he mistook me for a bear, or not say anything at all, just bury me. I found this out two years later when someone I knew from one of the Rand Point bars came through Reverend River. This guy who told me what Walt had planned said that he himself never thought I had done anything to the boy, but Walt sure did—and Walt also did not care about that whole innocent until proven guilty thing. Still, he never pulled the trigger. And I think about that a lot, how close I had come to being killed. I think about how in-the-dark I was to all that transpired around me.

And concerning Walt, I think he had no problem with killing me in a moral sense; I think he thought someone may have seen us leave town together, and simply did not care for life in jail.

I sat in the back of the bus praying for the driver to show. I had bought a hat for slanting over my face, and now checked out the passengers close to me to see if they were checking me out. I was back in time, waiting for Pat and his choice of weapon.

There was no reason to stay and tell the world that I had not committed that crime, though I would get Lucas to declare my innocence on Face Book or whatever. For now, I was for avoiding all scrutiny. I curled up against the window, determined not to show myself until Reverend River.

Someone bearing false witness against you, as Pat had surely done, is just not understandable by decent spirits—and it's as scary as the boogie man; a crazy child could put you in the jail without lifting a small finger. Anyone could say anything and with the use of good people ruin a good person's life. The old wound oozed its blood and angst.

The driver backed his bus out and brought a full crop of travelers to the interstate. I sighed beneath my new hat.

The trek up the coast dragged on. The long state of California seemed much longer than the maps claimed. We stopped in San Francisco for two hours. I always wanted to check out Kerouac's old stomping grounds but I stayed in the station. Oregon didn't skip by, either. Many desolate moments, numerous doubts about the future, past regrets tied about my shoulders as anvils. Hostile notions came and went with the day's light, but the dense, dark night held only one emotion: loneliness. Wait, there was another: pointlessness. I momentarily lost all perspective, so memories of glowing sunsets and children's smiles were pushed aside with a shrug. The world had looked on me, knew me now, and I was a hero who molested children in the old days. I suddenly felt like an animal pacing pointlessly back and forth in a cage.

The trauma had knocked something loose, but it was yet out of my reach. It rattled around somewhere low and in the back. I would have to find a point of perspective, tear off a panel and find out once and for all what pinged and panged so annoyingly, yet held the truth and thus a release from the whirlwind.

My mom says that every moment is complete—meaning, I guess, that closure is in every moment, or that no closure is required, or that every action, every moment is complete on its own, with no need for bows and ribbons to call it a package. Or maybe I should say it as a mantra that I don't have to comprehend: Every moment is complete. Every moment is complete. Every moment is complete.

Halfway across Washington, my back began to ache and each mile got longer. The crowd within me applauded as we pulled into Spokane. I had not wanted to bother anyone with a phone call, thus having to talk about it all, so I sat on a bench, the dawn's misty light at the bus-cave's opening, trying to get myself to call my dad. This seemed very hard for some reason. Then I struggled too long, and knew he had a log before him, creating a beam.

I did something I hadn't done since I got the Swinger from Lucas' mom: I hitched. I first asked a few in the terminal if they were headed toward Reverend River, having to explain to most where Reverend River was. They either weren't going there, or had heard enough stories about bus stop cons not to risk a bite. I walked beyond town, which took about an hour or slightly more. I had lost track of time, so I really couldn't say. I just kept moving, switching the suitcase from one hand to the other, pushing my thumb out at the rare passing vehicle. I took to talking to myself: "I wasn't a hero and I sure am no pervert." Things like that. A wind ripped down on me and I secured the top button of my autumn coat. The bus ride had taken me from summer to a harsh winter season. I was thankful for the puffy white clouds, though, and the lack of rain. I found myself surrounded by grassy hills on each side

KILLING THE BIRDS

of the road, the dew burned off and the day fully afoot. I imagined myself coming across a tavern of some sort, getting ripped and sleeping in a hay loft. This is the type of vision that comes to you after a Greyhound and a couple of hours hitching.

A rusted 1960s pickup rolled onto the side of the road up ahead. I jogged but my legs were stiff, so the jog became hobbling.

I opened the passenger's door and said, "I'm headed to Reverend River."

"I'm going twenty miles up the road, if that'll help."

I nodded that it would and thanked him heartily and climbed on in next to a man who looked a little like my father: same age, slim, pointy nose, blue jeans and a blue work shirt—a uniform to be sure.

As he maneuvered the steering wheel back and forth to keep the old vehicle straight on the road, he said, "I guess that'll leave ya about thirty miles short."

"Yep. This is very helpful of you, though. Thank you. Sounds like you know of Reverend River."

"Passed through it once or twice. Does it have a movie theater yet, or is it terminally stunted?"

"No movie theater, sir. Just wood mills, laundry mats, grocery stores, a post office, and other perceived necessities."

"I have to drive an hour to the movie theater myself." He smiled at the homestead in his mind.

"Really? You're not from Spokane?"

"No, the other side of it an hour, and north."

"Takes me about an hour to get to the Rand Point Cinema," I said.

He glanced over at me thoughtfully. "I guess we're just the type of wranglers that don't know enough to get out of the mud."

"I guess that's right, sir—though every now and then I think of moving to Chicago where my brother lives."

"I been to Chicago," he said simply. My eyes rose in interest. "Yep, had to go there to inherit money from a well-off uncle. They made me go down there; couldn't do it through the mail. I guess I got to see a bit of the town."

"What did you think?"

"You can have it."

The kindly man who offered all of Chicago to me dropped me at a roadside store where he turned off. He said maybe if I hung around there I might get a ride, but he thought I'd be better out on the road where I could catch folks on the move. We agreed that wherever you were, you could catch a ride in ten minutes or not one all day; it was all up to the hitchhiking gods.

I grabbed a bite, a soda, and then found a chair set out in front of the store away from the door. I loved this country. I could see more of the sky hovering over the rolling hills. There were mountains in the distance, but ten miles up the road I would be surrounded by them.

Now I daydreamed that this store was actually my home, with me on the porch smoking a pipe, my pretty lady inside singing a song as she prepared lunch. I made her Sandra Bullock, a woman of great charm and intelligence, I thought. Only my Sandra Bullock wasn't the actress, but a clone. We were happy away from the cities and harried concerns. I wrote, now just taking a break before lunch, and was fairly popular, providing the funds for house, food, and security. This was one of my favorite daydreams. I rarely added kids, but if Sandra wanted them, then I wanted them, too.

I was stretching my legs when the woman who had served me came out. She said, "My husband's here now and I have to go ten miles down the road. If I get in a Christian mood I may take you all the way to Reverend."

She sped down the road at twice the speed of my lookalike dad. The car smelled new, handled nicely. The CD player played Christian pop/rock, and the middle-aged woman sang along whenever the mood hit her. I gripped the seat belt and forced a smile. When she came upon a slower car, she swooped around it like it was standing still. The mountains now owned us as the road swerved between them. I laughed once when she passed a car in a no-passing zone.

"Don't worry," she said. "The worst that will happen is that you'll wake up in the Lord's embrace." She paused: "Unless, of course, you haven't found the Father and have yet to be reborn, cleansed with the blood of Christ."

I forced a smile.

She squinted at me, leaving the road to God, and this agnostic fellow prayed fully, committed. A few minutes later she scrutinized me again. "Do I know you?"

"I don't think so, ma'am. I don't know you."

"This is so strange. Your face is suddenly so familiar, but you're from Reverend, and I'm rarely there." She kept searching her mental filing cabinet, and I felt sure she had it in there somewhere. "Wait! You're the reporter who caught the Bird Man!" The car cut over to the other lane for a tick, and as she brought it back I thought I might break down and ask to be let out.

"No, I'm not, but another person this morning thought I looked like him."

"Wait!" And this time the exclamation was part scream. She pulled the car over to the side of the road, knocking down someone's mailbox. "Get out!" she demanded. I didn't know what to say. I just sat there with my mouth open. "You diddled that boy in Rand Point! Get out! Maybe Satan will give you a lift!"

"I never touched that boy!"

She reached beneath her seat and came up with a shiny handgun. "I only know what I heard on TV. You're on your own."

She pointed the weapon at my head. I grabbed my suitcase from the back seat before getting out so this mad Christian wouldn't speed off with it. The second I was out she hit the gas, turning the wheel fully, racing back from where we came. God had another stunt driver.

I put my thumb in my pocket and determinedly marched toward

home. Too many people know just enough to be dangerous, that's what was wrong with this country.

I celebrated when I reached the police station by sitting on the cement stump that kept any fool from going down into the deep ditch. I felt better again; I had been marched the day away, was tired on tired, but I felt better.

"You're back," Richards said neutrally.

"I am."

"How was Los Angeles?"

"Warm and pretty. I was a hit on the Reno show, but you've heard the latest, I'm guessing."

"Sorry for your troubles, Dan. Still, you're a free man not charged with anything."

I stared up at him accusingly.

He said, "Well, you're home safe, anyway."

I said, "I'm home."

KILLING THE BIRDS

Chapter Twenty

Richards drove me home, where Ted Wilson, the newspaperman from Rand Point, caught me at the front door, a camera man struggling to keep up with his equipment. Wilson had abandoned the dying beast called the newspaper. I caught Richards chuckling as he drove off. So far, it appeared, Wilson was the only one who had made it for this part of the story; maybe the others thought I was still in Los Angeles; maybe the viewers told the media to drop it. Ted wagged his tail in excitement, looking young, like he had never looked like when he was young. He looked to make sure the camera was running and then dipped back to his dignified persona: "This Ted Wilson of channel 5, Boise. I'm here with the hero with a tarnished image, the Bird Man's nemesis, Dan Holdsworth, who had just last night been honored with a Later Reno Late Show appearance. Dan, how does it feel to fall that far so fast?"

I had one comment: "I never touched that boy, and they never even filed a complaint with the police."

I slammed the door in his face.

After I emptied my suitcase and began my shower, I rose above my hovel in my head and saw Ted Wilson and his camera man waiting in their van; I saw my neighborhood, then the town; then I watched the river wind away with a purpose only mindless nature understood fully;

I watched the trees bravely face the wind; I saw Rand Point, Boise, Los Angeles, and finally all of America—they were all watching each other on TV. I was a spaceship rising ever higher, gaining a fuller perspective. My fame, my fifteen minutes, thank God, were almost over. One over-the-hill Ted Wilson outside my door, and he would tire of me soon enough. He's out there talking to his camera: "The man who caught the Bird Man is in a cage of his own now. It seems the brother of a woman he had once lived with claimed that Mr. Holdsworth molested his sister's six-year-old boy. That was seven years ago. No charges were ever filed."

As bad as all that was, at least I sensed a declining interest in me. Well, I prayed for a declining interest. Maybe the American people were tired of having their heroes revealed as sexual misfits. They would shrug and say, "Whatever. They never charged him." But others would say, "Get the hell out of my car! Maybe Satan will give you a lift." Either way, I was home.

Jimmy Wagner was found dead without any shoes and Idaho's state bird carved into both his feet. So it goes.

Wait! There was a chance I would be in the public limelight forever, trapped, no way out, famous always, the Fates laughing heartily.

No, I would vanish from sight like most pervert heroes do. Of course, I would get looks around town, mostly by those who had been abused themselves. They'll say, "There goes my father, that son of a bitch!" Or, "There goes my pervert uncle!" My molester status may never wane in certain eyes. Maybe I'll move to Chicago. And you know, instead of losing my book deal, I might be able to get a bigger advance out of it.

I went to the liquor store and bought a couple of bottles and a couple of cases. I let myself in Lucas' place, managing the packages in one trip. Lucas sat, of course, before his computer.

"You're back."

"It's an illusion."

"I got on some websites of these TV magazine shows and released a statement for you."

"What did I say?"

"That you never touched that little boy, or hurt anyone in said manner. That Brother Pat is a twisted fuck, and that is proven by the fact that no charges were ever filed, that you lived with them three weeks after the supposed day of the molestation—a flagrant use of your popularity for Pat to become news and vent his warped anger."

"Yeah, that sounds like something I'd say."

"Seems you've been shopping."

"Ya wanna shot and a beer?"

"Naw, I'm recovering from the last couple of weeks."

"Well, I'll be in the game a while. Jump in when you feel able."

"We really have it bad, don't we," he said more than asked.

"Yep." I plopped into the sofa's arms with a beer and a bottle of Wild Turkey. I was living high while the money lasted. "You're saying we're sick, right?"

"Right."

"Yep."

"I been thinking, Dan."

"That can't be good for anyone."

He backed his chair to turn, thus fully facing me.

"It's about the case, Holdsworth. Remember when we were brainstorming, you, me, and Rosa?"

"Good times; the salad days." Beer, bourbon, wince.

"We were never going to find a needle in the haystack. Four murders, four states. Forget it. It's funny to think of our believing we could come up with something."

I said deliberately, "Ha ha."

"But then you began to think locally and you researched in that direction. You came up with the picture of Wilford Wagner."

"Yeah, yeah; I was there; get on with it."

"Relax. I need you to stick with me. It isn't complicated, but I have to take it slow."

I pulled out a joint. "Smoke 'em if ya got 'em."

He smiled, but only for a tick. "Let's try to move this along for you, Cheech. Let's say Wilford did not do it. Let's make that solid in our minds."

"Solid." Puff, beer, bourbon, wince, exhale.

"The killer set him up, but ended up framing Barde, but you've got it back on track to Wagner being framed."

"Oh, I'll track it back."

"So the killer planned on bringing a closure to his Bird Man's reign of terror. I don't think that was because he was afraid of getting caught. Like I told you before, this guy likes to watch the effect he can have on us. He sits there watching it like a show he wrote."

"He's like David E. Kelley, only meaner."

He wanted to laugh, but had to keep his train of thought.

"Dan, list all the people closely involved with the case."

"Busy." Puff, beer, bourbon, wince, exhale.

"Damn it! You were the one out there, Dan! I need you! Help me now!"

"What?"

"List everyone who had a seat for this unfolding drama, other than the TV viewers."

I rubbed my freshly shaven jaw. Then I digressed. "You don't even want to hear about L.A. I got a story for you. You're going to love it! Guess who I got drunk with? Hey, Rosa left a message for me at my hotel. How did she know I was there?"

"She emailed me and I gave her the info."

"How did she have your email?"

"The night you left us alone, we were 'working' the case. She thought she'd better have a way of contacting us from Boise as the thing kept unfolding."

"Funny." I surveyed the ceiling. "Hey! Guess who I got drunk with?"

"Dan! Think!" His eyes bulged.

"Okay: but I might not tell you now about what famous—"

"Dan."

"Okay, I won't think, I'll just say: Sergeant Richards was there from the Wagner boy's death, the FBI twins, me, of course. I'm not a suspect, am I? Okay, okay. Rosa showed up..." and then I added suspiciously, "rather conveniently." I raised my eyebrows and had a drink. The burning elixir flowed freely. Joy!

"Yes," Lucas said. "Rosa did show. Gabe was there, too."

"Yes, Gabe. I have a story about him."

"Think, Dan. You were out there. I'm here. I'm smart, but you're out there. You're good at getting out there. Who do you see watching you as you jump through hoops?"

I laughed. "I can see Max when I showed up at my house after shopping. The day Barde showed up and took the FBI agents' guns from them. The others were screaming out questions. Max had his tape recorder in the air, a smile so wide."

Lucas maneuvered the chair and typed out the list so far.

I said, "Come on... Max?"

"I don't think it's him either. Look, this person murders a boy and then remains in town until the story's echoes have finally died."

"Yeah," I finally joined in truly, "and the killings don't start the day he arrives either. He's there awhile before he kills, sets himself up as one of them, and probably uses a fake name in every town, if he's smart."

"He is."

"So it's on to another small town, where he can continue the Bird Man drama. It's a traveling show! His name grows, while he brings to a town a fear it has never known—no big city; he wants the virgin.

And always he lives in the town at least a year, maybe more, before killing."

"The Bird Man wants to up the ante," Lucas said. "He wants to watch his own trial! He soaks in our excitement as we exact our revenge. So he picks someone to frame."

"Jesus!" I declared. "Gabe directed me toward articles from our paper; he wanted to get the frame back to where it was intended."

"Gabe came to Reverend about a year ago. Six months before the murder he must have mailed the vest to Wagner as a gift from a secret admirer, the guise of a fellow NRA admirer, having already chosen Wagner's nephew to kill."

My mind raced through time, took in so many sights and facts.

I said, "The secret admirer suggests in an accompanying letter that Wilford wear it for his big speech on the gazebo, maybe pretending to be female, and of course Gabe is there to get the picture."

"That means Wagner did give the vest to Barde out of the goodness of his heart."

"Oh, fuck, Lucas! Wilford Wagner was a good man!"

"Well, maybe. He was going to kill you three, wasn't he?"

"To protect himself; he just wanted to be left alone on his mountain. When Barde was brought in and the vest was found to be connected to the out-of-town murders, Wagner knew he had been framed, that it was pure luck that he gave the vest away. Then we come up with the picture, and he knows his goose is cooked."

"And didn't you say Wagner was a racist?" Lucas continued his summation of Wilford Wagner.

"Wilford Wagner was not a saint, but to blow up his own world in fear of the all-encompassing world around him! To be cornered with a false judgment."

"What a coincidence: Barde wanted to be left alone on a mountain, too."

"Wagner called him a brother," I said, "someone separate from society."

"One mountain man had compassion for another."

"And Gabe is there with his camera, taking it all in, saying to himself, 'I got it all. I got it all.' And he also kept saying, 'This could get interesting.'"

I shook my head. Lucas located his glass of water and drank deeply from it. I had a good swig of beer and the same from the bottle. I thought that Lucas must really be hurting not to be drinking."

"Now, Dan, we need something more."

"We do?"

"This is not enough, not nearly enough. Is there anything you can think of that could incriminate Gabe? He's very careful, but there's no such thing as a perfect crime, or so I've heard."

We thought, had our respective libations, and even got into an argument about existentialism. See, I'd been on this witch hunt for a while now. I was not in a hurry to bring another innocent man into this mess. Suddenly it hit me:

"Lucas, he keeps the shoes."

Lucas screamed, "He keeps the shoes!"

"Yeah, but he probably has them buried somewhere, like a cemetery he visits. Remember, he's a smart man."

"Either way: you'll have to tell all this to Richards and they can see if he left anything behind at Mrs. Rhoads' boarding house."

"They won't find anything."

"Dan, I'm at least convinced we did the best we could. Gabe did it. It's up to the justice system to find him now."

"Well," I mused, "we still don't know for sure he did it."

"No, of course, we don't know for sure—but he did it."

"He fucking did it."

Then my eyes must have opened wide, for Lucas asked for an explanation.

I said, "Every time I picked up Gabe for an assignment he met me out front, and he was playing with this ball."

"So?"

"He tossed it to me once. It was heavy, not hollow. It was no kind of ball used for any game I had ever played. He had it painted as an eight ball from pool. You know, black, a white center with the black eight lettered in."

"Oh God," was all my old friend could muster.

"He melted down the boys' shoes into a boys' ball for play."

"The shoes," Lucas said.

"The shoes," I confirmed. Then I added, "Did I mention that Gabe told me he had killed his own brother?"

KILLING THE BIRDS

Chapter Twenty-One

I had a couple cups of strong coffee and reluctantly drove over to the station to tell Richards our Gabe speculation. The sergeant laughed and shook his head doubtfully and occasionally stared off as I spoke, but by the end of my explanation, he felt my words enough that we took a drive over to Mrs. Rhoads' home to see if camera boy had left anything behind—specifically a hard rubber ball made out of dead boys' sneakers.

Snow had come in earnest. The windshield wipers were put into high gear.

Mrs. Rhoads' porch had a thick dusting of the powder, so we watched our footing. The old house looked deserted, with abandoned objects in the yard, paint peeling from every surface and the stair rails slanting according to the wind. She usually had three borders at a time in the three-story house, if you count the attic. Apparently none of them were handy or neighborly enough to work around the old girl's place.

She opened the door in mid-sentence: "Late November snow and it looks resolved to make a fuss. What brings you to my home, Sergeant Richards? Don't tell me my son's back in town and in trouble."

"No, Ma'am; haven't seen Billy in five years."

"Me either. He's probably dead. That's what happens when you don't call your mother."

"Mrs. Rhoads, we were hoping to look around in Gabe Teplitz's old room. Has anyone moved in there yet?"

"No." She pulled up the spectacles that were hanging around her neck, and inspected me. "Is this a new deputy? He's not dressed properly."

She damn well knew me; she was a card.

"No, this is a reporter. Do you think we might take a quick look around Gabe's room?"

"Maybe... if you tell me what it's about." She kept herself up much better than her house and yard—a round, soft-looking woman in a clean house gown, gray hair neatly tied up in a bun.

"Mrs. Rhoads, this could be nothing. I don't want to smudge anyone's name before I have some facts. I would just consider it a great favor if you would let us have a look around."

She pulled back from the door and let us in.

All that was left in Gabe's old quarters were a bed, a dresser, a lamp-supporting nightstand and a small black-and-white TV on another night table.

Mrs. Rhoads said, "All these items are mine, except for the TV that he left behind. He boxed everything else up and mailed it out."

"He mailed it out?" Richards asked.

"He didn't know where he might end up, so he mailed it out to a friend, I think—I'm not really sure."

I ventured to say something. "Mrs. Rhoads, is there anything you can tell us about Gabe, having lived under the same roof with him for the last year or so? Strange noises... anything?"

She thought a moment. "Only that every now and then I had to check to see if he was still living here. I came in here once because the door was opened, didn't think he was in here, but he was watching TV with the headphones on. Of course, he had all kinds of video equipment hooked up to that little black-and-white. Still, the boy never made a sound, coming or going. I just never heard him. He never ate down at the kitchen table with the rest. And if you cornered him into a conversation, he got out of it as quick as he could. He always paid the rent on time, never asked one thing of me. I'd say that I'm going to miss the little guy, but it's almost as if he were never here."

We felt around the closet, checked under the bed, but he had left nothing of himself but the TV. Out on the porch Richards paused to button up his coat and said, "I guess we could dust it for prints, see what history he has, but if he's the clever demon you and Lucas make him out to be, I doubt he left prints." Richards pulled on his gloves, glanced over at me, and then looked out on the falling snow, saying, "Isn't that something? We arrest Barde, he escapes, we chase; then you find that picture of Wagner in the vest so we go to him, he kills himself; and all along it's our little Gabe, and we can't find one piece of evidence to charge him."

. . .

The wind howled for the next few days and the snow accumulated. It broke some kind of record for November, and everyone began stocking up on food and supplies. I stocked Lucas' shelves. Next I gassed up my snowmobile and had a blast riding up to check on my mom. The machine-creature bounced and chattered but kept slipping over the snow and ice and slippery roads like a champ. I had to wipe my goggles every half mile and dodge a pick-up here and there, but I was one concentrated grin. The final back road I accelerated and my back end slid to the right, almost landing me in a ditch. Mom must have heard my winding engine, since she was waiting at the door with a wide smile. She jumped on the back and I took her for a spin. She held tightly and giggled girlishly.

Back in the old homestead, the basement wood furnace kept us warm, crackling logs that Dad had brought up by the cord throughout the summer. We had tea and jelly on toast and talked our usual first big-snow talk: Was she all set? Was the CB in working order? Make a list for what I could bring her next time I came. My coat, gloves, and such hung near the kitchen woodstove to dry. I told her about Dad's new lady, and she dealt with it slowly, coming around to the inevitable gratefulness that he wasn't alone. I asked about the widower neighbor, and she said that their friendship was progressing. She did not appear comfortable talking about him either.

"Are you okay now, Dan? I know…" She paused uncomfortably and then plowed on. "I heard about Melissa's brother getting that story in the paper. It must have brought up a lot of trauma again." She gazed on me as only she could: soft yet searching, willing to deal with any mess of mine, hear my words, and be of all the help she could be. She hated that I had to go through such trials.

"I'm fine, Ma. It was a hard couple of days there, and what an odd autumn, but I rode my snow craft up here, you know, and that has me feeling normal again."

She shook her head. "I can't help thinking all of this insanity might be less disruptive to your soul if you fully accepted the Lord Jesus into your heart. I know He's in your heart, I know you're a Christian by nature and action, but I tell you, Dan: it's a whole new deal when you give yourself to Him completely."

"I bet you're right, Ma. I bet you're right."

"I thought the A.A. meetings would have helped you with that. You're still going?"

I hesitated telling her this: "No, I've been off the wagon."

She leaped into her old philosophy: "It's all this Mankind bull. The world makes a soul so confused. Dan, the Lord will ease your pain. You must go back to A.A. Or how about coming to church with me Sunday?"

Didn't she ever tire of being denied? She was one Christian soldier.

But that's not surprising. Back in the day she protested, gave to that cause through songs and deeds. Then she gave herself to the land full-tilt, and her family. Now it all ended in God. I wish I did know God, just to tell Him how lucky He was to have her on His side.

"I'm sorry, Mom. I just like being a part of the holiness in my own way."

"I'm sure I understand, Dan, but give me an example of that way."

"I'm the soul that doesn't go by the book, like the cop who doesn't go by the book."

We agreed to have Thanksgiving together, as usual, and I would bring leftovers to Lucas, as usual. Only this widower neighbor might be there this time, along with a few Reverend River losers that have come to depend on her for favors—orphans of a sort. And then there was Christmas in Nashville.

I and my snow dog leaped from one pile to the other on the way home. Mom didn't like my cruising in the dark, but that was a whole type of fun; the headlight revealed just a piece of the road's puzzle, the swift motion cutting through the country darkness, my machine an armed angel on a mission. The constant blaring of the engine placed me in a bubble, apart from the tranquil countryside that I barely viewed from the ruckus. Off the back roads I passed the lighted houses, some with wonderfully colored Christmas lights and decorations already displayed. My insides filled with warm winter memories and associations with the better human qualities. For a moment I and the country folk were brothers and sisters again.

I turned onto the bridge and slid into town a cowboy thirsty for drink and hungry to talk about my ride. Athens was empty except for a couple of young guys I didn't know and Max, who sat alone at the bar.

"I didn't see your snowbird out front," I said, and climbed aboard a stool. "Is it in the shop?"

"The wife had to visit her lunatic father," Max said; "Seems he's gotten worse. We might have to do something with him. Marge says bring him to our home. I say the nut house in Rand Point. Damn his wife for dying."

"So you're drinking your sorrows away?" The tender came over and I ordered a beer.

Max said, "Your penguin sounds better than it did when it went down last year."

"Damn right! I fixed it up. Man! You should be out there! One rush after another. God made snow after having a dream about snowmobiles. I had the whole beast off the ground coming down Boyko Trail; must have hit a swoop in the road."

Max smiled. "Sounds like a kick."

"Ya wanna take it for a spin?" I just got it fixed; now I'm offering rides.

"No—better not tonight."

"A little too much of the spirits?"

"Nah, I just feel so low I might pull an Ethan Frome into the biggest Douglas fir left."

"Yikes."

"I'll be all right. Hey, sorry to hear about that story out of Rand Point. Some of us here know that's just beyond you."

"Thanks."

"Did it blow all those deals you had—all those deals that made me insanely jealous?"

"All of them but the book deal. I sent back the contract signed. They don't think by the time the book is released that anyone will remember the non-charge of molestation. They think that the folks will still remember the Bird Man, and will want to hear about it. Only I have a twist at the end no one knows about yet."

"Good for you." He sounded sincere, but didn't have much enthusiasm.

"I just have to come up with a title. Unfortunately, the most honest title would be, The Bird Man Got Away. Better yet: The Bird Man

KILLING THE BIRDS

Flew The Coop."

"Why? Because he blew himself up?"

"I'm not sure old Wilford did it. Hell, I'm pretty damn positive that he didn't do it."

Max began chuckling, which grew to hearty laughter, which ultimately had him coughing while pounding the bar counter.

I said, "I know; it never ends."

"No, Dan, you never end. Or you don't want it to end."

"What the hell does that mean?"

"This is the biggest thing that has ever happened to you. Why would you want it to stop—especially with the last headline being about that molestation crap? But you're just going to have to accept it, buddy. Take your book deal and run. I mean, hell, if it really wasn't Wilford, well, that's not going to help the book's hero angle."

I was about to tell Max that the hero thing was over for me. It had been a wild experience, but was over. Now the elusive truth haunted me; Gabe haunted me. I had the "truth" but not the energy to make Max believe it. Then we all went out front to see who was screaming.

My Indian friend Raven was beating his chest and howling. He carried on madly. I mean, you couldn't keep track of what he was yelling about, only that he was using vile words. I tried to calm him down.

"Raven. Raven! It's me: Dan. Raven!"

He ripped open his shirt and climbed on my snowmobile. I thought I could just pull him off, but he connected to it with his raven claws. It took me, Max, and the tender to drag him off into the snow. Raven lay on the ground, howling and cursing at us.

"You white pigs don't know shit about shit! You wouldn't last a day out in the real nature with the bear and the eagle! And I know you all want me in chains, in prison, or dead! You raped my sister and mother and father! And now my grandfathers are being pulled around town tied to the backs of your snowmobiles!"

Max asked, "What in the hell is he talking about?"

The tender went back inside. One of the young guys I didn't know said something about "messing up the injun." I once again attempted to break through the teenager's illusions.

"Raven, do you remember me?"

"You're the one who dragged my grandfathers into town! Then you went into the bar to brag about it to your white pig friends!" He came to his feet, his eyes wide, his fists clenched.

I said, "Calm down, Raven. This is all going to be better in the morning."

He screamed at the top of his lungs and ran at me. I was terrified. I made fists and began to swing. Max grabbed Raven by his neck and pulled him to the ground, keeping his own body on top of the poor, crazy bastard. I knelt down to help Max, for he had helped me. The boy struggled beneath us. The two young drunks encouraged us to kick his ass. Max said that he thought we would have to pound him a few times to get him to settle down. I said that we should just hold him for a minute or two.

Max shouted over Raven's accusations, "I'm fucking freezing!"

"Me too! Just hang on. Just hang on a minute."

The tender was back in the doorway. He said, "That's how long until the cops get here. I called them."

. . .

I looked at Raven in the back seat of the patrol car, his hands cuffed behind him, crying now, still speaking senseless words. I asked Ellerth what they were going to do with him.

"He needs professional help. No more cell time to sleep it off. It's the booby hatch for Tonto."

"But he's just a kid," I protested.

"This is what he needs. They may be able to help him. What do I know? But he's not fit to be in the mainstream. He needs more than we can give him."

. . .

I drove the snow craft home as a robot being controlled by a part of myself that was in on all of this, pre-programmed, but could not let on to the rest of me. I parked alongside the shack and covered it with the tarp, another day taking various forms as it went; the good, the bad, the ugly. I trudged up the front stairs and checked for mail. There was nothing in the mailbox, but a beautifully wrapped package lay at my doorstep. Santa Claus and elves and bells made up the glittering paper. I smiled at the pretty wrapping. I took it inside and noticed there was no postage on it. Someone must have hand-delivered this. Who would give me something this early, just before Thanksgiving? As I thrashed at the paper and then the box eagerly, I thought maybe Rosa had left it for me, now waiting to surprise me. I pulled the round object out from the box.

It was the hard-rubber oversized eight ball; it was the same ball that Gabe had thrown to me before we went to Jimmy Wagner's funeral; it was the dead boys' shoes.

CHRISTOPHER SMITH

Chapter Twenty-Two

The words of the letter that accompanied the box with Christmas wrapping paper were cut from magazines and newspapers, like a ransom note. It was a fairly long note that must have taken forever to construct. It said:

Dearest Dan,

I could not live with you not knowing the truth of all this. In all my travels I have not been one to make friends, for I am the kind of scientist who only needs mice on which to experiment, and you can't get too chummy with mice. The enclosed ball may get you started. Have you got it yet? It's the sneakers of the Bird Boys. They called me the Bird Man but I wanted the mice to call them the Bird Boys. Well, experiments are for observing, not controlling.

The test did go many ways, did it not? I could never have predicted. And you became my favorite mouse. Every scientist has one. I wanted to force Wilford Wagner off his mountain and into a court room, but what happened was so much better. And though I appreciate the immediate mice, it was so satisfying to finally get the attention of all the TV mice. The experiment went grand scale.

I could not risk flaunting my presence any longer, waiting for you to take a firm hold of the fact that I lead you to check local stories in the paper. Still I wanted you to know; I wanted you to have the shoes. I look at you like a friend, and friendship is a most unscientific concept; abstract to be sure.

So all that is left now is to say good-bye to my star mouse, and then to go find my next experiment.

Don't go changing,

Gabe.

I can't tell you all the stupid and bizarre thoughts and feelings that raced through my mind and paused in my soul. Here are some in no particular order:

He did not need to cut out these words like a ransom note. That was all style, effort, and, if I might play scientist, insanity.

Also, I felt nostalgic about our time together. We had run up mountains, ran from FBI agents and almost gotten killed by Wilford Wagner, the mountain mouse with the compound. I missed Gabe—not serial killer Gabe, but the odd little fellow Gabe I drove around with in my Swinger, up and down and all around Reverend River; though that Gabe might not have ever truly existed, he was dead now; another case of the Blue Reality.

I cowered, as if he were there in the room with me. Convinced he was not, I still feared the day he might return, and sweated out the realization that we had been physically close to each other many times.

I wanted Gabe to know that I had figured it out—well, okay, Lucas and I had figured it out—that I knew the ball was the boys' shoes before it arrived at my doorstep. What a fucking stupid thing to want. The boys are dead, the killer free, and I wanted his approval.

I wanted to cry because I was alive. I wanted to cry because others were dead. I wanted to cry because God would be so nice to come home to and I knew that I would never let Him inside my door.

Then my blood curdled as my eyes adjusted to a sight, then registered a fact: I saw a camera lens about thigh-high pointed at me. Someone was crouching inside my kitchen doorway recording me. I jumped, and jumped again when I confirmed the camera man to be Gabe. I made a leap for the door and heard him shout, "Stop or I'll shoot!" I slowly turned back to see him pointing a handgun at me. I quivered like a bowl of jelly could only dare dream.

"Come back in," he said, letting a smile build. "Sit right back down where you were." I reluctantly lowered myself onto the couch. "Do you know your lips move when you read? What are you, ten years old?" He placed the video recorder on top of my TV and pulled his knapsack off and laid it on the floor beside the TV.

I said, "Don't kill me." I wanted to call him a sick fuck but I said the don't-kill-me plea.

He said, "Try not to think about it. I just had to get you reading that, your child-like lips moving. When I composed the note, I was on my way out; I knew I could not risk remaining in the river any longer. But you know, watching you take off in that snow mobile made feel playful. I even went driving around looking for one to drive around with, and what do you know, I finally found one in a front yard with the keys left in. No one locks their doors in this town. I parked it in back out of sight. Oh!" he exclaimed; "When you first saw the ball, what an expression!" Then he pondered. "But you must have just thought that was a present from me... until you read the note."

Like the big-mouth fool I am, I almost blurted out that Lucas and I had figured it all out, but that might have brought Lucas into this nightmare. I just stared at him, the gun, him, the gun, still wanting to call him a sick fuck.

He did not appreciate my silence. He eased over to the window to steal a peek outside, then leaned on the door and said, "I'm sure you have some questions, whether inane or insightful. Don't cheat yourself out of some sort of satisfaction."

"Gabe, I can't think of anything to say. I'm too scared."

"No, that's not it, Dan. Sure, you're scared, but you were shitting bricks when Wagner had us, and you came up with just the right things to say. Though, of course, you're right: with me, it doesn't matter what you say; so out with it; first thought that comes to your mind."

"I already said it: Please don't kill me."

He pushed himself off the door and scowled, uncharacteristic for him—but then so was that long paragraph about staying and going and being playful about snow mobiles. "The second thought, then, mouse Dan."

Yeah, he sure sounded different, talkative. Like the other Gabe was the scientist with nothing to say to the mice, only to deal with them, but this was the remaining human part of Gabe. This was the friend who wanted to share, wanted me to share. So I complied.

"Were you some other killer before the Bird Man?"

He almost leaped into the air, and then moved close to me, sitting on the small coffee table. "Yes, yes, yes... attaboy... that's my favorite mouse! Tell me how you knew this wasn't my first go-round."

My mind raced. I felt I needed to entertain him, be his friend, or something like that. I said, "Because the Bird Man was too organized, too good. Everyone stumbles at first."

He was impressed, waving his gun at the ceiling.

He said, "Absolutely correct! You are just the best mouse, Dan. I mean, you are stupid, but you make up for it with your curiosity. Yes, of course. The first go-round was messy. I was damn lucky not to get caught. I used to abduct them, which is really asking for it. Though I'm sure I could handle that now; still, not the way to go; noises neighbors can hear, constantly checking your home for traces of your past mice. Look! Let me show you."

He activated his laptop and waited for the file to come up. I almost rallied my courage to lunge across the room, since the gun was pointed to the floor. His face turned to me, smiling widely.

"Watch and learn, Daniel Mouse."

A boy, maybe ten or eleven, sat on a basement floor, maybe in a garage, his hands behind his back, gray duct tape over his mouth. Tears were flowing down his face. I heard a voice in the background. He was telling the boy not to struggle so. He never assured the boy of his safety, just told him not to struggle. It was Gabe, of course. It seemed to me that the camera was then placed on a tripod, and a few moments later a small man in a Bugs Bunny mask holding a butcher's knife came into the shot, crouched down and pulled the tape from the boy's mouth. I was terrified and transfixed; the image of the bunny with the knife was pitch-dark surreal. He said to the boy, "We can't all live forever, can we? Some have to die for the good of the rest." The boy began pleading for his life. "No," Gabe said. "This is too important, Kenny. You'll just have to accept your part in this. Well, actually, you don't have to accept anything." Then I saw the knife and closed my eyes.

"Dan, you're missing it!"

I heard the boy scream but a moment. Who would want to hear this story? Who would want to know that such a warped brutality existed?

I opened my eyes.

"Oh, I almost forgot," Gabe said, "I wanted you to see this." He opened another file and I saw Wagner's compound burning from above, the view of the drone. "Now watch carefully the left side of the screen, those bushes." The bushes gave way and out came Wagner and his Marion on the other side of the compound from where Richards and I were watching the destruction. "See, dummy, survivalists don't kill themselves; he and Marion are probably in Canada starting all over again; plucky survivalists building another compound."

It made me feel good to see Wagner and the woman alive.

Gabe said, "Now back to that boy who got sliced by Bugs Bunny. That was my first calculated mouse dissection, my neighbor Kenny. I watched firsthand as the Steinbergs worried; hell, I helped looked for Kenny. The police came, the reporters came. I was hooked right off." Gabe took note of my expression. "Say it. Dan, say it. DAN! Say it!"

I feared for my life but I said, "You are a cruel, sick bastard."

"Let's continue by going backward: Kenny wasn't the first, he was the first pre-meditated murder. No, my brother had that honor. I killed him when I was eleven. No love triangle. I was just so sick of him; so sick of his picking on me; so tired of his stupid face; so tired of his telling me that he could get away with whatever he wanted. So I grabbed the largest kitchen knife and stabbed him about ten times." He took a deep breath. "Wow—that was something. I was terrified, sad and happy. I didn't know even if I was still alive then." He strolled around the room waving the gun as a conductor's wand. "Then I returned to reality, whatever that is, and got to work at hiding the evidence.

"See, everyone needs a little luck in life. You don't just hear that you have to look both ways before you cross the street and then never get hit by a car your whole life. No!" he shouted. "You need some luck! And I had gotten mine. We had been fighting about who would take the first shower before our Boy Scout meeting. Mom had gone down to do laundry. So in my anger I stabbed Stan while he was in the shower; pure luck, no thought—all the blood went directly down the drain. I wrapped him in the plastic tarp Mom had used when she painted, and hid him in my closet, then cleaned the tub, then the knife, and then returned it to its drawer. I told Mom that Stan said he wanted to walk to the meeting by himself, that he had left without even taking a shower. Mom was very protective and immediately commenced to worrying, though she knew he'd be fine. I showered and we went to the meeting. Mom saw he wasn't there and waited. When he didn't show, she told me she was going to drive over to a couple of his friends' houses, her face already on its way to pale. After she left I sneaked home, dragged Stan down the stairs and buried him between our house and the neighbors.' Again, pure luck that no one saw me. Don't think for a moment that I was not fully aware of my fortune. When Mom found me at home, I said that I had gone to look for my big brother."

My eyes were on their way out of their sockets.

"Yes, some story. It was something, digging that hole. So I watched as my parents ran around crying and searching for their missing boy. The cops figured he had been abducted, not being the first to disappear between home and school, or church, or a Boy Scout meeting. They interviewed me quite a few times over the next few months, made me feel important. Thinking about it now, they suspected me every now and then, but really, my mom had just gone down for the laundry. Sounds more like a boy dodging a shower, doesn't it? What a game the truth is."

He stood very still then.

"Two years later I killed my neighbor Kenny in my parents' basement. Again, the stupid police never had a clue. They thought the deaths were related, but related to whom? I got tired of digging, so that's when I took to leaving the bodies to be found. It was fun to watch them endlessly search in vain, but even better to watch them find the dead, to see their horror, to know they knew." He sighed as if it were a nice evening wearing on.

"Eventually I began giving the killings textures, traits. See what creativity brought to the process. Next thing I knew I had it down to a science. It was true scientific experimentation."

My throat was dry, my forehead warm. I ran my fingers through my hair for the hundredth time since he had started talking. I asked, "Gabe, didn't you ever miss your brother?"

Don't ask me why I asked him that.

He stretched his neck, rolled it around his shoulders and said, "No."

I shook my head.

"I was on my way then," he said, continuing his success story. "Forward, not backward; curious in so many areas. I had always wanted to feel what killing would be like. I always wanted to know what I was capable of. I went on to be a very good student in school and in life. I would get bored easily, so I would move on; different towns, different jobs, different names. I realized that resourcefulness was the key to survival. It was also the key to my studies."

I blurted out suddenly, "You're just killing your brother over and over again."

"No I'm not!" He pointed the gun at my head. I waited to die, for a flame's flicker, relieved to be gone from this terror, this confusing place. Then he smiled. "You know I can't let you live."

"Why?"

"Because I've said too much, so you know too much. You know where Stan is buried."

"He's still there?"

"Sure, right there under where the folks store wood, or a wheelbarrow, or junk they think they'll use someday."

"I won't tell anyone."

"Whatever. You don't know my real name anyways."

"Please, Gabe. I'm your favorite mouse."

"I'm a scientist: even my favorite mouse gets it in the end."

To stall I said, "Why the birds, Gabe? Why the birds?"

"Oh good, you're still curious—curious till the end. Well, my brother Stan loved birds. First he took to watching them, and then he took to taking pictures of them, and finally studying everything about them. He would recite the state birds while trying to get to sleep. We shared a room and he drove me crazy with the birds. Just drove me crazy."

I knew I should go down fighting. As I came to my feet to the directional pointing of his gun toward my basement, I brought the coffee table up with me and pushed it at him. As he fell back I took hold of his arm and ripped the gun away. With the gun in my hand I must have fallen over the rocking coffee table. He darted out the back door. I saw nothing out in the dark backyard. I thought maybe he had run out front where a car was waiting, but then I heard a noise, a rustling; I pointed the gun in the direction of the rustling. Suddenly an engine turned over, and the lights of the snow mobile came on just as he was passing me and then gone out front. He really had stolen a snow mobile.

    I had to hurry or he would be gone and never seen again and another boy would die. I pulled the tarp off my snow mobile, jammed the pistol in the back of my jeans, and was after him toward town. I tell you true and clear that I was not chasing a story, that I was not chasing glory: I was desperately trying to stop another boy's death—and maybe even exact some revenge in the name of local boy Jimmy Wagner. Would I have chased if I did not have the gun? Well, as long as he didn't have one as well... sure I would have—what kind of a man would I have been if I didn't.

    I was going down Nog Hill fast, the wind and snow blasting against my coatless body. My goggle-less eyes squinted ahead to see Gabe slowing to make a turn at Main. I would also need to slow down, but I had to take advantage of his slowing to catch up, so the turn was going to be a close one for me. He turned left, not sliding much, for he really did take off the gas. He had never driven a snow mobile before and wished to live to kill again. I turned my body into the turn early and used the sliding sideways to slow down in time to avoid crashing into the post office on the other side of the intersection. Still, I did slide through the intersection, and I did bounce onto the sidewalk and smacked against the post office. I righted myself and was back onto the road out of town, seeing Gabe in the distance. Passing the gas station, the last business before the rock cuts, I saw Sergeant Richards getting into his patrol car after filling up. I called out over the winding engine, and I waved Richards to follow me if he saw me, took note of the lack of a coat and goggles and such and smelled trouble, but I did not know if he heard and saw me; I never slowed down.

    I closed some distance on Gabe and wondered if he were going to take us all the way to Rand Point. Then I saw the colored lights reflecting in my side view mirror and knew Richards had joined me in the slippery chase. There is no way he could have guessed I was chasing Gabe. He probably thought I was really drunk and racing all the devils in the world. The odds were high that one of us would slip right off the road soon and maybe even make it into the river that had not iced over this early in the season. I closed more space on Gabe and then knew why: he was slowing to turn onto a side road. I needed to follow, so I leaned early and often again but was pretty sure I wouldn't make it and prayed early and often that I would land in the softest of snow banks. I made the turn, but that was only because the turned ended up to be soft and immediately up hill, and then rising to be parallel with the riverside road—and that is how I saw Richard's squad sliding and spinning down the riverside road for having tried to make that same turn, a turn a car tires could not make at that speed. I waited for him to smack into something hard, but we were at a section void of rock cuts for a few miles and he landed in a ditch. He was stuck but fine otherwise.

The rising road turned away from the river and my headlights gave limited vision. It was not until the road bended again that I saw Gabe's lights ahead. That was fortunate, as I saw Gabe turn up another side road, and I could have missed that. I had gained on him again due to another slow turn and actually grabbed for the gun to risk a shot here in the middle of nowhere, but I dropped the fucking thing between pants and some cowboy aiming and the weapon was behind me in the snow as I gained some more ground. The road got steep and I hit the gas and the engine wound and the wind had me tearing up and then I did not see Gabe's lights up ahead. Suddenly I was on flat land, arriving at one of those large fields where folks would gather sometimes I bet. Gabe was way on the other end, his lights all I could see of him. He was trapped; there was nothing but thick forest on the other side.

I sat straddling the snow mobile, letting it softly idle, breathing heavy, and so caught up in the effort and energy spent and the involvement, that I was not thinking in terms of fear, but more like a football player feels in a playoff game out in the elements. The adrenaline was full bore. If I went at him, he would have all kinds of angles to slip by me. If I remained here trying to block him, well, the entry/exit where I took my mid-chase breather was too wide. Still, that was probably my best bet.

I heard Gabe call out: "Where's the gun, Dan? Are you afraid to come over here and use it?" I could not believe how clearly I heard him. We were probably surrounded by high ground and a mountain off to the side. "Did you drop it?"

"Why don't you try and leave here and find out!" I called back.

It was quiet again but for the idling engines. Then Gabe said, "Well then, if you got the gun, good luck with your shot as I go flying by! But if you dropped it, Daniel, I suggest a good old fashioned game of chicken! I'll gun mine and you gun yours and we'll drive directly at each other and see who's the man and who's the mouse. Come on! Let's see what kind of hero you can truly become!"

He cranked his engine and I responded by cranking mine, caught up in the playoff football hysteria, and damn if we were not heading right toward one another. I knew he would not blink; Gabe was fucking crazy. Still, I had to say I felt pretty fucking crazy myself. Maybe I would flinch and turn at the last second due to survival reflex, but that was not my plan, that was not my state of mind. I was screaming, "I'm taking you with me!" We were on each other so quickly, and with the vision so poor, I didn't flinch. I hit him at high speed, but a bump or a rise had my vehicle sliding on to his and crashing off the side of his windshield, and I flew into the air turning sideways awaiting a violent landing.

I gained consciousness choking on snow; I was face down. The snow mobile had my left leg pinned and as I tried to pull myself free I realized I only had one good arm—the left one was dislocated at the shoulder. The pain rose along with the nausea. Then I heard Gabe trudging through the snow toward me, and I knew if I did not get free I was dead; there was no time for nausea and passing out. I rocked back and forth trying to twist out and I was free. I crawled atop my snow mobile not knowing if I could walk on the left leg yet. Gabe arrived into my headlights and stopped.

"My favorite mouse lives," he said flatly.

I tried to scold him but could not manage much but heavy breathing.

"You don't look too good, Dan. I don't have a weapon, but I'm not sure you can defend yourself in any manner at this point."

"You're a child-killer, Gabe. Even a half-dead man is too much for you. But I sure invite you to try. Please; rover, rover, come on over."

"I would really like to kill you, Dan, but I think I'll let the elements take care of you. Because if you could move, you'd be attacking me, and I don't think that snow mobile is in much better shape than you. But maybe I'll make it back here some day to Reverend River, and if you do live, well, I'll get to kill you; so you'll have that in your dreams; every night will be a dare for you to close your eyes."

"I pray you come back for me, you piece of shit. We're all going to die one day, but to have another shot at you before I go—yes, please come back, you child-killing piece of shit."

I think he was about to take a shot at choking me to death but instead disappeared from my headlights and I heard him drive away.

My left leg was not broken but the knee was wrenched. I rocked the snow mobile until I got on its sleds again. It did not turn over after a couple of tries and I thought about the battery dying and the lights going out and how dark it would be then. I took a deep breath, preparing myself for some kind of walk in search of a home, and turned the key again; it came to life and thus I might have life for a while longer.

By the time I got back to the riverside road I realize my head was bleeding. I paused to wipe the blood out of my eyes and thus saw Richard's patrol car still in the ditch. I squinted and was pretty sure he was sitting in the front seat waiting for a tow he called in. I drove over to him and he finally heard me. He got out of his car and I rose from the vehicle to make a wise crack standing with him eye-to-eye, but then stars flashed and I felt myself falling.

. . .

I awoke in a hospital bed with Mom at my side.

I was told I had been mostly unconscious for a couple of days, waking to mumble and then fading to dreamland again. When I was fit enough, Richards came in my room and said he had gone through all the things Gabe had left behind at my shack, in such a hurry to leave town. The reason Richards knew to check my place was that some of my mumblings contained parts of the chase with Gabe. Richards thought it was fever babbling but went to check my single-floor dwelling just in case.

"I suppose you would want to cash in on this footage," Richards said, referring to the Bugs Bunny mask and the poor terrified boy.

"No," I said, "people can't possibly want to be disturbed at that level."

"Sure they do," Richards said, "but I wasn't going to hand it over to you anyway. It's for the courts and for folks to study."

"Did you see the Wagner footage, him and the woman slipping away from the burning compound?"

"I was really happy to see that, Dan."

"Me, too, Serge."

. . .

KILLING THE BIRDS

I spent a week out at Mom's convalescing. Dad came out a couple of times and we three had some good talks. Thanksgiving rang true: big meal, games, and songs. I had talked to Lucas on the hospital phone, but hadn't seen him since the latest incident with the Bird Man. Mom tried to talk me out of taking leftovers to Lucas, still worried I would relapse. I said that I needed to check in on him.

Gabe got away clean, leaving his ball and note behind as evidence. The prints he left behind that night led nowhere, but the story of a missing brother—the time and place of the cold case—led the authorities to finding his true name: Adam Goodman. His parents finally got to properly bury Stan. That closure brought the knowledge that their other son was a monster.

Dad dropped me off at my place and I took the trusty Swinger over to Lucas'. I smelled death as soon as I walked in the door. I almost vomited and then covered my mouth with my sleeve. Lucas was face-down at his computer. I pushed his right shoulder just as a way of getting myself to absorb his departure. There were no new marks on his body. This was no dastardly murder, but a long, hard-fought journey to death—nothing new about it. One of his organs had finally had enough. His face lay against the computer's keyboard. The screen saver was on, had been for days, I guess. I turned off the computer. I wanted to lift his face but he wouldn't look any better or feel any better no matter how I placed him. He was far too heavy for me to do much with him, far too heavy for me to haul him to his bed. I called Sergeant Richards and then waited on the couch I had sat upon a million times and looked at my dead best friend. So many images flashed in my mind: Lucas and I hanging in the lunch room in high school, Lucas kissing a girl at a party when he was jock-fit, save for a little baby fat, and all the hours we drank and laughed together.

This was no mystery; he had been consumed by his own appetite. He had eaten himself to death. The mystery was why had he not been able to stop himself? Why had I, his best friend, ceased trying to stop him all those years ago? Hell, I was bringing him his beer and junk food! I got up and began grabbing beer and food from the refrigerator, tossing them against the walls, sink, and ceiling. The beers thudded, some opening and spurting their contents. The light boxes of cupcakes barely made a sound no matter where they landed. I was screaming, but I can't remember what I was actually saying. Then something broke through my madness.

"Dan! Dan!" Sergeant Richards and Ellerth stood just inside the door. I had left it ajar. I stood very still, as did they, other than Ellerth's pulling a hanky out and covering his mouth. Richards eased past me to inspect Lucas, Ellerth following close behind while stealing glances at me along the way. I saw Ellerth's eyes widen when he got a good look at Lucas. He could not stop himself from speaking as he stood over my Lucas.

"Jesus H. Christ. Look how big he got. I haven't seen him in years and years. I had no idea he got this big."

Richards motioned for him to zip it. Then the sergeant asked, "Are you okay, Dan?"

I shook my head that I was definitely not okay.

Richards sighed. Someone was dead. Life was always moving toward death. Gabe had made a ball out of death. I made tears. I just wanted to find a safe place to hide, and I didn't know of one. Not even the old homestead.

I called the sergeant by his first name for the first time that I can remember. I said, "Cole, I have to go somewhere and get myself together. I'm so sick and tired of questions, so please don't ask me any."

I went home and sat in the dark and saw plenty there.

· · ·

Lucas' mother did not come home for the funeral. Ends up she was in jail for forgery and other con activities. We spoke on the phone. I gave her someone to cry to. She wasn't such a bad lady, and she deserved to cry all she wanted, as did we all. She thanked me for paying for the funeral and for being Lucas' friend. She apologized to Lucas through me. I wonder if he heard.

My mom and dad dressed in solemn clothing and came to bid their eldest son's best friend farewell. They gave me someone to lean on, emotionally and literally; I limped but I still helped keep the over-sized specially-made casket afloat with the help of nine other strong men. Not only was the ground white with snow as we stood at the gravesite, but the trees were as well. The night before, a wet snow had fallen and the temperature had dropped, freezing the snow and ice to whatever it landed upon in the midst of the storm. Forevermore, Lucas' departure would be remembered for its crystal landscape.

We who came to listen to the preacher's words—the same preacher who helped say goodbye to Jimmy Wagner—watched our breath take misty forms before our mouths.

I spent Scoop TV money on a hearty reception. I had said that we couldn't just go our separate ways from the graveyard, that Lucas merited one last fling. I saw my dad smile as I said this to the folks who had gathered around Lucas. We all met at Max's, for he had a big house near the cemetery. I was grateful that he agreed to let us congregate there.

At one point Max and I held court in his living room, recounting many Lucas stories. Max took great delight in unfolding the yarn where Lucas ran into Mrs. Walters' burning house to retrieve her missing cat. He must have been fourteen. I thought he was crazy at the time. I mean, it was a cat. But who am I to say what's worth what? It made him a hero in Mrs. Walters' eyes.

I reminded Max when Lucas got forty points the night we beat Newport in the sectional finals. Man, that guy had a jump shot! When he got going, he just did not miss—like he had arrived at an enlightened place and knew how to stay there; or maybe to say that when it came to basketball, Lucas could get out of his own way.

It was always funny to see Sergeant Richards in something other than his uniform, let alone a suit. I had never seen him drink before either, but he was throwing them back. He was respectful and responsible but he understood the need for celebration. He had known Lucas through the sports, knew his mother, for she had been a hell-raiser around town. I went to Richards as he told fishing lies to Max and Ellerth. They were near the pile of beer cases, and it was then that I had my first drink. Part of me just didn't want to go that way. Suddenly the choice vanished, completely forgotten, and I cracked open two at once, ripping right into a complete fabrication about my dad's last record-setting catch. We laughed.

Max eventually went off to tend to his wife, and Ellerth sneaked out for a smoke. I asked Richards, "Why an eight ball?"

He had a buzz on, so he answered me as a comrade. "Dan, you're a veteran of the crime business now. What do you think?"

"I can't think anymore. Tell me what you think, Sergeant."

"I think he chose the eight ball because it can win a game for you when you get it in the hole, and it can lose a game if you knock it in the hole too soon."

I pondered that: "As good as any explanation."

"As good as any," he replied.

"So, what else did they find out about camera boy?"

He pushed the beer down his throat and came up pressing his lips together. "Well, Dan, a lady recognized his picture where the Wyoming boy was killed. No beard then, but she knew him. Ends up he stocked shelves at a grocery store near where the boy was found. In Oregon he worked for next to nothing at a newspaper. His name there was... what was it? Steve Landsberg. The editor said he was the most resourceful photographer he'd ever had."

Richards stopped, so I pushed him. "What else?"

"He may have been a serial killer in the east called Killer Bugs. He left Bugs Bunny masks on his victims. Why do you care, Dan? What does it do for you to know?"

I felt flush suddenly. I looked around the room, at the floor. Then I faced the sergeant. "I don't know. I'm just curious. Like everyone else in this world except my father."

After an awkward silence, Richards asked, "Will we ever hear from camera boy again?"

"No, I don't think so. All this exposure; Gabe Teplitz is gone, along with Adam Goodman."

"That's my say. Maybe one day he'll get caught in the act, go too far. We'll hear about it on the news."

"Yeah, the world will keep in touch."

. . .

I tried to get myself to call Melissa's boy Colin to ask if he remembered the truth of our friendship, and if he knew what a dick his Uncle Pat was, but the truth darted like a squirrel near the road, so I would let the story be.

What I did do was to go get Lucas' computer, because I knew he would want me to have it. I knew he would want me to check the files for all evidence of his existence, thoughts he might have written down, stories—who knows? I was for him and he was for me. Life gave us that, as we gave to each other. The papers wouldn't cover that story because no one cared about him but me.

Christmas in Nashville was very nice. I got quite emotional with my brother and sister due to all that had happened. Life's quiet times are lovely but the drama does remind us of our priorities and values—like how the ones we love mean so much.

Their children were wonderful, so much energy and humor. They also performed tantrums, but that's the way with tornadoes. Children always reminded me of how afraid I could get. How I had taken to writing because there was less on the line than actual reality. My brother and sister were far braver people than I.

Well, maybe we just have to want things so badly that we're willing to pay that particular price. I guess if I really wanted to be a father I would be a good one. I looked at my life and could not tell for sure what I wanted, other than money for expressing myself. You know, so I could express myself full-time. My mom says I will have children one day. She's certain. I don't know.

She has God. I don't know.

With the last of my Scoop TV money I holed up and wrote this book, the one you just read. When I ran out of money the publisher advanced me some more. That was so cool! I write; they pay. That was as amazing as anything else that had happened to me. I had snags here and there, but kept at it. Interestingly enough, I finished the account of the Bird Man at the exact same time that it had started: early October. I can write fast when I'm left alone.

The publisher didn't like my title, and they fought me tooth and nail.

This is one title they wanted: Bird Man Watching.

Not bad. But I got my way.

I sold the movie rights before I finished the book. I'm sure Hollywood will make some exciting changes. Rosa will be kidnapped by Gabe and I'll have to save her. The snow mobile chase will get much bigger and have multiple explosions; maybe they'll kill off Richards. They won't like the idea of letting the Bird Man escape, so I'll knock him out and then say something clever like, "Time for you to get back in your cage, Bird Man."

Rosa and I have a steady email exchange which is very rich, but she's in Boise and I'm in Reverend River when not publicizing the book. We talk about meeting in New York. Maybe we will meet. Who knows?

I haven't had a drink in six months. I'm not sure how I got back on the wagon, other than to say that my whole life is invested in that action. All my past attempts to quit, successes and failures, thoughts with answers, hopelessness, faith and cynicism—it all bleeds into the new effort. One guy in A.A. loves to say this to new members when they remark on his being sober for twenty years: "We've all been sober the same amount of time: today."

As for my old drinking buddy Lucas, I visit his grave regularly. I tell him what's going on in my life, what I did that week that I'm glad for, what I didn't do that I wanted to, and what I did that I'm ashamed of. It does me good. He's my priest.

The Bird Man story is about a killer of boys, and I will always see the man I knew as Gabe Teplitz clearly in my mind—but right now, for me, the story of the Bird Man is about how knowing what's true, who really did what, who is really capable of what, is tricky business. And thus you'd better take your time deciding what you believe. Or maybe never decide, never know anything. Just be nice and try to enjoy life; knowing things makes people crazy. Still, as someone with a mother on a mountain, staying away from town, being her son, a man of the media, another point to the story might be that we people are separate entities that are endlessly tied to each other.

I came up with my final title—the one you see when you look at this front cover—when sitting by the river recently. I remembered a moment in time. It came so clearly that it startled me. I was nine years old, sitting on the cement steps of my grandmother's two-flat, where we lived just before we left for Reverend River. Dad was building a wooden fence to tell the neighborhood kids to stay off the lawn. I was helping, but then took a break to sit and have a drink of lemonade with my mom. Dad had a big gulp and went right back to work. Mom was in a goofy mood and we were recovering from a laugh. A plane rumbled across the sky and descended toward O'Hare, seeing we lived on the northwest side, twenty minutes from the airport. I said something like this:

"When the planes get that low, do they ever hit the birds?"

I can remember Dad smiling and staying to his chore. Mom said, "Try not to think about it, honey."

"But I want to know, Mom. I want to know. Doesn't somebody know? You think you'd hear about it, all those birds getting killed by planes."

Then my dad's voice rang out as he smiled brilliantly. "You won't hear about planes killing the birds, but let one bird take down a plane: Front page!"

. . .

When night falls and dust settles on my ambition, I think of Jimmy Wagner and all the other angels that didn't make it home for dinner, and I pray there's another kind of home, another type of dinner table, and that they all made it there just fine.

Purchase other Black Rose Writing titles at www.blackrosewriting.com/books

and use promo code PRINT to receive a 20% discount.

BLACK ROSE writing™

Made in the USA
Middletown, DE
25 August 2015